Best wishes to Margaret

Michael Dickel

CLASSIFICATION: FICTION

This book is sold under the condition that it shall not, by way of trade or otherwise, be lent, resold, hired out or otherwise circulated without the publisher's prior consent in any form of binding or cover other than that in which it is published and without a similar condition including this condition being imposed on the subsequent purchaser.

A CIP catalogue record for this book is available from the British Library.

Printed and bound in Great Britain.

Paper used in the production of books published by United Press comes only from sustainable forests.

Published in Great Britain by
United Press Limited.
2004
ISBN 1-84436-078-4 Paperback
ISBN 1-84436-011-3 Hardback
© Michael Shocket 2004
All Rights Reserved

www.unitedpress.co.uk

KNOW ME TOMORROW

by

Michael Shocket

This book is dedicated to Irène

Contents

One	11
Two	29
Three	36
Four	46
Five	57
Six	72
Seven	80
Eight	86
Nine	91
Ten	110
Eleven	116
Twelve	128
Thirteen	136
Fourteen	141
Fifteen	149
Sixteen	155
Seventeen	164
Eighteen	173
Nineteen	181
Twenty	192
Twenty-One	203

Acknowledgments

My thanks are due to Uncle Joe for Fireman Goldberg's recollections of the Blitz on London Docks. I wish to thank my cousins, Sacha and Albert, and my sisters-in-law, Dora and Olga, for sharing with me their childhood memories of life in Paris and Brussels under Nazi rule.

I also wish to thank my grand-daughter, Jo, for her technical assistance.

ONE

It's five o'clock in the morning and I don't feel as if I've been to bed. A large part of the night has been spent hunting and squashing swarms of insects, or pushing intruders out the door and throwing them down the stairs. I mopped up the bathroom floor, to clear up after the creepy crawlies. Then I checked under the bed - and had a hell of a job getting back on my feet. It wasn't easy, but I managed to lassoo - and eject - the cowboy galloping round my bedroom on a white horse.

Two hours ago, Irène asked me to take her out for a walk. It happens to be snowing. With commendable self control I resisted an impulse to throttle her. (And she's the person I love most in the world). A few minutes later she was fast asleep. Not I.

Have you ever suffered from insomnia? When it happens to me the effort to drop off to sleep is comparable to an attempt to achieve an elusive erection, when the harder you try the softer it gets. So I gave up trying - to doze off, that is. There was no question of the other.

Thank goodness she, who demands prompt and obedient attention, is now in the land of dreams. Judging by previous experience I can postpone all insect and unwelcome visitor hunting for a couple of hours until tablet time. So I make myself a cup of tea and compose a heart rending plea for help to our consultant. Having considered and dismissed thoughts of homicide, suicide or both, here am I in front of my computer. Let the screen in front of me be the recipient of my wicked thoughts. I might even indulge myself in the luxury of self pity. In fact, I'm following the social worker's advice:

"Do your own thing," she said. "Do anything you fancy."

That's all very well, but the only time I have available is in the small hours. What I'd like to do is thump on the piano and sing bawdy songs out loud. There's my grandson's football, and I want to kick that through the closed window. Or how about banging my head against the wall? But we live in a flat, and only moved in recently. I don't want to upset the neighbours.

Last night, during my wakeful hours, I had an idea. Although I couldn't stop thinking, there was no pattern to my thoughts, just a tangled skein of memories I was unable to disentangle. So I wondered whether I might achieve some coherence by attempting to sort it all out in print... I'd write a book!

As an alternative to counting sheep I tried to select a pen name: Martin Shawcross? Timothy Hardcastle? Phineas Duckworthy? Sebastien Pinkerton? I soon realised I was barking up the wrong tree and asked myself a few questions:

"What's the main subject?"

"Me."

"Why are you doing it?"

"I don't seem to know who I am any more. I don't know where I'm going. I can't remember properly where I've been. Maybe putting it down on paper will help."

"Do you intend to be entirely truthful?"

"Oh, yes."

"Well, how can you do that in the name of Oscar Wilberforce? Could George Cuthbertson-Smith have a brother like our beloved Alan? Expelled from Hebrew classes for telling an autocratic rabbi to go fuck himself?"

"I suppose not."

But it isn't easy for me to reveal my identity. I don't like myself enough - and never have. Since puberty I've been reluctant to face my real self. In vain I peered into the mirror to see the person I would like to be - some version of a fictional or screen hero.

But if I'm not happy with who I am, do I really want to be anyone else? Perhaps, after I've finished unravelling the thoughts tormenting me last night I'll find the answer. Apart from all that, the children have been pestering me for some time to write down all I know of the family history. It's not such a bad idea to leave them some record, before I go, and it's lost forever. Above all I want to leave a message for my grandchildren, possibly best achieved by a love story... mine.

I hope they'll never feel impelled to run away from home, as I did, at the age of ten.

I didn't get very far. My father had a shop, behind and above which we lived. It was a seamen's outfitter's establishment, close to the gates of West India Docks. Originally it had belonged - one of a small chain - to my maternal grand-father. His main store was in Leman Street, in the same line of business, close to London Docks. Just across the main road was his home, number 82 Chamber Street, which housed my grand-parents and the seven most wonderful aunts and uncles - as far as I was concerned - in the whole wide world. That's where I ran, over sixty years ago - a distance of two miles.

Why? Because my father, in one of his rages, threw a knife at me.

Sounds dramatic? Well, I needed that as an excuse. In fact the incident was trivial, compared with other times he'd beaten the shit out of me. And usually:

"What was that for?"

"I felt like it."

In this case it had been a glancing blow, which didn't even leave a mark. It was a table knife, with no point or serrated edge, quite blunt, and simply the nearest thing he could put his hand on. I might just as well been struck with a plate, bottle or napkin. But a knife? That was just the kind of example of murderous intent I subconsciously needed to justify taking a runner. There was only one place for me to go, and I ran nearly all the way.

Booba, the Yiddish name for Grandma, the person I most wanted to see, was out shopping, and Zeida, aka Grandpa, the next in line, was in the synagogue. Only Uncle Ulla was home, and I blurted out my tale of woe. With a heart of gold, he had a very cool way of dealing with difficult situations, and he listened impassively. When I got to the end of my story, my grandfather came in. My uncle met him and took him into the kitchen, where I heard them talking. Then Zeida shouted:

"That Litvak! (a pejorative term for a Lithuanian Jew) I'll kill the momzer! (bastard)"

Good. My journey was not in vain. The conversation continued, too quietly now to be overheard. Uncle Ulla went to the telephone in the hall, and I gathered he was talking to my mother. Grandpa came in to me, outwardly calm, but his nostrils were slightly flared, usually the only sign he gave that he was angry. He took me on his knee, and, whereas I had shown some restraint talking to my uncle, I gave in to my emotions, and poured out my heart to him. We had a very special relationship.

"You know," he observed finally, "I didn't like your father either."

"Really? Then why...?"

"I threw him out the door. He came in through the window."

"So why didn't you throw him out the window afterwards?"

He smiled.

"Maybe I should have."

After a pause: "But then you wouldn't have been born."

The smile broadened to a grin, and the gold caps on his back teeth glinted merrily through the grey bristles of his small beard.

"Nu? So it was a *mitzva* I gave in and let him marry your mother after all."

Uncle Ulla came back in.

"It's all right now. I'll take you home."

A few minutes later we were on the 77 tram on its way to the terminus at West India Docks, opposite my father's shop.

So Zeida Goldberg thought it was a good thing I'd been born.

I came into the world - with some difficulty - seventy six years ago. According to my mother I had to fight my way out of her. Her pelvis was small, and my top half unusually large. As a consequence of squeezing my way out of her, I emerged with my head moulded to the shape of a cone. Could it have been a presage of my role in life as a clown?

Happily it didn't take too long for me to become a normal looking baby - although I do take a small size in hats. Furthermore, the trauma of birth must be the reason for my claustrophobia. In recent years, while medical staff were attempting to perform a scan, I had to be hauled out of the tunnel - fast. I'd experienced a panic attack. Another result of my struggle to see the light of day is that I suffered - on rare occasions - from temporal lobe epilepsy.

First years were extremely pleasant, due to the fact that my father was rarely at home during my waking hours. In those halcyon days he was out first thing and came home after I was tucked up in bed. I had my wonderful mother all to myself. Furthermore, I was the first grandchild in the Goldberg family and they all spoiled me rotten.

On reflection the phrase is misleading. Can you "spoil" a child with too much love? No. It's the other extreme which does the "spoiling," and I had more than my fair share of that later on.

My mother was the second of eight children. She had five brothers and two sisters, all of them so remarkable that they deserve a book all to themselves. I have to give the extraordinary Goldberg family - to which I'm so proud to belong - a considerable part of this one. The Shocket family - paternal contingent - will receive scant mention, reflecting their interest in me. There are, however, a few notable exceptions. As far as my father himself is concerned, I quote my brother, Alan, always prepared to face the truth, particularly if it could be expressed in outrageous terms. He confided to Uncle Mike, Mum's oldest brother:

"He may be my father, but I hate his guts."

When I read "David Copperfield", I squirmed in delicious horror over passages involving Mr. Murdstone. He was the embodiment of the man who terrorised and thrashed me regularly - until I was big enough to make him think twice. Before I actually ran away, nobody knew. Even then I was reticent about the worst, because, inexplicably, I was ashamed. Unlike Mr. Murdstone, my old man never wielded a cane. That would have counteracted the urgency of his need to lash out. He used his hands or the nearest object he could grab.

I fantasised that - in some mysterious way - he was actually my step-father. I wanted to deny any biological link to a man who not only abused me, but also. unknown to the rest of the world to this day, treated my wonderful mother with what I shall euphemistically call "disrespect." For some extraordinary reason I could never fathom, he always verbally abused her in Yiddish - a language he never used for any other purpose except to curse customers who had the *chutzpa* to leave his shop without making a purchase. Invoking the heavenly powers to afflict them with plagues, he asked that they should contract unspeakable diseases, "stink from the head", or hobble crippled to a premature and painful death.

Yiddish was not a language which came readily to the Shocket family, perhaps because they lived outside the East End ghetto. But it was mother's milk to the Goldbergs, and has always been sheer music to my ears.

The title reserved for me by my father was in effect a sort of boomerang: *momzer ben anider* (bastard son of a whore.) He never cast aspersions on the paternity of my brother, possibly because Alan rapidly grew tall enough to tower above him. Moreover, he'd inherited the old man's knee jerk reflexes and was capable of retaliation - as the saying goes - in spades.

The favoured epithet of that runt of a man for the elegant exquisite lady he had the effrontery to marry, and whose boots he was unfit to lick was: *"grobbe gemayne dreck"* (fat, coarse piece of shit) Why didn't I tell my grandfather? How could I? He really would have killed the bastard. After all, I felt, his *tallit* was the appropriate adornment for Zeida's neck - not the hangman's noose.

The extraordinary thing is that I'm convinced the old sod loved my mother. He never showed any romantic or sexual interest in another woman. Of that I'm sure. Even more amazing is the fact that, apparently, she loved him. Looking at the case today, with the passage of time, I have the impression that he was mentally sick - unable to control a deep-rooted rage. It simply took charge of him. He had to vent it on whoever was in range and, I must add - incapable of retaliation. By the same token, despite his actions - and he did have a cruel streak - I've come to believe he may even have loved me.

Apart from Mr. Murdstone, I could identify him with Mr. Hyde. I didn't see anything of Dr. Jekyll. That was the character he showed the world outside home. Also, basically selfish, he denied pleasure to anyone but himself - and was frugal even there! And that's where Judaism or his concept of it - supported him.

By his own rules he was a religious man - in other words when it suited him, and justified his warped philosophy. I cannot use the term orthodox, applicable to my grandfathers on both sides. Jews have more than their fair share of prohibitions, and my father enforced most. The most solemn day of the year, *Yom Kippur*, the Day of Atonement, he claimed to enjoy. If he did so, it was not because it affords the opportunity to devote oneself entirely to spiritual cleansing. That is its significance to the truly pious. To many of us, and certainly to me, it's simply the most miserable day of the year. If my father was, as he said, happy, it was because he saw most people around him suffering from withdrawal pains. He was longing for a cigarette and a sandwich, and, if inside the stuffy synagogue, bored to tears by a tedious mediaeval chanting which went on and on, lasting all day. The more wretched others became the more pleasure it was for him.

Not for him was the real joy Zeida Goldberg could not contain, and had to spread around him. I remember him beaming as merry as any Santa Claus when he gave out *Chanukah* presents during the December festival - a practice outside my father's repertoire. Throughout our childhood he never gave my brother or myself a gift of any kind. But Grandpa relished the fun in every *Yom Tov*. Piety brightened his existence, whereas practised in our home it blighted mine.

We greeted the Sabbath every Friday night with a traditional *kiddush*. Significantly my father omitted a charming ritual I saw Zeida perform when I spent the weekend with him. Grandpa always concluded the Sabbath prayer by blessing his children - and me. On the other hand, once, upset after an unwarranted explosion of rage against my little brother, my mother lost her words in the traditional prayer for lighting the candles. He snarled at her, and I think it was at that moment I made up my mind that orthodox Judaism was not for me. For him it provided reinforcement for masochistic and sadistic inclinations. It fed his psychosis. Incidentally, he did actually spend the last years of his life in the geriatric ward of a mental hospital. But more of that later.

School I hated. Nevertheless, Saturday was the worst day of the week, unless I was with the Goldbergs, when I felt as if I were in Fairyland. At home the mosaic law was invoked to ensure life was as unpleasant as possible. I was not allowed to play football, partly because it involved travel. Unfortunately that prevented me from being in a team. The radio was not allowed. It meant the use of electricity. Writing and drawing were forbidden, and about the only activity permissible was reading. Even there a rigorous censorship was enforced. Characteristically my father never suggested any of the pleasurable activities which do not break the law. It was left to our mother to brighten the day with specially prepared, mouth-watering *shabbas* meals which defy description. Now that I have learned to cook I attempt in vain to repeat her recipes with equal success. It saddens me that she is no longer with us to sit at my table, and sample a plate of my *lokshen* soup. It might not be up to her inimitable standard. Still, she'd be thrilled to bits that I made it.

When our shop still belonged to my grandfather, it had to be closed every Saturday. Hypocrite that he was, as soon as he acquired the business for himself, my father broke one of the most sacred religious laws by keeping it open. He left my mother in charge while he marched me off to the synagogue.

To a child this was a veritable marathon - a distance of a mile, which he covered with gigantic strides. Desperately trying to keep up, I part walked, part trotted, and for the most part limped in pain, at his side. I wondered then, as I wonder now, to what extent his relentless turn of speed was motivated by an urgent need for spiritual communion, or simply a subtle form of punishment for me. Recalling those forced marches I feel again the pain at the back of my calves. We passed three churches on the way. By the time we reached the *shul* I was a prospective convert to Christianity.

Inside the synagogue other kids freely employed the subterfuge of going out for a pee. It was less to relieve themselves than to relieve the tedium of a three-hour service, for the major part of which they were free to play in the yard. But not I. My young friends - we knew each other from Hebrew classes - would chat during brief spells inside. Even adults seemed to spend more time in conversation than in prayer. Not my father. The *shamus* (beadle) was responsible for maintaining a measure of decorum - a word for which there is significantly no Yiddish equivalent - during services. He was a remarkable man we shall meet again later. A shabby, impoverished appearance, and juicily accented English, failed to disguise the underlying gentleman and scholar. Well respected, in his unobtrusive way, he was most influential in holding together a straggling and largely indifferent community. In the interest of keeping reasonable quiet in *shul* he never objected to the boys' repeated absence during prayers. The old chap was pleased to see the back of them. But how I envied my friends, as I was compelled to sit beside my father all three hours long. Furthermore he embarrassed me. The loudest worshipper in the place, he was also the least musical. Vocalising with an excruciating nasal twang all through what I consider a painfully out-of-date ritual, he combined the noisy enthusiasm of a football fan with the yammering of a sexually aroused hyena.

I have never known hands move as slowly as those on the clock placed on the bleak wall of Poplar Synagogue. It bore little resemblance to Zeida Goldberg's place of worship, a beautifully ornate and ancient building in Great Alie Street. My father, at prayer, cut a ridiculous figure in sombre surroundings. My grandfather, on the other hand, filled me with affectionate pride. He was a veritable pillar of the establishment, which had a magical charm. I wonder: is it still there? The *chazan* (cantor) at that time was a handsome individual, sporting a tiny beard and moustache in the style of the Three Musketeers. He was opulently robed, and had a name I can't hope to spell accurately, but which sounded like "Shapotchnik." He was constantly smiling, and was gifted with a lyrical tenor voice which would have graced the stage at Covent Garden.

At that time, we were living in the dock area of Limehouse. It was a neighbourhood housing thousands of Chinese - they called it "Chinatown" - hundreds of anti-Semitic dockers, whose sons waylaid me in the street and at school with taunts of "Jewboy". In fact, there were actually very few Jews. These were mainly shopkeepers, a minority group, whose domestic and commercial lives followed a course very similar to that of immigrant Asians at the end of the twentieth century. Indeed, the tram which took me to school in the thirties went past shopfronts displaying names like Ginsberg, Cohen, Grossman, Silverman, Goldstein. Now they show Patel, Shah, Singh, Nathwani and Gupta. The wares and trades involved are very much the same. Another similarity is that, as they prosper, the families move outward from places like Bethnall Green, to form communities in outer London and the suburbs.

When we lived in Limehouse there were not enough Jewish residents to justify the construction of a synagogue. The nearest place of worship was an ugly recently constructed building in Poplar. Even here the congregation was too small to merit the customary employment of both rabbi and cantor. One minister had to fulfill both functions. He was a worthy gentleman indeed. Sadly he possessed a voice which did not match the quality of his learning.

Saturday morning services were tedious, and I particularly resented being stuck in the stuffy atmosphere.

I can smell it now, rather like stale mothballs - especially if the sun was shining through the windows, half glazed in unimpressive stained glass. By the time we arrived home for Sabbath dinner - we didn't call it "lunch" in those days - my legs were aching badly, and the master of the house was experiencing withdrawal symptoms, due to being deprived of his cigarettes. Smoking, which involves fire, is strictly forbidden on most holy days. At other times the old man didn't exactly "smoke." My grandfather did this rather elegantly, favouring Turkish cigarettes, puffed from time to time through an amber holder. Dad, on the other hand, had a fag-end wedged in the corner of his mouth - not a pretty sight - only removed when it began to singe the Hitler moustache he wore - an appropriate adornment - yellowed with nicotine at the edges.

Occasionally we arrived home earlier than expected - or perhaps Mum had been busy in the shop, and dinner was not ready. I was quick to pick up the signs. Tobacco deprivation allied to the pangs of hunger meant that all hell would break loose. I made myself scarce. But if I was slow off the mark the ensuing fracas left me wondering why on the seventh day it was a sin to tear toilet paper, but considered O.K. to beat the living daylights out of *me* for no reason except that I happened to be within range. At a tender age I asked myself if the world wouldn't be a better place without this "God" to whom I'd wasted the morning mumbling a load of rubbish, *created in my father's image - terrifying, angry, vindictive?*

At that time I was ambivalent about religion, of which my father and grandfather were at opposing poles - one negative, the other positive. For the former Judaism provided a rationale for the darker side of his nature, whereas for the latter it gave meaning to the joy he experienced in living. Zeida was a fulfilled and happy man. Orthodoxy was a confirmation of his basic integrity and a formula for the upbringing and education of the family which he loved above all else.

I have cherished memories of him: profiled at the window in the early morning, swaying gently as he *davened*, massive gilt-edged prayer book in hand, well worn *tephillin* round his arm and forehead, enveloped in the white folds of his praying shawl, and with an expression of utter peace. I picture him coming home from *shul* on a winter morning, pink-cheeked, his breath frosting from the bitter cold, bearing a huge brown bag brim full of warm, fragrant rolls for the family breakfast; practising with his *shofar* - he had the honour of blowing the ram's horn on high holy days. The most precious memory of all is of him presiding like a king at the head of a magnificent festival banquet, resplendent in his ceremonial robe, a snow white *kittel*, liberally pouring wine into glasses of all shapes and colours - with a superb silver chalice for himself.

Twenty two year old Marks Goldberg disembarked, as the saying goes "from the onion boat." At the end of the nineteenth century England offered the young *yeshiva* student freedom - from pogroms and the prospect of military service in Poland, where he'd left his wife, Miriam Leah, in charge of two young children, Michael, my namesake, and his baby sister, Pearl, who, two decades later, would become my mother. They were to follow him as soon as he could make suitable arrangements. Coming from a deeply orthodox background, and with only a religious education behind him, Grandpa was completely unprepared for practical living in London. The fact that he had distinguished himself as a talmudic scholar was unlikely to put butter on his bread. It did however ensure him a warm welcome within the ghetto of East London. Friends persuaded him that the only way to scrape enough money to keep body and soul together, and put a roof over his head, was to engage in the demeaning occupation of selling second-hand clothes from a barrow. Faced with Hobson's choice, and anxious to bring over his wife and children as soon as possible, with the assistance of new friends, Zeida gritted his teeth, and literally put his back into it. Dragging himself up by his bootlaces, and by the grace of God, to whom he prayed with renewed fervour, he acquired a shop. It had living accommodation above, admirably suited to his requirements, and became my mother's first home in England.

In the words of his beloved bible: "And the face of the Lord smiled down upon Marks Goldberg. He begat five sons and three daughters, and prospered in the land of England." He now had three stores, with new clothes on display. The family had outgrown the living quarters above his original shop, so he bought two newly built houses in a side street, just opposite the business.

Although I haven't seen 82 Chamber Street for over sixty years, I remember it vividly. The happiest days of my childhood were spent there. How I wished it could be my permanent home. A fine house it was indeed, proudly boasting three lavatories in the backyard, and their doors, side by side, formed the backdrop for family photographs for many years. At the back of the yard was a workshop, filled with rolls of cloth, and opposite was the cellar door, leading down to a bathroom, installed by Grandpa at a time when private domestic bathrooms were a novelty in the East End. There was also a massive cooker, exclusively for frying vast quantities of fish.

On the ground floor was the dining room, which contained one of the largest mahogany tables I have ever seen outside a mansion. Expanding with removable leaves, it could accommodate family banquets, table tennis, or synagogue committee meetings to fit the occasion. There was another enormous table in the kitchen, with a plain wooden surface scrubbed almost white, invariably covered with American cloth. Other items of furniture I recall clearly include a dresser - in a recent dream I saw the rose patterned cups hanging on its brass hooks - and in the living room to match the mahogany table and leather upholstered dining chairs, an ornate chiffonnier running almost the length of the wall. A hairbrush, hurled at my father - no doubt with good reason - by Aunt Sophie, with more anger than accuracy, permanently scarred it. In the corner was a bureau of the same wood. I was allowed to rummage among its mysterious contents. On the first floor stood a fine piano. My mother and my Aunt Bee were both musically talented, and I loved hearing them play.

Whenever I stayed the night, I slept at the top of the house with my two uncles, Ulla and Joe. The bedroom was at the back, and had an intriguing view of the rooftops. Prominently featured was the skylight of Bonn's, a popular venue for weddings and *bar-mitzvahs*. Loud music - for the most part lively *klezmer* and invariably happy - poured out across the rooftops and entertained me until it melted into my dreams.

My grandparents' home was always full of people: uncles, aunts, their friends, later their husbands and wives, *machetoonim*..and there's a word which requires a little explanation. The Goldberg family was certainly "extended", collecting not only spouses for the eight children, but also their respective parents. The latter we call call "*machetoonim*". The male of the species is the *"mechitan"* His wife is the " *machetenista*," traditionally the butt in Jewish humour, mocked for being over-dressed, or clad in "shmutters," teetering on heels too high, hair dyed like a peacock, or looking like something the cat brought in and creeping around like a *"shnorrer."*

Occasionally she is considered a fit mother-in-law for the son or daughter in question but not very often. Given its connotations to the brethren, the word "*machetenista*" is untranslatable.

When they arrived in London my grandparents knew no English. They attended an evening class to learn the language. A Hebrew student of standing, Grandpa was the slower learner by far. Booba, who'd always lived in his academic shadow, left him standing. Zeida would take me on his knee to regale me with traditional bible tales and folklore, but Booba introduced me to Dickens. She became a frequent visitor to the library, borrowing one volume after another written by her favourite author.

At first glance the couple were an ill-assorted pair. He was large, ebullient and distinguished looking, immaculately dressed with wing collar, perfectly adjusted tie and gold pin, *a watch chain* stretched across his ample waistcoat. He sported a small beard, in the style of George V, and neatly parted grey hair looped rather low on his forehead. He had a selection of amber cigarette holders, and on the days when smoking was not permitted, he filled his waistcoat pockets with sweets, which he shared with any children in his vicinity. Zeida walked tall, briskly on his own or with friends, but considerately moderating his pace when Booba, tiny Booba was hooked on his arm. Not for her the submissive few paces behind her husband, favoured by her contemporaries. A feminist before her time, she proudly demanded the rightful place beside her man, who would have wished it no other way. Quoting her esteemed author she used to say to me: "Look. Darby and Joan." She walked slowly, in tiny black shoes, polished like glass. They were hand-made, to accommodate feet which gave her trouble throughout her life.

Although Grandma intellectually repudiated any ritual in conflict with her rational philosophy, she dutifully maintained an orthodox home. With too sweet a disposition to revolt openly against her husband's authority, she did, however, on a few memorable and hilarious occasions, take a stand. In these rare matrimonial conflicts all family bets were on Booba. The "Guv'nor", as the children called him, would get on his high horse, puff himself up, grow taller, carried away by his own rhetoric... He backed up his argument with words of the prophets and quoted chapter and verse the exhortations of *Moshe Rabbenu*, Moses our teacher. Booba waited impassively until he ran out of steam, then crisply told him what he and Moses could go and do. Floored by one of his wife's devastating one-liners, Grandpa withdrew with his tail between his legs.

At festival banquets, however, he reigned supreme - undisputed monarch, as he and my grandmother presided over the large family, for every single member of which both would have unhesitatingly laid down their lives.

Booba and I were on the same wavelength. Although extremely affectionate, I don't remember her ever speaking to me as to a child. Not only did I confide in her, it operated in reverse. She talked confidentially about her scepticism concerning the very things she practised, discussed her reading, and the reflections it inspired, her worries - and above all, people we both knew, usually satirically, but in appropriate cases, encouraging my admiration and respect. Throughout her long life I turned to her for advice, and since she passed away, there have been many times when, not knowing what action to take, I hear her voice: it's usually a phrase in Yiddish, and provides a solution once and for all.

Just between ourselves she admitted her aversion to my father, and, in contrast, was outspoken in her delight at my choice of wife. My grandmother and I were so close that I make no apology for giving more than a passing reference to someone who exerted a great influence on my philosophy and my life. Zeida had learning. Booba had wisdom.

She was quick to laugh and quick to cry - but sorry for the plight of others, never for herself, and the first with practical help. No doubt she was following the example set by her father, Michael, after whom her first-born and I have been named. My great-granfather died prematurely, knowingly exposed to infection as he tended the sick in an outbreak of cholera.

On one occasion I remember Booba laughing so much that tears rolled down her cheeks, she collapsed to the floor and her false teeth fell into the cat's dinner. She'd just come back from a funeral. It had been the burial of a distant relative, unlamented, by dint of a propensity for defrauding those nearest to him - including Uncle Lew.

A word now about this latter gentleman, who was married to Grandpa's sister, Aunt Bessie. A kind and lovable man, he was nevertheless a family joke. Booba called him the "*lange loksh*" - an elongated streak of vermicelli - due to his excessive height, unfortunately accompanied by a pronounced stoop. Endowed with a high-pitched voice, he had a tendency to end his sentences on a note at the top of the falsetto range. Furthermore, his speech was impaired by the absence of all his front teeth. To crown it all, Uncle Lew was the supreme example of a "*shlemuzzel*," in other words the hapless victim of every conceivable disaster - an accident waiting to happen, and that day of the funeral was no exception.

Punctuated by peals of laughter Booba recounted the event: the coffin was lowered into the grave, and, *nu*, the men stepped forward to shovel earth (in accordance with tradition), and who was first in line? Of course, it was the *lange loksh*. He must have been thinking of the money the *ganef* down there had stolen from him, because he couldn't hide his *fargeniegen* (pleasure) at throwing the dirt on him. He started shovelling with such *naches* (the most intense pleasure), that... well, you know how bent double he is, over went the *shlemuzzel,* head first into the *loch.* The *potz* buried himself! When they hauled him out, he was yelling "*Oy vay!*" over and over again ... Booba mimicked his falsetto to perfection... he was plastered from head to toe in mud. And what do you think he was yelling about like a *meshigene*? His head was uncovered - a grievous sin. Why uncovered? Because his bowler hat was perched on top of the coffin.

Booba told the family, enraptured by her recital, that she was afraid she'd done herself a mischief preventing herself from laughing out loud. Now she'd have to excuse herself to go and change - including her underwear. And that started her off again.

My mother told me that, while she was still a young girl, she was asked to take food to a neighbour, an impoverished widow with five young children.

"Talk to her a bit. Give her my regards, and hide this *peckel* (bag of goodies) under your coat. As you go out, leave the food on the hall table, but try not to let her see you do it. She's a proud woman. Don't embarrass her."

According to my mother this was but one example of charitable acts on the part of my grandparents. It's called a "*mitzva*" - for righteous Jews a sacred obligation - indeed literally a "command" - to be sought out and welcomed as a privilege. Although I find much orthodox practice difficult to accept, there is a considerable part of our traditional moral code by which I was raised, and which I'll always admire. I won't "throw away the baby with the bath water."

In the early years of the twentieth century Jewish families in the East End organised their own efficient welfare service. I know that Zeida scrupulously set aside one tenth of his income for charity, in accordance with religious law. It was a self-imposed tax.

But is the so-called "*mitzva*" actually a command from "God" or the concept of a wily old prophet? I asked my grandfather if Moses simply put the fear of God into a superstitious rabble to keep them in line. Couldn't he have made up the whole works himself?

I half expected Grandpa to be cross. But he was quite

unperturbed.

"*Nu?*" he said. "So, if he did - and I'm sure he didn't - who do you think put the idea in his head?"

The dear old chap was just getting into his talmudic stride, and began to elaborate on the theme of man having not only a body and a mind, but a soul...

Booba wouldn't let him have the last word. Piling more of her delicious pie on my plate, she told him - in Yiddish - to stop "banging on my tea-pot" (talking my head off) and let me finish my lunch in peace. Behind her back Zeida winked.

One particular "*mitzva*" performed by Booba near the end of her life had a long lasting effect. After the war ended, to the amusement of my aunts and uncles, I was asked to supply my grandmother with a number of what she persisted in calling French letters. Her sister, a resident in Paris, had perished during the holocaust with almost her entire family. However it was discovered that there were two surviving children, the younger of whom was in an orphanage.

"My sister's grandson," she kept repeating tearfully.

The boy's name was Sacha, and Grandma had me constantly translating letters. She wouldn't rest until Sacha was in her arms. Eventually he was officially adopted by Aunt Sophie, and is the apple of her eye. I'll tell his story later.

I may have drawn the short straw in my choice of father, but I won the jackpot in the maternal stakes. Furthermore, due to my close relationship with the Goldberg grandparents I acquired fluent Yidish, a fact which was influential in my winning a beautiful bride.

I was just about to tell you more about that, but I hear a little bell tinkling in the bedroom. It announces that my wife is now awake, ready to get up, and requires immediate attention. So, until this time tomorrow...

TWO

The clocks in Israel are two hours ahead of ours at this time of year, so I am not unduly surprised to receive a phone call from Dora, who lives in Tel Aviv, when it's only seven o'clock over here. She knows our routine, and that her sister will be asleep after being given her morning medication.

She tells me that she'll be in London in a few weeks, to spend some time with her daughter, Tali, and the grandchildren. I'll try to arrange for the other surviving sister - the youngest - Olga - to come over from Brussels and stay with us at the same time. The rare occasions when the three of them can be together are so precious that it would be a shame to miss an opportunity. To my delight, whenever they're under the same roof they revert to childhood, bouncing on the bed, throwing pillows, dancing along the pavement to French songs they sang as kids...

Dora's plans are good news. She ought to be able to supply me with details about the girls' life in Belgium before the war, and during the German occupation. I've never been able to prise much information on the subject from Irène, who's always been either unwilling or unable to reminisce. When pressed she's on the verge of tears, and I haven't the heart to persist. But she and I are the main characters in this "Tale of Two Cities". If I'm permitted to delve into my own family history, I can hardly avoid researching hers. Hopefully Dora and Olga will remember what she claims to have forgotten.

I know that it begins with a similar story to my mother's, but with a kind of generation slip. My father-in-law, Chaskiel Rusak, left his birthplace, Lodz, some thirty years after Marks Goldberg emigrated from Poland, and more or less for the same reasons. He, too, left behind him a wife and children - in his case three little girls - who were to follow as soon as he could establish a home.

Chaskiel was a man of strong character and integrity, with one serious flaw. He was throughout his life an inveterate gambler. Bad enough. Worse - he was just about the unluckiest man who ever placed a bet. With the world to choose from, he threw the dice, and decided to stake his future in Brussels. Little did he guess that he was taking his wife and children - with two more girls soon to be born - straight into the jaws of the holocaust. My grandfather began his career with a barrow. Chaskiel was good with his hands, and started to make a living as a cobbler.

We'll take up his story later. Now it's time for me to prepare breakfast.

I can't squeeze a word out of Irène except one or two monosyllabic replies to my questions. Well, there's nothing especially unusual about that. She always takes a long time to wake up properly - to "come to myself" as she says. I do make an effort to stick to Winston Churchill's recipe for a long and happy marriage:

"Never talk to your wife before breakfast," is sound advice.

But this morning I think she's sulking. And that always gets my goat. Then all of a sudden she initiates a discussion - and from her tone it will probably develop into an argument if not a full scale row.

"How can you sit there calmly after what happened last night?" - in a combative tone:

"?"

"You disgust me!"

I'm sorry to disappoint any reader whetting his lips in anticipation of some intimate and salacious revelation, but, for the life of me, all I remember is getting out of bed the usual half a dozen times to manoeuvre her towards and upon the commode, and wrestling her back to bed again. I'm frankly puzzled.

"What happened last night?"

"You know perfectly well."

"I do?"

Sniff.

"Remind me."

"That old woman again."

"Which old woman?"

"The one in the bed."

"There was no old woman, darling. You were hallucinating."

"No. I saw her."

"You think you saw her..."

"With her horrible little black dog."

Does she hallucinate in colour or just black and white? The doctor was curious, but we had no answer. "What was she doing?"

"You know quite well what she was doing... Tying pink ribbons round your balls, and you were wearing a silly, green hat."

Aha! So the hallucinations are in colour. I laugh.

"It's not funny. I was going to dial 999 and call the police."

I stop laughing. She's right. It isn't funny.

"How on earth do you think I could be involved in anything like that?"

"Why do you keep bringing those creatures in here.. when you know how I hated it last time?"

"When was that?"

"You know. They were just outside the window."

"How the hell could they be there? We're on the third floor, and there's no way up outside. All we can see are the rooftops and trees."

"I saw them."

"No, dear. You *think* you saw them. It was an illusion."

"And I tell you that's a nasty little dog. Why do you encourage them? And in the bed of all places...

"How do you think they got in?"

"Through the door, I suppose."

"But it's double locked. See for yourself. It still is."

"You must have opened it."

"No way."

"Then they came through the window."

"But they're all closed and locked too."

"I saw the creatures. And it must be you encouraging them."

It's a losing battle and I give up. I realise it should never have started. Then I notice that special look on her face again.

"What's the matter?"

No reply, but there's no mistaking that expression.

"Come on, you can tell me."

A shake of the head is her only reply.

"Are you seeing things again?"

"Over there by the door. It's the same one. She's back again."

"What's she doing?"

"She's got one of David's toys. Can't you see her playing with it? It's a yo-yo."

Oh, well, if you can't beat them, join them. "Shall I throw her out?"

"No, no, no! If you're aggressive with them they'll turn vicious. Just hide the photographs of the children. She might harm them."

Casting all reason to the winds I meekly do what she asks, and wish I could learn to do so unquestioningly more often. What I have learned is that in these circumstances diversion is a good tactic. Would she like to go shopping? No. Shall we take a shower? Good idea? Fine.

We have a large double shower in our new flat. It's a feature I would strongly recommend for matrimonial delights. Yes, it can be a lot of fun, and, after I persuade her that there are no creepy crawlies in there, in we go, and frolic so outrageously that our grandchildren - if they saw us - wouldn't believe their eyes.

As I dress her afterwards, while she is still in her underwear, how can I resist a long, long cuddle? Old women, their dogs, uninvited guests, vermin, insects ... all forgotten. How perfectly she fits into my arms, exactly the way it was that first, unforgettable time I held her close, when the sky was a network of searchlights and anti-aircraft gun were hammering in the distance. Her lovely head nestles snugly where it belongs, tucked into my left shoulder. She smells delicious from the shower, and still, after all these years, my heart feels as if it's turning over.

"I must be the luckiest man in the world," I tell myself.

"If only," I think, "if only this could go on forever."

I've always loved the fair sex - not, I hasten to add, with a string of affairs, although, maybe if I had the nerve and the spirit of sheer devilment of my brother... He really did play Casanova... Enough of that. I'm talking of a more sublimated, less sensual kind of "love." Honest - hand on heart. On the other hand I admit to having an eye for a pretty girl. I always have, and, yes, still do at my advanced age. An expression of my grandmother's springs to mind - as they do so frequently, about so many things: "*Kennst kicken mit die oigen - nit cheppen mit die hend.*" It's O.K. to look with your eyes, but keep your hands to yourself." Sound advice, as always.

Darling Booba. I adored her.

When, aged over eighty, she died in my mother's arms, she'd just put on one of her coquettish hats, dressed for the synagogue. It was New Year - a sacred day for the pious. Heart-breaking though it was for all of us, it was a fitting end to the life of a righteous woman. My mother was ninety four years young when she, too, died, like Grandma, with merciful swiftness and in full possession of her faculties, to the last, full of the joy of living. The fact that she'd been with me for over seventy years did not lessen my grief. On the contrary. It was like losing a limb.

These are stolen hours. I'm free to work on my manuscript today, because Irène is at her Day Centre in Edgware. It is frequented mainly by the widowed, elderly and disabled, and organised by Jewish Care. We're acting on the advice of our social worker, who made the necessary arrangements.

When I first drove my wife there two weeks ago I was convinced we'd made a mistake. Apart from the voluntary workers, everyone looked so old! I sensed Irène's reaction from her tightened grip on my hand. In fact, had I but realised it, quite a few of the ladies were actually younger than ourselves. It's just that my wife is so pretty people think she's still in her fifties.

Invited to stay with her for the first day, I was served

coffee and biscuits at her designated table. Then a strange phenomenon occurred. When faces became familiar, it was as if the wrinkles faded. Eyes became a more prominent feature. They twinkled and shone. We were also more aware of voices - often youthful - and of what our neighbours were saying. I could see that Irène was increasingly more comfortable with her environment, and began to relax myself.

When subsequently we took the lift, I couldn't believe my ears when I was informed that we were going upstairs for *aerobics*! Half this group were scarcely able to *walk*, needing sticks, zimmer frames and wheelchairs. *Aerobics*? This must be a joke. Anyway I knew Irène would never participate actively.

Before lunch we joined the discussion group, where we were warmly received; the gentlemen were clearly delighted to welcome an attractive new arrival and another member of the Goldberg clan. In the discussion which ensued I suppose they expected me to play a prominent role as the nephew of Manny, whose memory and knowledge of scientific subjects were legendary at the centre. Aware of my shortcomings, however, and impressed by the intellectual level of the group, for the first half hour I kept *shtoom*, but was able to redeem the family honour when we focused on embryonic cloning, featured in the morning's broadsheets.

It so happens that this development holds out the hope of a cure for Parkinson's Disease. It is therefore of particular interest to me, and I have gone to some length to understand the subject. So I put in my two cents, and Uncle Manny's ghost smiled down approvingly.

We were then treated to an excellent three course lunch, after which the day was rounded off with entertainment provided by a singer, with piano accompaniment. But there was another surprise in store for me on this quite remarkable day.

Sitting beside me was a dignified, handsome lady, about eighty years old. She was too frail to feed herself, and a trainee was helping her, chatting the whole time The old lady could only reply with smiles. Then the audience was invited to join in with the singer, and I heard an exquisite voice behind me. It was my neighbour. Unable to use knife, fork or spoon, to walk or take part in normal conversation, the old darling sang like an angel.

Not for the first time that day, I thought to myself that there's a lot more in these old people than meets the eye.

Contrary to all my expectations, Irène thoroughly enjoyed her day, completely untroubled by hallucinations. She was so stimulated by the social atmosphere that my daughters were impressed by its lasting effect in dispelling the apathy which had begun to cloud her personality.

THREE

I suppose it's a matter of temperament, but my life has always been on an emotional see-saw, exemplified by my childhood and my present situation. Although my early years were blighted by a tyrannical father, they were also blessed by such a wonderful collection of uncles and aunts, that I viewed the family with the wonder given to myths and fairy tales; it was as if my grandfather was King Arthur, but less remote, my grandmother a more lovable Queen, and their children knights of the round table and the most beautiful ladies in the kingdom.

Sir Michael - a gentle knight was he, of smiling countenance and wondrous courtesy, Sir Emanuel, whose magic and science rivalled that of Merlin himself, Sir Isaac the fastest knight in the kingdom - on four wheels, Sir Aaron, master with *physick* and the doctor with healing hands, Sir Joseph, whose acrobatic and athletic skills were admired throughout the realm, the Lady Rebecca, fairest of the fair - except, of course, for Mum, and the Lady Sophie, famed black-haired beauty whose flashing eyes glowed brighter than those of a tigress.

As a child I venerated and adored them all. As I grew older my feelings never changed.

A few years ago, at the wedding of one of my cousins, I was asked to propose a toast to the Goldberg family, and, in the course of my speech I praised them in turn: "Uncle Mike sadly the only sibling to die young was the kindest man in the world; Uncle Manny was the cleverest man in the world; Uncle Ulla was the most conscientious doctor in the world; Uncle Joe the best athlete, and my aunts the most beautiful... "

At this point a voice piped up from the back of the hall:

"How about me?"

That was Isaac, nicknamed Pop.

"Ah, that's Uncle Pop. He pops up everywhere."

There have been four cases of dementia with which I have been closely involved: Irène's sister, Ida, turned into a vegetable, suffering according to her doctor (whose diagnosis I question) from atrophy of the cortex; Irène has Lewy Body Disease; my father had Alzheimer's, and Uncle Pop, as the result of a stroke, had about thirty years wiped completely out of his memory. In a way, his was the most tragic case of all. Apart from forgetting the previous thirty years of his life - he was eighty, and thought he was fifty - he appeared to have a brain functioning normally at first, until it became evident that he had completely forgotten the previous part of a conversation. The poor old chap kept asking for his "beloved (a constantly repeated adjective) wife," and learned over and over again that she had died ten years back. We saw him suffer the torments of appalling grief time after time.

My aunt had been like Irène a victim of Parkinson's Disease. The illness is progressive. In Aunt Sadie's case deterioration was rapid, and she soon became completely incapacitated.

One day I found Uncle Pop washing the kitchen floor, and unrestrained tears were mixing with the soap suds.

"I don't know what I'll do if anything happens to her," he said.

At the time I was deeply moved. Now I echo his feeling, which is counterbalanced by:

"I don't know what she'll do if anything happens to me."

A pitiable factor in all this is that, under a prickly surface, Uncle Pop was the biggest softie in the family.

"Who's pinched my braces?"

Yap! Yap!

Booba had nicknamed him "The puppy".

"Somebody's nicked my bloody braces! Who did it?"

Yap! Yap!

"I'll bet it was Mike. I'll kill him!"

Pop was half way up the first flight of stairs on his murderous mission, when his mother's voice stopped him short.

"Just look!" cried Booba. "The puppy's got a tail!"

Trailing behind him, fastened to the back buttons of

his trousers were the "purloined" braces.

To his credit, the puppy was the first to laugh.

The name of his older brother, Manny, was not, as I used to believe, an abbreviation of Emanuel. Originally Menachem, he was called "Menny" by his mother, and became "Manny," particularly appropriate in his case, because it was evocative of the incessant humming he produced in most of his waking hours. Booba used to say fondly: "*Menny boorchet.*" He was forever humming quite tunelessly as he took things to pieces, repaired them, put them together again and created wonderful things out of bits of rubbish, or humming as he drove his car which was confiscated by his daughters after he turned ninety, and had been endangering himself and the general public for several years. The vehicle was replaced by an electric invalid carriage, supercharged in his garage-cum-workshop in an attempt to reach Formula One class, and enable him to race around Tesco's.

At the age of ninety one he saw off a burglar demanding money, and threatening him at his front door with a knife. No way was Uncle Manny parting with any of his cash, so, in some unbelievable way, he wrenched the man's knife away, tripped him to the ground... and sat on him! A neighbour, watching in amazement, phoned the police, while, in the meantime, the thief wriggled free and took to his heels.

Shortly afterwards, a policeman was taking notes.

"Name?" he inquired.

"Date of birth?"

Uncle Manny told him. The copper did some arithmetic, scratched his head with the pencil, and asked him to repeat it.

"H'm," he said. "Tough old sod, aren't you?"

His younger brother, and childhood co-conspirator, Isaac, *aka* Pop, was equally enterprising and mischievous - they actually made a gun together, and it worked - but had an entirely different character. Manny was almost as even tempered as the oldest sibling, Michael, whereas his younger brother, basically the most affectionate of them all, had a short fuse, and was nicknamed by his mother as the *"hoondel"* (puppy) because he was constantly barking. Then she renamed him again. He was forever "popping" in here, "popping" in there, and one day, to the family's delight, Booba said:"Pop, pop, pop... You'll turn into a pop..." which is exactly what happened to him. From that moment he shed the name of Isaac, and turned into Pop for the rest of his life.

Uncle Pop taught me about cars. Eventually he ran a fleet of vans, and, when he heard I was about to buy my first car, he dropped everything, "popped" round and spent an hour and a half in and under the vehicle before he pronounced it O.K. Uncle Manny taught me to draw, and how to make model planes, though never with his expertise. Out of a matzo box he created an aircraft, complete with fuselage, powered by elastic, which made its maiden flight launched from an upstairs window. It flew gracefully the length of Chamber Street, but unfortunately completed its voyage nose down in a fresh pile of steaming horse manure.

Uncle Joe, the youngest, taught me how to swim and dive. He tried to teach me to box, but - alas - I am either too gentle by nature for the sport, or, most likely, too scared of getting hurt. Joe is only ten years older than I, and we have always been more like brothers than uncle and nephew.

Now nearly eighty years old he goes dancing three times a week, and takes his grandchildren ice-skating.

Older than Joe by just over a year was Aaron, who, of course, had to suffer a name change. Booba called him by the affectionate diminutive "*Aarele*." That became "Ulla", and stuck to him for the rest of his long life, which sadly ended just two years ago. He was a doctor of the old school much loved by his family and his patients, and always at their disposal.

My two aunts, Sophie and Bea, were always very close to my mother, and virtually inseparable in old age. The latter was a talented pianist, and the former, as the one surviving sister, now in her nineties, and in full possession of her faculties, has naturally assumed the position of matriarch, holding open house to all my cousins. She attends the day centre together with my wife, and has instinctively adopted a characteristic protective role.

Nobody ever had uncles and aunts like mine.

I have such wonderful memories of them all... memories...What a precious possession is memory.

Irène and I visited Uncle Pop in hospital shortly before his death. The nurses were fussing over him.

"He's such a poppet," said the ward sister.

My cousin, Ruth, was standing beside the bed with a box of Kleenex at the ready, dreading the inevitable question:

"Where's your mother?"

He recognised me immediately, and was clearly delighted to see me. Then he stared wonderingly at Irène. He'd always been especially fond of her.

"Who's this lovely lady?"

Together with a large part of his life she had been completely obliterated from his memory.

I find little comfort in the thought that Irène has to lose not thirty - but over fifty years of her past, before in her diseased brain - I disappear into oblivion.

Tomorrow Irène goes to her Day Centre, so I ought to be able to continue my story. However, the Centre is in Edgware, and I learned that a dear old friend from my schooldays lives nearby. We haven't seen each other for many years, and I was distressed to hear that he's suffered two major strokes recently.

Pip was my best friend between the ages of eleven and fifteen. Then the war separated us. We were no longer in the same school, his large family remained in the East End, and my parents had moved to the suburbs. We were in different units in the army, and our lives followed separate paths. Unbelievably we didn't see each other again for over half a century. I can't wait until tomorrow.

Although he's been expecting me with equal anticipation, when Pip opens the door our eyes tell us that we are looking at two strangers. His wife, Eve, told me over the phone when we arranged my visit, that I'd find him considerably disabled from his last stroke, and that I'd be shocked by the distortion to his features, so I'm agreeably surprised by the appearance of this elderly gentleman with twinkling blue eyes (they at least are familiar), rosy unlined cheeks, and a broad smile, undiminished by the droop to one side of his face. Words fail us. We just throw our arms around each other, and I note the tears in his eyes as he leads me, shuffling on his zimmer frame, into the lounge, littered with the paraphernalia required by his disability, but immaculately clean, with evidence everywhere of a delicate feminine touch.

Eve is in the garden, which is just as well, because when she comes in five minutes later our conversation is transformed into a monologue. Eve takes over, without seeming to pause for breath. From her frequent sidelong glances in Pip's direction, I soon realise that she is dominating the gossip, due to anxiety that her husband, if allowed to get a word in, will betray his mental deterioration. Of course. I do exactly the same thing. I'd like to tell her that what she's doing is unnecessary, but can't think of tactful phrasing. In any case, there's never pause for a possible interruption.

Before Eve's arrival, however, I established that, although he remembers much of our years together, there are significant gaps. Pip recalls best the early years, having been evacuated to Fakenham, that the town is in Norfolk, we were studying for what we called "matric," but has completely forgotten how we were, as best friends, billeted together over a baker shop, that the family's name was Ogelby, the heavenly smell of fresh bread being baked at four o'clock in the morning, that we shared a room, actually slept in the same double bed, and assisted at the ceremonial funeral of the family dog.

At long last Eve runs out of steam, expresses interest in my own experience as a "carer", permitting me to touch briefly on the subject before she seizes on the opportunity offered by this particular turn in the conversation. It so happens that I am fascinated, and given much food for thought. Clearly there's no scrap of resentment in her caring for a disabled partner - even in disagreeable areas, which she has no hesitation in describing cheerfully in graphic terms. She actually considers it a privilege! I note the way they keep looking at each other, and I'm delighted by the obvious fact that my dear old friend, with whom I shared many a romantic youthful dream, has, like myself, a marriage made in heaven.

Pip and I used to be inseparable, at first in school hours only, because we lived two miles apart, and in those days, for boys without pocket money for tram fares, and without the luxury of bicycles, the distance was enormous. Then, when we were thirteen, he introduced me to his club, where we were able to spend about four evenings a week together. Unfortunately, we attended an all boys' school, and belonged to a club in which the sexes were separated, and I wonder to what extent, this segregation, allied to the fact that I had no sister, was influential in providing me with an idealistic view of women, enhanced by my good fortune in possessing wonderful female relations, and turning me into the incurable romantic I have always been.

I regretted not having a sister, but was able to rectify this disadvantage by the acquisition of three sisters-in-law as dear to me as true siblings. In fact... But more of that later.

Until I was six years old, and then for a further ten relatively colourless years, girls were a complete mystery to me. But when I reach the age of six Uncle Lew comes back into the story. He was married to my grandfather's sister, Aunt Bessie, who, by the way, lived to be nearly a hundred years young.

Bessie was brought over as a teenager from Poland by my grandparents. She became one of the family - a kind of big sister to the eight children. Dexterous and creative, she also happened to be pretty and sweet natured, and therefore was not lacking in suitors, mostly introduced to her by my grand-parents, and all rejected, as they apparently failed to come up to her standards. Apart from that she was quite fulfilled in her self appointed role as "nanny". She adored children, with whom she always had a natural affinity.

It was quite a shock to my grandparents when she presented a suitor of her own choosing to the family, and especially since the object of her affections happened to be Uncle Lew.

Asked for her opinion after meeting the young man, Booba was characteristically forthright, asking her sister-in-law in graphic terms of Yiddish I can't possibly translate, what on earth she saw in that ungainly "*lange loksh.*"

"He's such a *gentleman*," said Bessie.
"*Nu?*" A short Yiddish expression, indicative of incredulity, impatience, and a request for amplification, with also an undercurrent of contempt.

"He's never laid a finger on me."

It came as no surprise to my grandmother when, even after the act would have been legitimised by the duly executed marriage contract, no finger was appropriately laid. For the moment she contented herself with raised eyebrows, a suspicious sniff and the comment:

"Maybe, Bessie, such a *gentleman* you don't need."

It was a cruel twist of fate that Auntie Bessie, who so much loved children, and was invariably so much loved by them, should find herself married to a man who was totally impotent. Grandpa was enraged, and regretful that his suspicions hadn't been aroused by that high pitched voice. He urged his sister to obtain a "*get*" - justifiable ritual divorce. When she remained obdurate in her refusal - Bessie always had a mind of her own - it almost caused a rift between them. He certainly had no time for his brother-in-law.

The newly-weds set up house in what was to become the wrong end of the London Northern Line underground. Whereas about seven years later a large proportion of the Jewish East End community migrated to the opposite northern terminus, Lew and Bessie selected the southern extremity, Morden. All the rest of my mother's family, including eventually my widowed grandmother, settled with a huge number of Jewish families in the suburban ghetto of Edgware, oddly enough, with the exception of Uncle Pop, who bought a pretty house just a few doors away from his aunt.

When I was six years old, I had never been outside the city, and rarely seen a blade of grass. I was thrilled at the invitation to spend a week of the school summer holiday with Auntie Bessie, who actually had a garden! What I didn't know before my arrival was that she also had another guest.

Frustrated by the gap in her childless existence, the dear old thing had decided to foster orphaned children, and my companion was to be six-year old motherless Sylvia, who became my first sweetheart.

Cupid has claimed me three times as a victim, and here I was, at the age of six, the target of his dart. It was eleven years before I was struck with a second, and then at the age of twenty, smitten for the last time ... but with a sledge-hammer! And that wallop still hurts.

The week with Auntie Bessie proved to be a stay in paradise, and, in all honesty I have to say that it was to some extent due to the family joke, Uncle Lew. I visualise him now, esconced in his armchair in the corner, forever reading a newspaper, glasses perched on the tip of his long nose, or pushed up on his forehead, collarless - in the days when shirts were incomplete without a collar - and a stud peeping out of the top buttonhole. When he did become involved with the rest of us, he was invariably smiling. I grew to respect his great gentleness which held his marriage together. Figure of fun he may have been, but I would have liked to see some of his virtues in the character of my father.

Any activity Bessie undertook with children was inevitably a source of fun, and, either it was her influence or a genetic link between us, which had an effect on my career. In front of classrooms of teenagers or lecturing to postgraduate students studying for a teaching diploma, I found laughter to be a valuable catalyst to the learning process. However, here was I, at the tender age of six, about to receive my first lesson in sex.

It was hot in the garden where Sylvia and I were playing, and Bessie brought out a zinc tub, which I had previously seen filled with masses of homemade mustard pickles. She unceremoniously whipped off all our clothes and plunged us both, screaming, into the bath now containing cold water. Having more fun than either of us had ever known we soon began to show interest in each other's naked bodies. Amid peals of laughter Bessie named the unmentionable parts with extraordinary words of Polish or possibly her own invention. I'm not sure whether Sylvia had a "*khayospa*" or a "*khalloppel*", and, no doubt because I found them of less interest, I've no recollection of what she called my naughty bits, but I do remember that we found it all absolutely hilarious. I hasten to dispel any suspicion by the reader that we were involved in an activity, prompted by a perverse impulse on the part of a sexually frustrated woman. Bessie was as innocent as we were and had provided us with as wonderful an initiation into sex as I can imagine.

A few months later, Sylvia and I were bridesmaid and page-boy at my Aunt Bea's wedding, where we played at being husband and wife. Shortly after that, her widowed father reclaimed her, whisked her away into the unknown, and I never saw her again. Sad!

FOUR

"Boyfriends? What's all this with the 'boyfriends'?"

Booba was listening to a conversation about one of her granddaughters.

"This business with the 'boyfriends' I don't understand. By me a young man comes to the door - maybe with flowers, or chocolates - he's a *choossen* (prospective bridegroom). So what's this with *noch* another boyfriend? If he came to see *my* daughter I'd soon give the pair of them "boyfriend'!"

Wise as she was, my grandmother couldn't come to terms with mid twentieth century morality... not where her family was concerned.

"*Feh!*" would be her comment.

In her book, one could certainly have a free choice of future partner, but some conventions were obligatory. The one selected - provisionally, of course - would have to be formally introduced, and discreet enquiries made by the Jewish bush telegraph about antecedents; if these were acceptable, parents - when not already acquainted - would arrange a meeting... Boyfriends? Who knew from boyfriends?

The Goldbergs accepted whole-heartedly the young men chosen by their three daughters but, as far as my mother was concerned, only at first. The Shocket family background was good, and the young man's conduct in the early days - perfectly correct. But soon he said things which got right up Zeida's nose and Booba found that something about him didn't quite ring true. It wasn't long before he found himself *persona non grata*. Still, according to Grandma, he'd "cast a spell" - *kishoof* - over her daughter, and there was precious little could be done about it.

On the other hand, each of her other girls made a choice, of which she thoroughly approved at the time, and never grew to regret. Bee married Uncle Manny's best friend, Sender, loved and admired by all who had the good fortune to know him, and Sophie's husband, Dave, was sufficiently valued by Booba to be sent on her behalf to Paris on a rescue mission I'll write about later.

Shortly after her wedding, at which I was a page boy, and my first sweetheart, Sylvia, was a bridesmaid, Aunt Bee celebrated her birthday. It so happens that it occurs on the same day as mine. When he learned this, Uncle Sender, in a characteristic gesture, sent me the first birthday gift I had received in my life - and the most wonderful that I ever would. I still remember unrolling the brown paper round the frame of a magnificent two-wheel bicycle, and being thrilled to bits at the unique mother of pearl paint. He won a place in my heart for all time.

I'd like to tell you more about this remarkable man, but Irène is restless. It's time for me to prepare her for bed.

Things have been a little better... until tonight.

We're trying a new anti-hallucinatory drug - *Quetiepine* - in a small preliminary dose, and, although so far the effect on distressing illusions has been minimal, the drug acts most efficiently as a sleeping tablet, meaning that, instead of being roused by the tinkling of her handbell six or seven times a night, disturbances mercifully number just two or three.

It's now four o'clock in the morning. I've been enjoying a deep sleep, into which the bell has intruded, probably having been waved around for some time, because Irène has managed to get out of bed without assistance, and is staggering unsteadily towards the door.

"Where are you going?"

"Next door."

"?"

"You won't do anything about it, so I'm going to ring their bell, and ask them to help me."

One matter of concern is the nocturnal hour, and another is the fact that all she is wearing is a flimsy pair of knickers.

"My darling, it's two o'clock in the morning, and what on earth...?"

"I keep telling you to get rid of her, and you just lie there and ignore me."

"What... Who...?"

"That creature... That woman... That - thing - in the bed!"

So far we've been able to keep our difficulties private. Apart from seeing us use a wheelchair, and occasionally seeing Irène almost falling, our neighbours have scant knowledge of my wife's disability, and we'd very much like to keep it that way. but now....

Thankfully Irène is not sufficiently mobile to make it to the front door - which she couldn't unlock in any case - and I succeed in coercing her back into bed.

It goes against the grain for me to enter into her world of fantasies. I feel I am endorsing her belief in their flesh and blood existence, which I take such efforts to repudiate and disprove. But sometimes, either through weakness, lack of resourcefulness, or - as in this case - simply in order to get back to sleep - I am forced into collusion. So, without further discussion, I just put on my dressing gown, make a show of pulling nothing out of the bed, take a pretendedly resisting invisible woman by her non-existent scruff of the neck, and, ignoring her silent protests, unlock the door, tell her our flat is henceforth off limits, and throw her down the stairs.

Instead of showing gratitude or relief, Irène says:

"Now you've upset her, and she'll bring back the others."

"No she won't. I think I killed her."

That wasn't a clever remark, and it takes me a quarter of an hour to calm things down, tuck her in, give her a kiss, and discover that I'm now much too wide awake to go back to bed. So I make myself a cup of tea, and here I am at my desk, typing away like mad. There's no way I can try to sleep, and I'm not sure whether I'm happy or bloody annoyed that my beloved is apparently in dreamland, and smiling like a baby.

I am now in deep shit.

My beloved wife, who hadn't read a line of what I'd written so far, has just read the last few pages, and is furious. She says I make her sound like a raving lunatic, and insists that I remove all reference to her from the book, unless acceptable amendments are made. Now, for her benefit, I make this solemn declaration:

Apart from occasional hallucinations Irène is of sound mind, and quite able to take her part in a perfectly normal and intelligent conversation.

So, having shown her the foregoing half-truth, and resolved not to leave my manuscript lying around again, I shall pick up the story with another declaration - not for her, but for the reader:

With my hand on the bible I swear that my account of last night's nocturnal activity is the truth, the whole truth, and nothing but the truth.

I must admit to being more than a little concerned at the escalation of absurdity, so I refer to a leaflet I have on Parkinson's and Lewy Body Disease. Here's the bit I'm looking for:

"If, despite the balancing of drugs, hallucinations continue, this may sadly denote the rapid progression of dementia."

I start to think about her older sister, Ida, her descent into darkness, only relieved by final - merciful - oblivion; I think of the delightful girl Ida was when I first knew her, and the vegetable she became.

If I'm allowed only one adjective to describe her, it will have to be "immaculate."

I loved Ida dearly, and with good reason. Not only was she our staunchest ally in the earliest days of our courtship - yes, that's what we called it in those days before we had "relationships" - not only did she save Irène's life during the holocaust, she managed to keep my fiancée out of mischief during our prolonged separation after the war... no mean task, when it involved protecting the virtue of a gorgeous blonde in a city intoxicated with its freedom after Nazi occupation, and teeming with randy young American soldiers.

Ida could be led through a field of manure, and emerge smelling of roses; she remained untouched by filth, be it material or moral, and her inner purity was matched by the appearance she presented. She was chief salesgirl in a prestigious lingerie boutique in the Rue des Fripiers, and unaffectedly dressed like a model. I never saw her with a stain on her blouse, a crease in her clothing, or a lock of raven hair out of place, and the feature I remember most was her radiant smile. My wife has the same shape to her lips, and the identical smile, which lights up the world on a gloomy day, and makes your heart turn over.

It is a cruel irony that about ten years ago she was smitten with an alarmingly progressive disease causing severe dementia, and fate dealt her a vicious blow, when this most fastidious of women fell victim to double incontinence, was reduced to wearing nappies, and became oblivious to the condition of her hair, what she was wearing, understood nothing of what she was told, and didn't even recognise the sisters she'd loved and protected.

Shortly after the liberation of Belgium Ida was expecting to marry the young man who'd been her first - and only - boy-friend during the war ... much to the disgust of her father, who found it difficult to accept for his exquisitely refined daughter a suiter with the manners of a pig. It was no consolation to Chaskiel that on the credit side, Bernard was the soul of generosity. In conditions of extreme poverty the shoemaker and his wife had raised five daughters fit to grace the court of a monarch, and here was this...

"He's very generous," I said, pouring oil on the troubled waters.

"Oui, Michel," grunted my future father-in-law - we were good friends - and then added in Yiddish:

"Like a cow which gives milk, then kicks over the bucket.'

The proposed union was very reminiscent to that of my parents, equally unwelcome to grandpa and grandma Goldberg, and, like my mother, Ida appeared not only to submit to repeated verbal abuse, but actually respond with loyalty - and something I'll never understand - a perverse kind of affection. Does this kind of man have some supernatural power over women?

In stark contrast to the sophistication of his fiancée, Bernard had manners which would discredit a tramp. His chain smoking (of foul Belgian cigarettes) between, before, after and during copious meals and snacks, caused him to cough, hawk and spit indiscriminately, provoked a constant thirst, which made him drink whatever liquid was available, and consequently over-stimulated his bladder. So he seemed to be forever urged by an irresistible necessity to piss, wherever he happened to be, and whomever he happened to be with. The most favoured receptacles for the public voiding of his bladder were, for some reason, the hub-caps of parked cars ... vehicles inexplicably selected for their pristine condition. He'd stop in mid stride, swivel to the curb, and, regardless of dismayed companions or an intrigued audience, bestow his gift on the chosen wheel.

Now this may have been all very well in his native Brussels, where, after all, they have their famous Menneke Piss on prominent display, but when, on a visit to me in London, Bernard relinquished Ida's arm as we were strolling down a crowded Kensington High Street, swivelled, gazed admiringly at a gleaming Rolls Royce and began unzipping his fly, I was moved to intervene - in the nick of time. I observed as tactfully as possible that this was not a tolerable form of behaviour in the streets of London, whereupon he shrugged his shoulders, spat on the pavement and said, in an inappropriate tone of contempt:

"*Oh, vous autres Anglais!*"

As far as he was concerned, all Englishmen were misers, hypocrites, over submissive to authority, undernourished and - above all - sexually naive.

Before we became engaged and Irène informed him that, after graduation I intended to train for a teaching career, he was outraged. No sister-in-law of his would he permit to slip into a life of penury and starvation. No, she had to forget about her English soldier. Out of uniform he'd be shorn of attraction, a nobody, and she'd find herself washing the underpants of a pauper in some miserable hole... No, there was no need to cry... not while he was around, and it so happened that he had a good friend in Antwerp - a diamond merchant, no less - who walked around with more wealth in his coat pocket than a lousy teacher could hope to make in a whole year. Fortunately I had Ida fighting in my corner, and, although it was uncharacteristic of her to disagree with anything said by her prospective lord and master, she secretly told her sister to follow her heart, which Irène insists was what she intended to do anyway.

In fact Bernard ought to have eaten his words, when, after a few years of financial hardship - offset by marital bliss, enhanced by the arrival of wonderful children - I was enabled to augment my pathetic teacher's salary to a level he might consider acceptable by having a series of books published. Ironically, about the same time, his diamond merchant friend suffered irreversible brain damage, bludgeoned by a ruffian who relieved him of the jewellery he was carrying.

Incidentally I am happy to reassure the reader that eventually my delightful sister-in-law married not Bernard, but a dapper little gentleman called Maurice, who was one of the most generous men I have ever known, and, incidentally, who, notwithstanding a period of comparative poverty on my part, always evinced towards his schoolteacher brother-in-law the utmost respect and affection.

Despite the dire forebodings of Maurice's predecessor, my choice of career remained firm. However, before launching into an account of my own contribution to education - don't be alarmed, I've no intention of doing any such thing - I'd like to reminisce a little about my early schooldays and childhood ...in Docklands, to be precise... at 100 West India Dock Road.

"The Bargain Stores" was the uninspired name my father gave to his shop. The parent establishment, founded and more profitably run by my grandfather, was near to London Docks in Leman Street. Both were "seamens' outfitters". Grandpa concentrated on clothing, but my father widened his scope to cater for all of the incoming sailors' needs. Some of the merchandise I found intriguing: frilly sets of ladies' underwear as gifts for wives, sweethearts and the numerous prostitutes who flocked to the pubs in search of drunks who'd come ashore, their pockets bulging with swollen pay-packets. Openly displayed in the shop were cartons of condoms, which sold like hot cakes, and, for even more questionable use, handsome sheath knives, and discreetly concealed knuckle dusters!

I never had the slightest interest in buying and selling, but was fascinated by the clientèle. As ships docked, the shop was often packed with crew members from all corners of the globe, of all nationalities, with skins of all imaginable shades of white, yellow, brown and black. My father had no sales staff, and, whenever the shop was full, my mother was expected to help. Strangely enough, even the coarsest sailors, who'd already over indulged in Charlie Brown's, the pub just a few yards away, behaved well in her presence. She was indeed beautiful, and had a personality which brought out the best in all men - except unfortunately the one she'd married.

Our premises were in Limehouse, about a hundred yards from the huge gates of West India Docks. We were in the heart of Chinatown, with the infamous Pennyfields just across the road, the street with a reputation dating back into the nineteenth century, for opium dens, secret societies, gambling, robbery and murder. It was actually a warren of tiny hovels, apparently filled with dozens of Chinese, all the men smoking, and all the women chattering shrilly. There was a persistent clatter of Mah Jong tiles, and pungent, rather sickening smells of unfamiliar cooking emanating from dark, mysterious interiors, into which, it goes without saying, I never ventured. Occasionally I chose to walk through Pennyfields on my way to Hebrew classes. The experience was both exciting and frightening. Of course I never came to any harm. It was on the alternative route that I was waylaid by a gang of young white thugs, and beaten up with taunts of "Jewboy."

This couldn't have happened to my uncles, brought up in the area of Leman Street, where my grandfather's business was located, and *non-Jews* were the minority group. The Goldbergs were right in the centre of the Jewish quarter, close to Hessel Street market, which specialised in kosher food, where ragged old men bearing sacks and baskets chanted: "*Drei a penny bagel!*" Bagels three a penny!

Herrings were sold out of barrels, chickens on barrows and stalls, fish of a dozen varieties packed in ice and even carp still alive in water. Booba loved shopping there, and, when bombed out of her East End home in the war, she was almost forcibly moved to the relative security of Edgware, she suffered severe withdrawal pains, missing the hubbub of her beloved market and the companionship of former neighbours. Her comments about the new environment were in venomous Yiddish that would defy translation, particularly after the death of my grandfather which occurred at that time, and aggravated her feelings of isolation.

She had brought up eight children cocooned within the security of their East End ghetto. On the other hand, when I went to my primary school in neighbouring Poplar - there was no school in Limehouse - I found only one other Jewish pupil. He happened to be in my class. His name was Max Glassman, and we became close friends. Sadly we went on to separate grammar schools, and haven't seen each other for over sixty years. If you read this, Max, and hopefully are still with us, please get in touch.

We actually *lived* in "The Bargain Stores." Our main room was separated from the shop by a glass door. Since trade was sporadic, my father would inflict his bullying presence on the family for a large part of the day, looking into the shop for the odd customer and woe betide us if he'd been disturbed without making a sale. He was dependent on incoming ships for making a living, so the shop was either deserted for hours or swarming with seamen, all trying to be served at the same time.

During quiet periods - and that's how it was most of the time, while the boss was eating, going to the loo, or simply having a nap, I was frequently told to "watch the door," in other words stare through the glass on the look-out for the rare customer, and call my father. I hated this chore, and, except when it was freezing cold, preferred sitting out in the shop with a book.

If I felt unobserved and secure, I would sometimes rummage among the more intriguing items of stock. Although sorely tempted, I dared not unwrap any of the condoms - in those days better known as "French letters." Then one day I surreptitiously removed a packet of three from a half empty carton, and slipped it into my pocket. Feeling guilt written all over my face, I kept a low profile until I locked myself within the privacy of the bathroom cum lavatory on the first floor. Of course I tore open the wrapper and tried one on. I must have been very young at the time, because I remember how it hung pathetically loose from a very limp and insignificant organ, and I wondered if condoms came in sizes, and for what kind of a giant - or perhaps even a horse - that particular item had been designed. Terrified of being discovered, at the earliest opportunity I disposed of the article, which seemed to be burning a hole in my pocket, down a drain.

Behind the living room was a small kitchen, where my mother conjured up wonderful meals, and much of the food was kept in the backyard, in what we called a "safe." It was a roughly hewn wooden cupboard, faced with wire mesh, and was a fore-runner of our first refrigerator, acquired years later. In the same back yard was an outside lavatory, mainly for the use of our tenants, who occupied the third floor, above our own bathroom and two bedrooms.

My most persistent memory of our home is of the winter cold. Floors were either of bare wood or covered with linoleum. Needless to say there was no central heating, and the dark corridors were full of drafts. There was also a coal cellar, the door of which we had to pass to reach the stairs. My mother and I gave it as wide a berth as possibly. I was ridiculously scared of ghosts. Mum was justifiably terrified of mice, which we kept at bay with two cats.

At the top of the gloomy staircase were two tiny rooms occupied by our tenants, a policeman and his wife. He stood well over six feet, and, accentuated by his uniform, had an enormous belly, which he used to shunt forward whichever hapless individual he happened to be reprimanding. This gigantic, red-faced and bewhiskered copper was stationed at Limehouse Police Station, about a hundred yards down the opposite side of West India Dock Road. His wife earned part of her weekly rent cleaning for us. She was a shrivelled up skinny woman, hook- nosed, thin lipped and sharp featured - needing only the broom to complete her startlingly witch-like appearance. We referred to her only as "Mackie" the name given her by my baby brother as an abbreviation for Mrs. Mackintosh.

There were nights when Alan and I would cling together in terror, as the couple in the room above ours became over-active, and Mackie began screaming - not, I hasten to add, in the throes of wild amorous abandon.
"No, Alec, no!" she yelled. "I'm sorry, Alec. I'm sorry!"

Her shrieks were invariably accompanied by strange noises, which we later understood to be the sounds of thrashing the wretched woman with a heavy belt until her screams died down to a pitiful whimper. One morning, after a particularly noisy session, she was sporting a black eye.

Then there were nights when our slumbers were disturbed for a different reason. Occasionally the front door bell would ring in the small hours. A ship had docked, the crew come ashore with money to burn, and my father was only too anxious to relieve them of a portion of their accumulated wages. So he'd pull trousers on over his pyjamas, and hurry down to open the front door, followed shortly afterwards by my mother. They would then take more money in two hours than they could sometimes achieve in two weeks, and this really was good news for the family. My father would be in a good mood for at least two days, and we'd be spared the fear of abuse - for a while.

FIVE

Limehouse Church was situated about fifteen minutes walk from our home. I must confess that when I was told it was a creation by Christopher Wren I was unimpressed. Perhaps today my more sophisticated eye might view the landmark with more admiration, but, at the age of seven, I derived no aesthetic pleasure from its square cut design. I was much more fascinated by the building opposite, to which I would regularly make my way like a homing pigeon. It was a veritable palace of delights - the public library, and became my refuge until I left the area at the age of fifteen. And when I was over fifty, engaged in research for a thesis, some of the happiest hours of my life were spent at the British Library in the centre of London. If I close my eyes, and concentrate, I can smell its dust-laden atmosphere, and have my finger-tips tingle with the sensual pleasure of carefully handling the frayed, yellowing edges of ancient pages containing the thoughts - still fresh - of wise men long gone.

Of the many acts of vandalism committed by the Nazis, not the least barbaric was their burning of books.

I remember that, at the funeral of Uncle Abe - a worthy gentleman I'll introduce to you in due course - a dignitary of the synagogue poured into his grave a heap of old books, which, like the man being buried, had reached the end of their highly valued life. It would be unseemly to consign them to a rubbish dump. I found this to be a charming Jewish tradition, whereby the ultimate respect is shown equally to a righteous man and the source of his wisdom.

Whenever I've selected a place to live, a prime consideration has been the location of the nearest library. When I was attending primary school, my tastes were chiefly devoted to literature where the setting was in boys' public schools. Needless to say, in no way did they reflect my own education at that time.

I had many reasons for hating school. The one which springs most readily to mind was the appalling condition of the lavatories. In an area which consisted mainly of slums, the school itself was a gigantic slum. Its toilet facilities were a public disgrace, crudely constructed, and inviting abuse. There was a constant supply of organic material to begin with, not always consigned to its appropriate receptacles, and this, with the addition of all sorts of other debris, created a colourful - but noxious - mass, which might perhaps qualify for an award in a contemporary art exhibition, but sensitive souls avoided like the plague. Not once, during my five years at this establishment, did I permit my delicate bottom to make contact with the heavily encrusted seating accommodation available. One afternoon, however, I paid the price for my fastidious refusal to use the school lavatory. After exercising heroic restraint all afternoon, when I was half way home, nature took command. In the circumstances it was with the utmost difficulty that I ran the rest of the way, to arrive home in disgrace and, as they say in Yiddish "*mit fille hoisen*".

Another reason for my hatred of school was the daily ordeal of "assembly."

"Hands together, eyes closed."

For me, and the one other Jewish boy in the school, this simple act was a betrayal. It was all very well for everybody else. They were Christian, but we hadn't been conditioned to pray that way. The heresy was further compounded by the prayers and hymns which followed. The name of Jesus kept cropping up - and as far we were concerned, to utter it was a dire sin. Throughout the ordeal I kept my eyes wide open and my lips sealed, except when a member of staff looked in my direction, when I would mouth the words without uttering a sound.

The very beginning of the day determined my isolation, duly confirmed by the remainder of the session.

At that time, apart from books from the library, I was an avid reader of two comic periodicals: "The Gem," and "The Magnet." Normal conversation between the public school characters contained phrases like:

"I say, you chaps..."

Terminology included the "mater", the "pater", the "beak", "prep", and everybody played "rugger."

I never heard any of this in my school. More familiar

would be:

"Oy! 'Oo's nicked me bleedin' ruler?"

When they misbehaved in class, sons of the privileged received an "imposition." Our lot had the benefit of "a clump round the ear'ole."

I can't recall the inmates of Whitefriars or Greyfriars suffering the indignity of a "head inspection." Regularly a fearsome nurse in starched white uniform descended upon us, and we lined up to have our hair examined. Wherever infestation was discovered - not infrequently - the affected child experienced the ignominy of being stood to one side while the examination proceeded. Fortunately I never had to endure the disgrace of segregation, or I'd have died of shame. I attributed my immunity from opprobrium to my mother's assiduous shampooing, and regular attention with a small black object of torture called a "tooth comb." Only in later years did I learn that I'd simply been lucky, and not all the children I avoided after the inspection were necessarily "dirty." Head lice have a tendency to leap from one head to another, and are no respecters of persons.

With the majority of children coming from impoverished working class families, Thomas Street Junior School provided a sound basic education as far as numeracy and literacy were concerned, exacted respect where it was due towards a conscientious staff, but did little to fill the cultural void created in most of their pupils' homes - except in one respect.

As far as we were concerned, the headmaster was just one step down from King George and two from God. He had the capacity to exercise an enormous influence, when he had us all assembled in the hall. The man could have introduced us to Mozart, shown us reproductions of great art, read poetry...

He did none of these things. One wall he covered with a massive map of the world, a considerable portion of which was coloured red. These areas he proudly presented as "The British Empire."

One particularly distressing event which occurred at this time was what was probably an entirely *unnecessary* operation - the removal of my tonsils. In those days a tonsillectomy was performed as a routine procedure, in as perfunctory a manner as the basic vaccination against smallpox - in my case, at the Poplar Clinic. With about half a dozen other terrified children I sat, awaiting my turn on a bench outside the operating theatre. We were all enveloped in coarse, brown woollen blankets, unaccompanied by anyone except a sour faced nurse. She did nothing to allay our fears. Nobody had given us any idea of what to expect. All we understood was that something was going to be cut out of our throats.

"Will it hurt?" one little girl asked the nurse.

"You'll just be a bit sore afterwards," the woman answered curtly.

At that precise moment a shrill scream came from inside the door. No doubt it was only a cry of fear, but we didn't know that. I exchanged an eloquent look with the boy next to me, and he started to shake visibly. I decided to do a runner. When only a week old, I'd allowed them to slice the end off my penis. At that time I had no say in the matter. But I was a big boy now. I got to my feet, but the nurse must have anticipated the move, and forced me back on the bench.

"Don't be such a coward!" she hissed.

At that moment an unconscious child was wheeled out of the operating room on a gurney.

"Blimey! 'E's dead!" exclaimed my shivering neighbour.

I was next in line.

I've always suffered from claustrophobia, and, when, without any explanation or warning a mask was thrust over my face I panicked. When I kicked out with my legs as hard as I could, I'd like to think I caught one of my "assailants" on the nose before blacking out.

For months after this barbaric assault, according to my mother I was more or less a nervous wreck. One lasting effect has been that I like to give doctors and hospitals a wide berth. It was probably a coincidence, but since my experience at the clinic I started having occasional - and fortunately minor - attacks of what I later knew to be temporal lobe epilepsy. Scared stiff of surgical intervention I never told a soul about them. They followed a set pattern: the first sign was a feeling of unease, followed by a unique sinking feeling, and a strong sensation of "déjà vu." My eyes would invariably fix on some object, which would then be seen as through the wrong end of a telescope. These "funny turns" usually only lasted a few minutes, and had, at that time, no after effects. Two far more serious "turns" would occur years later, and I'll describe them in due course.

"Did the children enjoy the chicken soup I brought yesterday?" I ask.

Mandy answers with a broad grin.

"What's the joke? You didn't give it to the dog?"

"You know dad, you're turning into a real Jewish mother."

Interesting thought. I suppose I've been conditioned by the women in my life. For my mother and my grandmother - neither of whom was given to effusive displays of affection, food was an offering - an expression of love, and, as far as Irène was concerned, the offering took on an almost religious quality. Her own mother had risked her life under the Nazi occupation to obtain scraps of pathetic nourishment out of which she magically conjured up extraordinarily tasty family meals. I always found the women's attitude towards a basically simple animal function amusing, but now, according to my daughter, I've acquired it.

Before my wife became ill I never boiled an egg, or felt the slightest urge to do anything constructive in the kitchen, which was always Irène's exclusive territory, where I set foot at my peril.

Irène and I are incompatible in so many ways that even we can't understand how our marriage has survived for over half a century. Presumably the few things we have in common are powerful enough to outweigh the differences. I'd like to feel that the links are entirely spiritual, based on a kind of pre-destined union of souls. Coming down to earth, however, I am reluctant to admit that one of the tightest bonds between us could be quite mundane - a passion for food.

Tentatively, I made my first few meals in the microwave. I graduated to the hob, then the grill, and eventually the oven, bought a cookery book, then another... This was fun, especially when the rest of my family began to clamour for "grandpa's cooking',' and grandpa had found a new hobby.

This is one area in which my present attitude has been pre-conditioned by childhood experience, but in others, early memories have pushed me in the opposite direction. Having been abused by my father, I was incapable of ever raising a hand to my children; as I seethed at similar treatment meted out to my mother, hopefully I was prepared to behave differently to my own wife. Violence in my childhood home in no way impelled me towards violence outside it. On the contrary, I've always gone out of my way to avoid it - even opting out of contact sports. Service in the army during the war did not "make a man of me," but merely confirmed my aversion to fighting - except in a clear-cut situation of self defence. Another sphere in which personal experience as a child had a completely negative effect was my education. I hated school. So it may be a matter of surprise that I spent my entire professional career teaching. My experience as a pupil could be compared to the years I spent in the army during the war; in both situations I felt like the poor sod behind bars scratching each slowly passing day on the wall, waiting... waiting... waiting for release. And whoever heard of an old lag becoming a screw when he'd eventually got out of nick? Yet, on reflection, it could be an ideal way of perpetuating the horrors of our penal system. But I have to say that I never had the slightest intention of inflicting on unsuspecting children the tyranny and boredom I had endured under the tutelage of certain sadists, cynics, time-servers and - in one or two cases - plain lunatics.

I began my secondary education with one serious mistake - the choice of school. Two of my uncles, Mike and Ulla, had been pupils at the Central Foundation Grammar School, familiarly known as "Cowper Street", where it was located. Ulla Goldberg left quite a reputation behind him;

he'd been an outstanding wicket-keeper and batsman, an excellent footballer, a prefect, and a good student who'd gone on to study medicine. He'd been equally well liked by staff and students. I knew he'd been happy at the school, and, foolishly, I hoped to follow in his footsteps, not realising that, much as I would have liked to be like him, I was an entirely different kind of human being.

It was something of a miracle that I ever qualified for a grammar school place. In those days we had to pass the notorious eleven plus examination in both English and Arithmetic in order to "win a scholarship" and avoid relegation to schools taught by non-graduates, following a curriculum which could never lead to education beyond the age of sixteen, or any hope of a professional future. My problem was that, although I was considered outstanding in English - having won a national award in essay writing at the age of ten - I happened to be a complete idiot in arithmetic.

"How are you getting on in maths?" Uncle Ulla asked me a few months before the decisive test.

"Fine," said I. "I'm now doing pounds, shillings and ounces."

Whereupon my uncle took me in hand, gave me a few weeks of coaching, and, doubtless by the skin of my teeth, I contrived to satisfy the examiners.

My grand-daughter, Jo, is fortunate that her brain does not function like mine, which operates smoothly on the literary side, but, when called upon to deal with any form of numeracy, is quite dysfunctional. Jo has the kind of all-round brain which satisfied all her teachers, of arts and sciences alike. I was cursed with a one-sided intellect which put me at the top of the class in English, French and German, would have done the same for me in art, music, history and classics, if only I'd been taught them - either properly or at all - whereas I was near the bottom of the class in the great volume of mathematics and science with which I was bombarded. This was the area in which Central Foundation School specialised, turning out one or two famous scientists, a creditable number of consultants, scores of general practitioners, hundreds of accountants, and even a criminal or two. When however I was eligible to enter the sixth form, pupils were offered not one single advanced course in Modern Languages or English.

At the age of eleven, in all innocence, I chose this completely inappropriate educational establishment, encouraged by my father, because about ninety five percent of its pupils were Jewish.

Unfortunately for me, Art was taught in the first two years only, and I was unlucky enough to be in a class where the master teaching this subject was a miserable, uncouth and completely unimaginative old man, who was actually in charge of woodwork. During the entire two years we were never issued with paints, but pencils - "H" if you please, not even "HB" - and given "still life" subjects, which had no life at all: namely chairs, tables, cones, cylinders, cubes and spheres...and to prove to us that he was completely mad, on one occasion, when I think he had spent the lunch hour imbibing too heavily in the local pub, he staggered into the classroom, took off his battered, rainsodden hat, flung it on the table, and growled:

"Right, boys. Draw my hat."

Incensed, I followed his instruction, but, beneath his misshapen headgear I added a caricature of the silly old bugger, bulbous nose, huge, drooping moustache, great, bulging eyes... I can picture him today... and I knew full well that he'd never even glance at the work, which did, however get passed round the class, was much admired, and marked the beginning of my reputation as a caricaturist. The subjects were always members of staff, invariably irreverently executed, from my favourite seat, at the back row, in the corner. Incidentally, when I was engaged in the training of teachers, I advised my students:

"Pay particular attention to involve the pupils in the back row - especially in the corners. "

I was speaking from experience. "Set a thief..." as the saying goes. To be a good disciplinarian, you need to be either an incorrigible sadist, or to have been a right little sod yourself - with a warped sense of humour.

There were two masters, rather like Tweedle-dee and

Tweedle-dum, who taught - or went through the motions of teaching - maths and history respectively. Both were short, bald, pot-bellied, and with tiny white moustaches; physically alike, and equally bad teachers. They did however have quite different personalities. Mr. Constable, the historian, was aloof, took no interest in his pupils or their work, and was apparently content with having the silence of his lessons broken solely by occasional sighs of sheer boredom, and the scraping of pens, as we slavishly copied verbatim the notes he wrote on the blackboard for the entire length of each lesson. There were headings, dates, underlinings, unexplained events, which left no impression on our imagination, had no bearing on our lives... with no explanation of the society which produced them, and no discussion of their positive or negative effect on civilisations, past, present and future, depersonalised wars... fact upon fact, with no question of ideas, and not even an anecdote.

But, even if he bored the pants off us, the old codger was polite, whereas the maths teacher, who could have passed as his twin brother, had the manners of a pig. On one occasion he was standing behind me, at the back of the class, where he had squeezed himself, unnoticed, into the corner. I was putting the finishing touches to a caricature of the gentleman in question, exaggerating his pot belly, and with his trousers round his ankles:

"No wonder you're such a duffer!" he roared, frightening the life out of me, before gleefully giving me a detention.

"What are you laughing at, Shaps?" he asked my friend, Cyril. "What are you going to be when you grow up?"

"An actor, sir."

The old fool put his hands on his hips, his belly wobbling as he guffawed: "Haw, haw, haw!"

He was senile at the time, so presumably never lived to see my friend's name on programmes featuring Laurence Olivier, John Gielgud and Nigel Hawthorne, among others.

There is a belief that self-inflicted pain, discomfort and unnecessary suffering are good for the soul. That would be no problem if the loonies who held the idea got together on a remote island, and had a great time being utterly miserable. Unfortunately, not content with their own discontent, some of them decided to make thousands of kids - who might otherwise have enjoyed a happy childhood - as wretched as possible, and established prep schools and public schools for the sons of elite English families. First of all they were completely segregated from the female population, partly for fear that they might be distracted from concentrating on Pythagoras and geometric angles towards curves of a more exciting nature, but also in order to establish a more monastic environment, in which thrashing is the favoured means of developing social behaviour.

Limping in the wake of their more privileged brethren, boys' secondary schools in my day favoured the cane as the best legitimate method of maintaining discipline, although many less patient masters found a clump across the ear a more immediate and convenient resource.

Reminded of slippering, clouting and caning, whenever there is a discussion of discipline, many former victims will proclaim:

"Never did me any harm."

But they merely confirm the self-perpetuating nature of cruelty to children.

In the case of my own Central Foundation School for boys, the headmaster, Mr. Cedric Gibbons, whom most of us considered certifiably insane, made a hobby of fondling and thrashing boys' backsides.

I was about to elaborate on this theme, but thinking and writing about schooldays reawakens the longing - so badly suppressed at the time - for female company. Rain is pounding relentlessly on the window, the sky threatens to be a dirty gray for the rest of the day, and I need cheering up.

I'm going to join Irène in the bedroom for an afternoon nap.

She's half asleep, and looks beautiful From her peaceful expression I can tell that there are no unwelcome visitors - the old woman constantly brushing her long, white hair, isn't in the room, and there are none of her friends in their smelly clothes, no insects, no strangers in the bed.

We're alone.

There's no need to talk, repeat and rephrase sentences until they're understood, and there are no urgent requests... Irène starts up as there is clap of thunder, so I snuggle up to comfort her; we cuddle close, she smiles and her eyes close. I know she'll be fast asleep in seconds, and so will I...

The social worker suggested that she has an extended stay in a care centre - "to give you a break." No way. Nobody's getting my job. The social worker doesn't understand that not only does Irène need me. I need her. It seems absurd even to me, but I know that I missed her before we even met.

Outside our room the storm rages.

We don't care.

Half an hour later my wife is still sound asleep. I doubt whether she'll wake up before tea-time, so I tiptoe into my study and return to reminisce about my crazy headmaster.

Whenever the urge came upon him, he used to come out into the playground, covertly cast an experienced eye over the rear ends of the boys, make a selection, sidle up to the unsuspecting youth of his choice, fondle his arse, and, if it came up to his expectation, he'd lead the youngster to his study. Such was the old man's reputation, that the boy knew what to expect. Therefore, usually without persuasion, he'd place himself where indicated, present his posterior to receive the customary "six of the best," after which he'd be invited to rest his sore backside on a cushioned chair, and be regaled with tea and biscuits.

Amazingly the madman was able to indulge himself freely in this way for years, filling in the periods when there was a shortage of actual malefactors to be thrashed -- to keep his hand in, so to speak. Then one memorable day he picked the wrong boy.

"Dodger" Cohen was very nicely rounded - all over, and when the old man's gaze fell upon that beautifully moulded rear end, his eyes lit up. He obviously didn't know that Dodger was the most mischievous boy in the school, who, miraculously, had never been sent for a caning. The head went through his usual ritual; he prepared the tea and biscuits, smilingly invited the lad to take up the position, and selected a cane from his selection. He flexed the instrument, raised it with the flourish of an expert swordsman, and, at that precise moment, with admirable timing, Dodger farted.

He didn't get his tea and biscuits, but he didn't get walloped either.

The news went round the school like wildfire, and even the staff must have got wind of it, because, henceforth, even the strictest masters called him "Dodger" instead of Cohen - and let him get away with everything short of murder.

Early evenings have become a bad time. Yesterday was particularly upsetting. Irène hadn't spoken a word for about an hour. She looked strange, her expression fluctuating between sadness and something worse. I'd never seen her look like that before. Her mouth - one of her most beautiful features - had slipped to one side, was slightly agape, the jaw slack.

And I'd seen that look before... though I hardly dared admit it to myself. It was in the geriatric ward of Napsbury mental hospital. Was this, I asked myself, the beginning of a new phase in her illness? One that I've been dreading?

Then the awful look disappeared. Perhaps my imagination was playing me tricks. But she was frowning.

"Is anything worrying you?" I asked.

Then a complete stranger turned her head towards me.

"Where have you been all day?"

"Right here. With you."

She shook her head.

"You're lying - always lying to me."

For the next few minutes she continued talking complete nonsense.

"I never knew you were capable of such things."

"What things?"

"I know it was you who brought their cases in here."
"What the...?"
"How could you do that? Encourage them to move in? Into my home?"

My protestations of innocence fell on deaf ears, and she was now looking at me with open hostility, something new, and which I didn't like at all.

"You planned everything with them, and ..." she went on with a hysterical lift to her voice, "they're taking over the whole place!"

Vainly I tried to explain that this was all a delusion, but from her eyes I realised that it was a waste of breath. She wasn't listening. Then she started to cry. I went over to put my arms round her, but she pushed me away. First I had a sinking feeling of loss. Where was my darling Irène? Then there was a surge of anger against the impostor sitting in my wife's chair. It was our first period of full scale dementia, and one of the worst experiences of my life.

When we were in bed and she lay fast asleep, I tossed and turned. Was this how it would be from now on? Could I take it?

Now, this morning, she's her old self, actually singing in the bathroom. It's as though last night never happened.

But it did.

The singing stops.

I have the urge to go and hold her close. Looking deep into her eyes, I wonder: do I detect a dying light within them?

Although some of the teachers were awful, many we respected, some we admired, and a few we even liked.

Whatever else they may have forgotten, surviving pre-war pupils of C.F.S will remember our German master, Johnny Keegan, a veritable legend. He was not exactly a hopeless disciplinarian; it would be kinder to say that he had an exceptionally high threshold of tolerance. His lessons were riotous. We did what we liked, but, such was the genius of this man that most of the voluminous noise we made was in German. Johnny had a passionate love of the language, and particularly its wonderful lyric poetry. He taught from text books he had written himself, and which were years ahead of their time, but he was especially fond of having his classes recite in chorus - incidentally the best way to teach the oddities of German word order, where the *verb at the end of the sentence comes*. Poems of Heine and Goethe we declaimed, chanted and sang to invented melodies, accompanied by a thunderous percussion accompaniment on the desk tops.

Mr. Keegan, a charming Irishman, had the perfect teutonic image: stockily built, bull-necked, with close cropped hair and a wide, flowing moustache. My caricatures of him could have been of von Hindenburg.

We began learning German as a second foreign language at the age of thirteen, and nearly all of us had the advantage - before we started - of a good working vocabulary, namely in Yiddish, which is about eighty percent a bastardised form of German. Off to a flying start, we found it enormous fun to shout Yiddish like Hitler.

Whenever one of us overstepped the wide boundaries of acceptable behaviour, Johnny would point a stubby forefinger at the offender, and bark out his surname, reduced to one syllable: Silverberg became Sberg - with a silent "b" - Yadgarov would be Grof - without the 'g", and I... Shocket... alas, abridged to Shkit - with "k" silent as in "knitting." Inevitably "shit" was taken up in chorus by my delighted classmates, but, to my everlasting surprise and relief, the abbreviated version of my surname never stuck. Fate hasn't always treated me badly.

We played up the dear old chap mercilessly, yet, when he made a farewell speech from the platform on his retirement he broke down in tears. Johnny, bless him, loved his subject, loved teaching the language in its most sublime lyrical form, and - inexplicably - loved all the hundreds of boys, whose appalling behaviour could have driven a lesser mortal to suicide or murder.

One other member of staff I could never forget was Mr. J.E.D. Hollingworth - Holly - a perfect gentleman, accomplished actor - he was still performing on the amateur stage in his eighties - inspired teacher, and generally terrific guy. He didn't just teach Shakespeare, he acted it with us, and my friend, Cyril Shaps, and I were often his stars. I was usually cast as the clown.

One day he auditioned us both to recite a lengthy monologue in front of a wider audience than we usually had in the school plays. We read the piece twice.

"I can't chose between you," said Holly. "We'll have to toss for it."

Cyril won, of course. Who knows? If the penny had landed "tails" instead of "heads" perhaps I'd now be a member of the National Theatre, whereas Cyril would have gone to Cambridge instead of R.A.D.A. and ended up teaching. Strange how the turn of a coin can affect your whole life.

SIX

The phone rings. It doesn't wake Irène, and I hurry next door into the study to take the call without disturbing her. Fay is on the line. She and Harold are two of our oldest and dearest friends of over thirty years standing, and it was a matter of overwhelming joy to us when their son and our daughter married. Unfortunately the marriage was short-lived - but that's another story.

Harold was recently diagnosed with Alzheimer's disease.

A few weeks ago Irène and I were moved to tears when we saw him - formerly a progressive and innovative headmaster - dancing in a circle of fellow sufferers, with the facial expression of a young child. Fay and I often talk on the phone, deriving some comfort - most of the time - discussing shared problems, and she says I can usually make her laugh. Tonight I am less successful. She's phoning from the hall.

"Harold's asleep in front of the television," she says.
"So's Irène."
"He can't follow a film."
"Neither can Irène."
"I'm fed up."
"Me too."
"You're supposed to cheer me up."

I can't find an answer, and our conversation goes from bad to worse, culminating in:

"You tell me, Michael. What have we got to live for?"
Silence.
"What is there to look forward to? Yesterday he asked me: 'Who's Ashley?' when I mentioned him. He's our grandson, for God's sake..."
That hurts.
"It's like dealing with a child..."
"Well, perhaps that's the only way to..."
"No, it isn't. You know a child will grow up, understand more... not less. I feel I'm in a tunnel, with nothing at the end."

Without conviction I start talking about research into the rejuvenation of brain cells.

"Do you really think they'll last that long? Or we will?"

I must give Fay a ring this morning, and tell her what I should have said last night, but couldn't think of at the time.

Irène slept beautifully, woke up with a smile, enjoyed breakfast on our balcony, looking at a radiant blue sky, and agreed to make the most of a lovely morning, by a walk round our beloved Aquadrome nearby, where the paths are smooth enough to favour wheelchairs, leading round lakes and through shaded woods. The fact that this beauty spot is within walking distance and delightful in all seasons is one of the reasons we moved to our new flat, and I look forward to the time when Irène will be able to abandon her chair, and walk alongside me as in previous years, venturing further afield, where the pathways are too uneven for wheelchair access.

We had a wonderful walk. It was too early for crowds, the birds were singing away like mad, the surface of the lakes had scarcely a ripple, and shimmered merrily in the glorious sunshine, a family of swans floated by, followed by a mother goose and her tiny goslings... It was just perfect.

So I ring Fay, and tell her what a wonderful world we have. This morning she's in a more receptive mood, and says finally:

"I suppose we just have to stop complaining about all the things we can't do, and concentrate on those we can."

I couldn't improve on that.

All that was on Wednesday. Today is Thursday, one of the two days a week when Irène goes to her day centre in Edgware - a godsend. To my delight she looks forward to Tuesdays and Thursdays, and I find the stimulation she gets from people in the group who have become her friends has a marked positive effect. Above all, so far there have been no hallucinations in that particular location.

This morning, however, things are not so good - physically. It's that wretched "yo-yo" effect of the disease again, and she can scarcely move a single step. We all know she needs to use her zimmer frame, but she steadfastly refuses to do so. She prefers to use me, and that means my being available whenever the necessity - or too often an unreasonable whim - requires her to walk anywhere in the flat. Unfortunately there are also times when she is particularly restless - even agitated - and wants to get up every few minutes, and there are times when I'm simply not prepared to be a human zimmer frame, in a permanent state of availability. I'm digging in my heels. As the Americans say: "No more Mr. Niceguy." I put the frame in front of her, and say firmly:

"You want to walk - use that. Otherwise stay put. I'm tired."

Sounds simple? So far all I've achieved is to cause one row after another. But I'm sticking to my guns, despite the arguments, despite the sulks ...

We're sulking now, and, cutting off her nose to spite her pretty face she says:

"You can see I can't walk. I'm not going to the centre."

I turn a deaf ear, and fifteen minutes later I drive her, uncomplaining, to Edgware, where she is warmly greeted - especially by Simon, her gallant Russian friend, who promises me he'll take good care of her, and she flashes him a wonderful smile.

So here I am at my desk, picking up the threads of my story, memory winding back to my adolescence.

At the age of thirteen I became a man. That's what the crafty old bastards tell Jewish boys when they celebrate their *Barmitzvah*, but it doesn't take us long to realise that it's a load of sanctimonious bullshit - except, I hasten to add - for a select company of our truly righteous brethren, among whom I include my beloved Grandfather Goldberg.

When they told me I'd now become a man I imagined a new life ahead, but once the party was over I realised practically nothing had changed. I was still the kid who did what he was told, regardless of what I wanted. Freedom had beckoned, but I soon discovered that it was an illusion - except for one thing, and that was no small consolation. In our neighbourhood, which numbered several Jewish families, but barely a handful of observant ones, the Hebrew classes were poorly attended, and there was no advanced class to cater for boys after their *Barmitvah*. So henceforth, my evenings were no longer darkened by enforced boredom with nothing else on the curriculum but reading and translation from the prayer book and Bible, the history of the various festivals, and Hebrew education involving no use of the living language whatsoever.

So, in one way, I was wonderfully free.

But, in another, they got me. The real point about becoming a man is that you may be counted in the number of adult males to become a quorum for the purpose of communal prayer. The requisite number is ten, and our local congregation constantly had difficulty in becoming quorate for Friday evening, Saturday morning, festival services, evening prayers or the week of mourning following a funeral...

Nevertheless, apart from the tedium of Sabbath services on Friday evening and Saturday morning, I was freed of five sessions a week, devoted to repetitive, boring periods of religious instruction, which I was unable to reconcile with any rational or moral philosophy. I think I was sustained through the ritual *Barmitzvah* solely in order to please my maternal grandfather, for whom the occasion marked my acceptance into his exclusive club of piety, civilised behaviour and learning. After I'd performed to his satisfaction, he was beaming with pride, and then - bless him - he sat down with a bottle of brandy, and got thoroughly pissed.

Truth to tell, I had not shared his unquestioning faith for years. The deity he revered and loved was, as far as I was concerned, a complete fiction - a bad-tempered old man, with a penchant for sheer cruelty... At least that was what my enforced attendance at Hebrew classes would have led me to believe if I'd swallowed all the rubbish the rabbis fed me. The authority I *had* to accept in my normal daily life was my nutty headmaster. I was lucky not to have mortal dealings with the big boss "upstairs." If my mischievous friends and I were discovered making fun of our two bald-headed teachers - a not infrequent occurrence - we'd get our arses thrashed. The poor little devils in the bible who called Elisha "Baldy" were overheard by the Holy One, blessed be He, and gobbled up by a wild beast. Furthermore I was expected to revere the schizophrenic patriarch, Abraham, who heard "a voice", in response to which he was prepared to slit the throat of his son... And on the Day of Atonement - the holiest day of the year - the prayer book warns us of all the appalling tragic ends we might expect, but gives us the assurance that righteous living and prayer will avert the evil decree.

Even at the tender age of thirteen I'd come to the conclusion : if you believe that you'll believe anything.

My irreverent attitude I owe to my grandmother, and I've discovered the same wicked streak in my ten-year-old grandson, David, who is adept at asking unanswerable questions like:

"If God created us, who created God? He couldn't very well have created himself, could he?"

And on the same subject:

"Why did he make the world in six days before taking a break? Why six? He could have made it eight. Then I'd not only have time for homework, piano lessons, saxophone lessons, Beavers, drama, football and swimming, I'd have more free time with my friends..."

Carried away with enthusiasm: "We could have a week end of three days, instead of two..."

Bless his heart. Fortunate enough to be given the opportunity of developing so many of his undoubted talents, he appreciates the value of completely free, unprogrammed time, which had become available for me after my thirteenth birthday. So what would I do with the wonderful prospect ahead of me?

It was my friend, Pip, who had the answer.

But, before leaving what I considered to be the incarceration of Hebrew classes, I would like to ask posthumous forgiveness from two of my teachers there. I wish I could explain that my truculent attitude towards them was bereft of personal animosity or disrespect, but entirely due to resentment at being forced to spend valuable evening hours being force fed with unpalatable rubbish. Unlike what they were trying to force down my throat, the teachers themselves were likeable and interesting.

There was Lou Rinder, O.B.E. To earn a crust, the poor chap used to come straight to Poplar from a day's teaching at Cephas Street School, to be confronted by a group of boys compelled by their parents to be indoctrinated in the traditions of their ancestors. I have a suspicion that the teacher was as bored and fed up with it all as we were. But he was a scrupulously conscientious man, and did his best. A true professional, he gave his employers value for money, and, on the rare occasions when he closed the book, simply chatting spontaneously with us, perhaps without realising it, he was providing us with a finer moral education than we derived from all the jargon in the religious curriculum. We knew he had a cane in a drawer of the cupboard housing all the books, but I never saw him use it. He was what my grandfather would have termed a *mensh.*

I close my eyes, and see him clearly. He wears a well tailored grey suit, which has seen better days, and teaches wearing a grey trilby in place of the traditional *yarmulka.* With no time for a proper meal, during the break, he eats the sandwiches his wife has prepared for him.

Once or twice he'd talk about the war, never mentioning the O.B.E. he'd been awarded for gallantry, or how he'd been wounded.

That we discovered for ourselves. He merely told us that he'd joined up in 1914, when very young. In peace time he diverted the talent he'd acquired as a bugler to blowing the traditional ram's horn, or *shofar,* in the synagogue on the High Holy Days, and towards that time of year he'd entertain us with a demonstration.

When I was no longer his pupil, I was told that, in the days of trench warfare, Lou Rinder went "over the top" blowing his bugle defiantly at the German guns blazing away in front of him, until he was brought down by a bullet in his chest.

He must have thought me a cheeky, unpleasant little boy. I regret that I was never able to tell him how much I admired him.

This also applies to the teacher who prepared boys for their Barmitzvah, Mr. Lipschitz. This venerable gentleman was like an older version of Grandpa Goldberg; the same little beard, in his case snow white, a similar twinkle in his eyes, but reflected in tiny spectacles, and the identical heavily accented and mutilated English. Exactly like Zeida, he treated the synagogue as a second home, and handled the holy books with the same reverence used by my grandfather. It was a toss up which of the two was the greater scholar.

I could never fathom why he wore his peculiar little glasses - certainly not for reading. He had an extraordinary habit of holding a book high above his head - here again I never understood why - pushing his spectacles up on to his forehead, and squinting up at the text. Even when reciting from the Torah, a scroll too heavy to be scrutinised above his head, he would bend double, and read with his eyes turned upwards. Legend had it that he knew the whole five books of Moses off by heart... an absurd idea, but he certainly chanted from the Torah - no simple task, since the text has no vowels or indication of the correct tune, with consummate ease. Despite his eccentricities, he was respected and much loved as a teacher. And the congregation of Poplar Synagogue exploited him outrageously. Not only did he train all their sons - however thick-headed - to give a creditable performance at their *Barmitzvah*, not only did he officiate to perform the more difficult parts of the festival services, not only was he the official *shamus*, or beadle, but he also had the thankless task of paying all members a weekly visit to collect and record their contributions. I can see him now, in the front of my father's shop, with his little spectacles high on his forehead, squinting up at the kind of rent book in which payments were duly noted, chatting amiably as he counted the money.

Much as I liked and admired these two teachers, I was thrilled to bits at leaving Poplar Hebrew Classes for the last time. Freedom beckoned. How would I spend my

evenings now?
"At last!" said Pip. "Now you can join the club."

SEVEN

The very name, Oxford and St. George's, considering its location and membership, is a paradox, and, when I was introduced to its founder, Basil Q. Henriques, I was privileged to meet one of the most extraordinary men I have ever known.

I remember "the Gaffer" most vividly striding atop Highdown Hill, site of the club summer camp, his vast anachronistic black cape flowing majestically in his wake, his impressive height reinforcing the impression that a superior being from another dimension was leading us. An autocrat by nature - in keeping with his role as a magistrate - he was, on the one hand, austere, awe-inspiring, condescending, proud and uncompromising - and, on the other hand, one of the kindest and most generous men of my acquaintance.

His background, and the area in which he chose to work, were at opposite ends of the social scale. The Henriques family escaped persecution in Portugal in the seventeenth century and established itself in Jamaica with a thriving import and export business, which it transferred to England, soon acquiring wealth and prestige. Basil was born towards the end of the nineteenth century with the traditional silver spoon, enjoyed an elite education at Harrow and Oxford, and in early 1914 elected to make a career helping the underprivileged inhabitants of London's East End, where he founded the famous club, shortly before the outbreak of World War One.

Duty called, and he left the leadership of O. St. G. in the capable hands of his wife, Rose, thereafter known - with respect - as "the Missus." As an officer in the Tank Corps, the Gaffer served his country with courage and distinction, then resumed his activities in Berner Street, known today as Henriques Street.

Like many remarkable men, he had more than a streak of madness. Only a lunatic would have attempted to graft the mores of English public schools and the sons of patrician families on the pupils of Cowper Street,

Whitechapel Foundation, and the infinitely more sordid educational establishments which catered for less intellectually gifted children of what was generally considered the lowest class of British society. Only a madman would have tried - and only a man of exceptional character would have made quite a good job of bringing the finest aspects of the moral education of the English upper class into the lives of children from the ghettoes of Eastern Europe, bringing the noblest ideology of Oxford University into the hovels of Whitechapel. What man in his right mind would dare to attempt the introduction of Liberal Judaism into a ghetto whose inhabitants were deeply enmeshed in orthodoxy? Who but a complete nutter would expect to impose the ethics of Harrow and Oxford on the children of Whitechapel, offspring of Ashkenazi Jews from Eastern Europe who were frankly suspicious of their Sephardi brethren? The poverty stricken immigrant families from which his club members came had mixed feelings about the "*Langer*", as they called him, with reference to his stature, which, alone, inspired them with awe, apart from his status as a magistrate. But they were contemptuous of his religious beliefs, puzzled by his background and speech.... "This is a Jew?" Above all they were relieved that he was keeping their children off the streets and apparently out of mischief. Furthermore, the very naming of the club was enigmatic to gentlemen more familiar with the Yeshiva than with Oxford, and more comfortable with Abraham and Moses than St. George. No completely sane individual would have attempted his project. Only a great man would have succeeded.

Furthermore, smile as they might at his eccentricity, the *Langer* struck an answering chord. Grateful for being offered a home, freedom, the opportunity to earn a living and send their children to good schools, these immigrants earnestly wanted to belong, become an integral part of this land of their choosing. Above all they looked forward to taking pride in the contribution of their sons and daughters to national achievement in the arts, sciences, commerce and sport.

The odd thing is that the Gaffer in my opinion was

not an intellectual. I know that he had problems securing a place at Oxford, and ended up with a mere third class degree in History. His success might be attributed to an example of "fools rushing in..." but I prefer to think that success was due to his exceptional courage - noted in his war record - and that remarkable generosity of spirit present in all the great figures of the twentieth century.

As a magistrate he doubtless scared the shit out of offenders, but more than once I witnessed his kindness. On one particular occasion a friend of mine told me that his older brother, who was studying medicine, couldn't afford to buy books that he needed. It came to the Gaffer's attention, and, in a private meeting with the young student, the old chap simply put his hand in his pocket. The future doctor got his books, and this case was just one of many.

During the war, I was one of a considerable number of ex members to pay a visit to the club while on leave. We were warmly greeted by the Gaffer, and I'll never forget the look in his eyes when he said to me:

"It's wonderful to see our friends."

He was justifiably proud of the club's impressive role of honour, and had played no small role himself in preparing so many Jewish youngsters for service to the country which had provided a home for their parents.

Part of this preparation was the annual summer camp on Highdown Hill.

For youngsters like myself the club filled a great void. Not only did it provide an escape from existence bedevilled by our families' basic need to survive, it gave us the opportunity to develop social, athletic and artistic potentialities within a sound moral framework. But its main function was to teach us the precious nature of leisure and how to make the best use of it.

Even as I write these words, and as if to reinforce the point, Irène calls me. She has just awakened from a morning nap, and requires my immediate attention in the bathroom. My valuable hour of leisure this morning comes to an abrupt end. So, hopefully until she indulges in a siesta this afternoon, I shall postpone my reminiscence of summer camp - over sixty years ago - and venture back into present obligations... I must confess, with reluctance and just a touch of resentment.

Five hours later she is indeed fast asleep, and I can resume my beloved scribbling, a pastime I was able to enjoy to good effect at the club, where I won - for the second time in my young life - first prize in a national essay writing competition.

The Gaffer beamed down at me from his great height and shook my hand. Characteristically he had taken the trouble to read the effort, and said he thought it "first class."Although the club was essentially a "fun" place as far as I was concerned, it actually played a considerable part in my education: Uncle Manny had taught me to draw, and "the missus" taught me to paint; Holly had started my interest in drama, and the club gave me the chance - several times - to perform in plays and concerts on stage; Uncle Joe taught me to box, and at the club tournament I got the hiding of my life; however he also taught me to dive, and I came first in the junior diving competition. Somehow along the way, from talented older boys I learned to play the piano - by ear - and with some limitations. Fascinated by a chap's rendering of Rachmaninov's prelude, which he played in C sharp minor, I prevailed on him to teach me. Another time he entranced me with the first movement of Beethoven's Moonlight Sonata, which he performed in the same key, and again he was patient enough to practise with me. As a result, I now have my own considerable repertoire, all played without sheet music in one of two keys: C sharp - or D flat.

But whenever I think of O.St.G the first memory that springs to mind is that of the showers. Few of my friends enjoyed the luxury of a bathroom at home, and it was sheer bliss for us, after a workout, to shower at leisure with friends. And just as this simple pleasure was a delightful novelty we were determined to make an integral part of our future, so too was the new experience of nature provided for us at the annual camp, where I shall never forget our amazement as we all enjoyed our first sight of an incredible sunset - over the South Downs.

However, my recollections of the camp are not entirely blissful. The Gaffer apparently shared the belief, common in English aristocratic - even royal - circles, that unnecessary discomfort and Spartan conditions are excellent for character forming. I did not and do not subscribe to that philosophy, and a week at camp played no small part in turning me into a confirmed "five star" holiday maker.

On Highdown Hill we peeled spuds, cooked and washed dishes in primitive conditions; we slept - who slept? - on lumpy ground upon palliasses, which we ourselves filled with insect infested straw, beneath the leaky canvas of tents erected by us... and the ultimate ignominy: dug a trench for the "latrine" (I shudder at the very use of that word) over which was placed a long, roughly hewn plank, adorned with a row of companionable round holes of various dimensions. To my utter disbelief, Uncle Ulla, who was the camp doctor, despite his being the most fastidious man I have ever known, planted himself thereupon when the need arose. Furthermore, to my even greater astonishment, the Austere Basil Q. Henriques, with an amicable nod to his neighbours on either side, enthroned himself unconcernedly on the largest hole. Nevertheless, there was no way I was going to perch on that crude piece of carpentry to become part of a band in what I considered ought to be a private and solo performance.

Consequently I suffered from self- inflicted constipation for a week

One particular event leaves a poignant memory. It was a "route march," doubtless an echo from the Gaffer's military past. I shall have something to say about military marches later on in the story, but this one was really not a march at all, simply a prolonged hike. It started well, but, after about two miles the heavens opened, and we were subjected to one of the most violent downpours I had ever known. Of course we didn't turn back. Aghast at first we plodded on, getting wetter and wetter... until, wonder of wonders, we were so sodden that the rain no longer had any effect. Unbelievably we began to enjoy ourselves. Striding in the lead, with his black cape flapping defiantly in his wake, the Gaffer led his singing troop, mile after mile, and, soaked through to the skin, we made friendships that would last us all our lives.

The high point of this holiday was meant to be the Gaffer's speech - "man to young men." Actually I found it an anti-climax. He metaphorically donned his magisterial gown, and that put me off for starters. Despite the solemnity of the occasion, I had difficulty in suppressing the giggles at the most serious passages in his peroration, during which, among more acceptable moral obligations, we were enjoined not - absolutely not - to fart in the tent, and as for masturbation - for the life of me I can't recall the euphemistic term he used - but this was top of his agenda of filthy habits we should eschew at all costs.

Notwithstanding all this, I loved and respected this man. If there were such a place as "heaven" and an after-life in which we could actually meet again those who have passed on, the Gaffer is one spirit I'd want to find. He was a truly great man, who richly deserved the knighthood bestowed upon him.

EIGHT

It's upsetting the first time it happens.

I noticed that she wasn't her usual self in the shower, and literally difficult to handle. Her movements were even more delayed than usual, mostly in the wrong direction, and she had in her eyes that disturbing glazed vacant look, which usually only appears when she is very tired in the evening.

I went through the customary ritual: soaking her all over with clear water, then soaping her whole body, beginning, as always, with her feet, and toes, working my way upwards... I reached the back of her neck...

"Do my feet."

"I've done them."

"No, you haven't."

So I do them again, and return to her shoulders and neck...

"You haven't done my feet."

A few weeks ago I'd have started an argument. But I hope I know better now. I wash her feet once again, and this time give her a little tickle so that she'll remember.

"You're hurting me. Why can't you do things gently?'

She has a problem getting up off the shower seat we've had installed, then can't turn round. I do my best to help.

"You're hurting my arm. I'll have bruises all over!"

After considerable effort and quite a strain on my back muscles, I manoeuvre her out of the shower cubicle. She stumbles, begins falling, and I catch her just in time, feeling my back click. Damn! I'll be swallowing Paracetemol for the next few days.

"Stop being so rough! You're making me sore all over!"

I throw a towel over the loo seat, hand her a bath sheet, and go back under the shower, but, before I have time to relax, through the noise of the jet, I hear her crying. I switch off, hurry through the glass door...

"What's the matter?"

She tries to speak, then forgets what she wanted to say, so I simply take the bath towel from her, and carry on dabbing her dry. I begin dressing her.

Then it happens.

"Stop that. It hurts! Don't pull! My knickers won't fit any more, because your father hurt my stomach."

My father's been dead for thirty years and never touched her.

"When did he do it?"

"I don't know... In the shower. He hurt my arm - and my stomach."

"How did he hurt you? What did he do?"

"He pulled me."

"My father did that? How could he?"

"It was Dad! I'm telling you, Elaine. It was Dad!"

It hits me like a thunderbolt. It's broad daylight - and she thinks I'm my daughter.

I let it pass without comment, and complete dressing her. By the time I've finished her disturbing expression has disappeared, and she seems back to normal ... more or less.

Will you know me tomorrow?

If the primitive aspect of the O.St.G. camp in any way prepared me for army life, it was solely to confirm that, away from home, I am averse to any living conditions below those of a first class hotel; furthermore, I do not appreciate being deprived of female company. Clearly, I should not be in my element on active service. I'll be more specific later in my narrative, but at the moment I'm about to recollect the "march" of Oswald Moseley and his horde of Fascist thugs through the East End of London, and I'd like to linger briefly on the theme of "marching," of which I had my share of first hand experience during the war.

Drill, or "square bashing", as we called it, I always found ludicrous. The Sergeant-Major strutting about, pirouetting grotesquely, stamping his boots and screaming was - for me - less awe inspiring than comical.

During a stroll in the park, if I broke into a military

"march", stamped on the ground, and swung my arms fully forward and back without bending my elbows, they'd justifiably pack me off to the nut house. But in khaki, and on parade that's different, and I have to ask myself why.

Despite my cynicism about the procedure, when I was actually part of the "bullshit" involved in a ceremonial "march past", and swinging my arms with the best of them, I was infected by irrational pride - momentarily - until I was brought to my senses. Despots and war-mongering politicians must be well aware of the mass hypnotic power in "marching." With the addition of mass singing it becomes irresistible. Add the blast of a brass band, and you'll urge normal peace-loving men to murder and the slaughter of innocent women, children and the elderly, in the firm belief that they are carrying out the will of whatever god is invoked by their leader.

On one particular occasion it was "Eyes right!" for Field Marshall Montgomery. I came out of a sort of mesmeric trance - the arrogance of a strutting army is so infectious - just after the brasses behind me burst into an enthusiastic rendering of "Colonel Bogey."

"Blimey!" muttered a yob in the rank behind me.

"Blimey! They're playing 'Bollocks!' "

At the time I didn't know that the gentleman taking the salute - at that time every Englishman's hero - was, in fact, a spiteful, and, at times vitriolic, anti-Semite.

"Swing those arms! Left! Right! Left! Right!"

"Bollocks! And the same to you!"

I don't like marches. Irish Protestants put on bowler hats, march through catholic streets, and vice versa. The act is provocative, and usually succeeds in its purpose of causing violent confrontation between hyped up men, who ought to be sharing amicable pints of Guinness instead of beating the living daylights out of each other.

When I was in my teens I witnessed Oswald Moseley "marching" at the head of his anti-Semitic black-shirted hoodlums through the streets of the Jewish quarter of London's East End. At the time it was shocking; in retrospect it is something of a sick joke.

Thugs with scant respect for the law - or anything else - invoked "freedom of speech" in order to attack the freedom of law-abiding citizens who had the effrontery to be Jews. The bloodthirsty yobs demanded the protection of those responsible for the maintenance of law and order, to provide the force necessary to suppress all those who had the temerity to stand in their path in order to protect their democratic right to live in a peaceful society. I watched in disbelief at thugs in police uniforms charging their horses at unarmed protesters, lashing out indiscriminately with their truncheons, cheered on by the Fascist marchers as they bashed in the heads of Jewish men and women.

From the window above my grandfather's shop in Leman Street, the family had a good vantage point for what - had we but known it - was a preview of the beginning of "Kristallnacht." As the marchers came in sight, vast crowds of young Jews - men and women - and dockers who were unsympathetic to Fascism, attempted to block their path, shouting:

"They shall not pass!"

Behind where I was standing at the window with my aunts, their brothers were holding back Uncle Pop, who wanted to:

"Go down and fight the bastards!"

My grand-parents were huddled in the back of the room muttering about pogroms. Mounted police, supported by crowds of them on foot, tried to clear a path for the Blackshirts, and then, unable to hold the protesters back, began beating without discrimination the heads of men and women. That's when the real screaming started, and there were bleeding heads everywhere. Just below us, a well dressed man collapsed in a pool of blood. His lady companion cradled him, shrieking in a foreign language, we later discovered to be Swedish. Uncle Ulla, recently qualified in medicine, ran downstairs to give first aid. As the gentleman later confided in the family, when offered a cup of tea, they were visitors, sight-seeing, caught up in events they failed to understand.

At the time I didn't understand them either, but they

left an unforgettable impression, which, nearly three quarters of a century later, sends a shiver down my spine.

And this was a picnic compared to the experiences of my cousin, Sacha, in Paris, and Irène's family in Brussels, as we shall see.

NINE

The first sign that Irène had Parkinson's Disease manifested itself - and passed almost unnoticed - several years ago. My daughter, Elaine, remarked that her mother had developed a habit - she thought it was no more than that - of walking, swinging her left arm normally, but with the right hanging stiffly by her side. Vainly we encouraged her to move the other arm. Soon her walk developed another abnormality. She was beginning to shuffle slightly. So we sought medical advice.

Our G.P. at that time observed her - obviously concerned more with her feet than her arms - and diagnosed polymialgia. He prescribed steroids. The only effect they had was to provide my lovely wife with an unflattering puffy look. Realising he'd been barking up the wrong tree, the doctor referred her to a consultant physician, who made an immediate diagnosis of Parkinson's Disease "in its early stage." Furthermore, in the course of routine investigation, it was discovered that she had a tumour, and an immediate operation was recommended for the removal of her right kidney.

Concern about the Parkinson's gave way to the worry of surgery, and Irène was duly admitted to hospital, where she turned out to be the patient from hell. Apart from childbirth, she'd never had a stay in hospital, and I'm convinced that, if she hadn't been recovering from a major operation, they'd have kicked her out of this one.

The surgery, which took place early in the morning, was completely successful. During the afternoon, heavily sedated, she drifted in and out of sleep, and, as soon as she appeared to be settled for the night, I went home to bed. I was awakened by a telephone call from the hospital. No, there were no complications...

"It's just that she's asking for you."

I peered at the clock, and rubbed my eyes. It was a few minutes past one a.m!

"Asking for me?"

"Well - er - not exactly. She's screaming the place down - disturbing the other patients - and we can't calm her..."

"Tell her I'm on my way. That should keep her quiet."

Driving to the hospital under normal daytime conditions took about three quarters of an hour. This time I made it in fifteen minutes. She calmed down as soon as I arrived, then slept fitfully until the morning, when I was able to leave. We went through precisely the same procedure every night until, to the relief of the hospital staff, she was discharged.

The staff had given me the impression that she was the worst patient they'd ever had, and told her so when, to everybody's relief, she was saying good-bye.

She turned in the doorway, and with wide-eyed innocence proclaimed:

"I only wanted my husband."

Then we had to deal with Parkinson's, and, in due course, I took her to see a reputable specialist in this field at the National Hospital for Neurological Diseases. He confirmed the diagnosis, but, after a series of tests, gave me the additional information that she was suffering from an accompanying condition known as Cortical Lewy Body Disease.

Then he stirred up a hornets' nest. Going into Irène's family history, he unearthed the information that, on the maternal side, apart from her older sister, no less than five cousins, living in various parts of the world, had suffered from some kind of severe neurological disorder. Only one, living in this country, and under the care of one of his colleagues in a neighbouring hospital, had been diagnosed with both Parkinson's and Lewy Body disease. This gentleman's sister had recently died in a residential home, suffering from what was thought to be Alzheimer's - an illness with comparable symptoms of dementia.

The professor, I could tell, thought that all this appeared to be more than mere coincidence, and asked whether I might provide him with details of Irène's sister's physician. I explained that he was in Brussels, but offered to send him the information he required. And that's where we stirred up the proverbial hornets' nest. I touched a raw nerve, both with the family members I contacted, and, above all, the Belgian practitioner. Relatives proved over-sensitive to any suggestion of a genetic flaw, and the doctor invoked professional etiquette in his refusal to co-operate. He said he was unable to send reports, x-rays and whatever without the patient's consent. Unfortunately the patient was unable to agree, since she was now deceased. I wonder whether our consultant shared my unspoken hunch that his colleague in Brussels was covering his own rear end. On the other hand, reluctance to face facts by the family is understandable.

It was time for some personal research. From a mass of mostly incomprehensible scientific jargon I crystallised a simplified layman's explanation. It was a chastening experience, and not very pleasant. Everything I read made me more aware of what an unfeeling bastard I'd been.

Some Parkinson's patients are afflicted with "the shakes", others like Irène, experience rigidity, occasionally appearing to be glued to the floor, exhibiting a characteristic shuffling of the feet without moving a centimetre, as they attempt to become "unstuck." All actions become extremely slow. The disease is due to an excessive loss of brain cells which produce dopamine, the chemical which transmits messages from the brain to the limbs required to move. It's as if the brain says: "Walk", but the feet don't get the command. The same problem occurs with everyday movements familiar in normal circumstances, like doing up buttons, dressing generally, using a knife and fork, spreading butter on toast, sitting down, actually planting one's bottom where it needs to go, standing up, turning round, going through a door A strange feature of the disease is that it fluctuates. and this has led me to be particularly unkind, thinking: "You know you can do it if you try. You're playing up." Not so. They call this "up and down" aspect the "yo-yo effect".

I can be selective enough in self portrayal to give the impression that I am patient, considerate and kind. But the truth is I can be a right pig at times. Reading about the effects of Parkinson's Disease, I realise how thoughtless and cruel so many of my remarks have been. Several spring to mind:

"Do you realise you've been standing on that spot for five minutes without moving?"

"For goodness sake, finish the sentence!"

"The only answer I need is a simple 'yes' or 'no.' Can't you understand what I'm saying?"

"But I only just told you that a couple of minutes ago."

"You know perfectly well that's the wrong direction."

Why can't I simply accept what she says or does - however absurd - and simply say: "Yes, dear"?

As far as Cortical Lewy Body Disease is concerned, even the average G.P. who qualified over ten years ago has never heard of it. The sickness involves abnormal brain cells causing symptoms similar to Alzheimer's, with progressive loss of mental functioning: confusion, inability to sustain a thought - Irène has long been prone to unfinished sentences, words trailing off into nothing, forgetfulness of what she intended to say, disorientation - she has for some time completely lost her sense of direction, occasionally even within the flat-hallucinations - these were yet to come-memory-loss... eventually complete dementia.

I was reeling under the impact of all this, when I received the "coup de grace."

"The progress of the illness may be more rapid than seen in Alzheimer's disease."

I wish Mandy were less impulsive. But that's her nature. My older daughter, Elaine, is reflective and will consider all options carefully, sometimes taking so long that she misses the boat. Mandy, more like my late brother, Alan, than like me, goes off like a firecracker; no sooner does she have an idea than its execution is immediate. Both my girls thought I should see the doctor - for myself. Vehemently, I protested. The doctor and I are sufficiently involved with Irène without clouding the issue, pestering the man with trivialities and diverting our attention from the main problem. I can't afford to have anything wrong with me ... and even if I do, there's no way I can find time to deal with it. However, Mandy made the appointment for me. So off I go, while Elaine stays to look after her mother.

The appointment is for ten thirty, and I eventually

find myself face to face with him at eleven. He's so conscientious that we always have to wait while he spends ages with the previous patient, and I begin to get agitated because Elaine has to pick up young David at twelve. Fretting has no doubt sent up my blood pressure...

He asks about Irène, and then wants to know the reason for my visit. All I can tell him is that I feel perfectly well, but my daughters made the appointment out of concern for what they call "chronic fatigue." This is a practitioner of the old school, less interested in his computer then your actual person, so he gives me a good going over, satisfied that my elevated blood pressure is circumstantial - though he'll take it again before I leave. As I said: he's the good old-fashioned type of "hands on" family doctor, who doesn't cut corners, and I turn down his kind offer to stick a finger up my backside - "No problems there"- liar that I am - and he settles back in his chair for a chat.

"Are you sleeping well?"

"No."

"Last night?"

"Not really."

"Tell me about it. Right from the moment you turned in."

"We went to bed about half past nine - as usual. I fell asleep straight away. The hand bell tinkled at seven minutes past eleven. Yes, I can be precise about the times. I've a large clock on my bedside table, and I have developed the habit of noting the time we take over the night-time disturbances. Under protest she allows me to raise the head of the bed mechanically - preferring me to yank her upright. How does she get up from the sitting position? With great difficulty. I have to swing her feet round, and then haul her to her feet. She then leans on the commode, which we use at night, and last night, each time it was used, it took us nearly five minutes to turn her round, and get her seated. The problem was reversed to wrestle her back on the bed, and position her comfortably. How long did that take? Four minutes, I can tell you exactly, because I made a mental note of the time I put myself back into bed: it was eleven fifteen. I know, but that's about normal. We went through the same procedure, taking more or less the same amount of time, four times. No, I don't usually go straight back to sleep. The longer the job takes, and whenever one of us gets cross, or we engage in a wrestling match, the longer I stay wide awake..."

We pause, while, aware of Elaine's problem of collecting David, this lovely man phones her at my flat, and she says she has already arranged matters.

"Was it only to use the commode that Irène disturbed you?"

"No. At five o'clock she woke me up to throw a dog out of the bed."

"What did you do?"

"What I was told."

"And?"

"Well, she said that it was covered in fleas, and there they were, crawling all over the bed. The bed-linen had to be changed."

"So what happened next?"

I would so love to say that I complied meekly with her request. But I can't. This is confession time. I shan't pull the wool over your eyes. I'm not really the person I've presented, not always the sympathetic, understanding individual presented in these pages. I can be unsympathetic, mean, intolerant, bad-tempered, explosive - downright horrible. But I've hidden all that. The kind husband I portray to you is only half the story. And I cannot lie to the doctor. Shame-faced I tell him:

"I lost it."

"What did you do?"

"I shouted at her... told her I was fed up with pretending those bloody hallucinations existed anywhere outside her own brain... there was no way any dog could find its way into a third floor flat, where the doors and windows were all locked, I had no intention of changing the fucking sheets... She could do what she bloody well liked... Imaginary fleas, dogs, horses or elephants... I was going back to sleep for what was left of the night."

"And did you?"

"Of course not. I stayed awake hating myself for losing my temper and behaving like an absolute bastard."

"How about this morning?"

"I still don't like myself."

"What time did you get up?"

"Half past six."

"Is that usual?"

"Yes. I make breakfast and give Irène her tablets. She's unduly concerned about taking them at precisely seven."

There is a long pause, and I hear the clock ticking.

"I think we both know what's wrong with you, don't we?"

"Well yes. I'm just bloody tired."

"Exactly."

"Right. I'm sorry to be wasting your time..."

"On the contrary. It's a good thing you came - before you both find yourselves in real trouble. You need help."

"Any suggestions?"

"No, but I'm sure social services will have a few. They ought to be able to arrange for you to have more time for yourself."

He picks up the handset where he dictates messages for his secretary, and I wonder whether it hasn't been a wasted morning after all.

"Incidentally, how would you like to spend any free hours we can give you?"

"Actually I'm writing a book."

"A novel?"

"It's an autobiography."

"Really? Am I in it?"

"You are now."

One of the most wonderful things that ever happened to me was the birth of my brother, Alan, when I was six years old, and one of the worst his death from cancer fifty years later. He came into the world on the second of March, and to mark the occasion the sky outside our window was brightened by a heavy fall of snow.

I can only remember him laughing, even in the hospice where he lay terminally ill, and most of the nurses were in love with him. The fact that not one was ever discovered under the sheets in his bed was proof enough that he was close to death. Aware of his condition a rabbi paid a mercy visit, and met me as he was leaving. He was wiping his eyes. "Nice chap," I thought, "to be so upset by the imminent passing of a man he'd never met before."

"Your brother?" he asked.

Then, as I nodded, he added in a choking voice:

"Your brother!"

Whereupon I realised that the tears on his cheeks were of mirth.

"First of all he informs me that I shouldn't bother with any Jewish equivalent of the last rites, because he's going to the other place. Then he tells me two of the funniest, filthiest Jewish jokes I've ever heard."

He composed his features into the serious expression befitting his dog's collar and the occasion, and shook my hand, murmuring appropriate words of consolation. But a glint came back into his eyes, and he failed to stifle the chuckle making its way through his beard once again:

"Your brother!"

How often have I heard those words uttered with the same mixture of shock, disbelief and sheer admiration?

A few minutes later Irène and I were at his bedside, and a pretty nurse brought his medication. She leaned over him. No. It wasn't the tip of her right breast almost touching his nose that brought the seraphic smile to his face; his one remaining eye glinted as it focused on the bottle she was holding.

"The cancer's not so good," he said to Irène, "but the heroine's fantastic."

On one occasion I said to him:

"I met a friend of yours yesterday."

"Oh, who?"

I gave him the name. He looked at me oddly.

"You didn't say you were my brother, did you?"

"Of course I did. Why shouldn't I?"

"You're lucky he didn't punch you on the nose... I was having it off with his wife."

Our mother used to say that her prematurely white hair was due to aggravation caused by her younger son. That's as may be, but, in fact, she spent more time chuckling than fretting over his escapades.

"He had the devil in him from the day he was born. I don't know where he gets it from."

Booba told me.

Several times she was summoned to the headmistress of Mum's school, where she was constantly in trouble for rebellious and mischievous behaviour. At first I found this difficult to believe . Although she was always good fun and had a great talent for comic mimicry, until he was permanently out of the way, my father cast a shadow over her personality.

Two years after Alan was expelled from Christ's College at the age of fifteen, our cousin Stuart Shocket arrived for his first day as a pupil at the school. Before he took off his coat he was summoned to the headmaster's study.

"Shocket?"

"Yes, sir?"

The head barked at the new arrival:

"Any relation to Alan?"

'Yes, sir. He's my cousin, sir."

His face now purple, jabbing a forefinger in the now quaking first former's direction, the man roared:

"I'm going to have my eye on you! Watch it!"

Fortunately a law abiding citizen, Stuart was a model pupil, academically gifted and well behaved. He went on to university and graduated in medicine.

As a child Alan sang like an angel, but according to his teachers, was the incarnation of Lucifer. Although quite clever - as a four-year old, before his first class, he was reading quite fluently - he avoided homework on principle, and spent all his time in school being a clown... except that he was absent as much as possible, forging notes from his parents, and, in his last year of formal education, spending the time he should have been working at his desk watching the most lurid trials at the Old Bailey.

Via Uncle Manny my brother inherited the gene of manual dexterity, and the technical curiosity it inspired. In other words he loved taking things to pieces, as he said, to find out how they worked... All very well, but he lacked our uncle's persistence in putting them back together.

"A bright boy," said his less vitriolic reports, "but lacking in concentration and staying power."

One day Mum came home from a shopping trip, and was taken aback to find her newly acquired vacuum cleaner in pieces over the kitchen floor. After my father had nearly killed him - for once not entirely without justification - my brother invoked the god of vengeance to avoid reassembling the machine - although he would never have done that anyway.

A few years later he took to stripping down a couple of cars - and a hearse -which he was going to rebuild in showroom condition. They remained fragmented in the garage.

But he did successfully make and put up single handed new kitchen cupboards for our mother. They collapsed a few months after his death, and it was fortunate that they did so, because each time Mum opened the doors to take out crockery she began to weep.

As a boy, he was always surrounded by friends, but his main partner in crime (an appropriate term) was a youngster almost as evil in mischief as he was himself - Cyril Wax.

They were particularly villainous to their rabbi, who once remarked to me, as he pointed a shaking finger at Cyril:

"Dat boy... He's a *buggair*."

Unbelievably, the last time I saw Cyril, a few years back, he told me he was now known as "Reverend Mitchell Wax," and he was a lay preacher.

I still don't know if he was pulling my leg.

Alan never realised his ambition to fly. Having been successively expelled from Hebrew classes and school, he completed the hat trick by being kicked out of the R.A.F.

Apparently he was insubordinate - he'd never accepted any kind of authority - but this and his role in a scandal involving the C.O's daughter were disguised under the title of mental instability.

My fiancée and my brother took to each other from the moment they met, and, as Irène spoke very little English at the time, Alan kindly offered to give her lessons - with interesting results. Accompanying her on one of her first journeys on the Underground, with which she was fascinated, I was aghast when, handing in her ticket at the barrier, she proudly said to the startled official:

"Up yours, Charlie!"

According to her "teacher", that was the polite English equivalent to: "S'il vous plaît, monsieur."

Fortunately, it was several hours before we returned home, and I'd had time to simmer down before confronting the culprit.

"It could have been worse," he said. "I was going to tell her..."

"I'd rather not know."

True to form, at the age of eighteen, Alan got the girl next door pregnant. It never ceased to amaze me that, however horrifying the scrapes he got into, my brother had some kind of angel watching over him to turn disaster into good fortune. This was the case here.

Sally and he had a successful, fun-filled marriage for nearly a quarter of a century - until he was caught (after a long run of luck) with his trousers down in the wrong bedroom.

Before that event put an end to his married life, our families had grown up very close to each other; we had children of more or less the same age, and took many wonderful holidays together - two hilarious ones on the river, when we hardly ever stopped laughing. Needless to say, my children adored him.

Alan's fatal illness began when he had a detached retina, caused by a tiny malignant tumour. The eye had to be removed, in a vain attempt to prevent metastasis. Sporting an eye patch before he received his glass eye, he made the most of his resemblance to a pirate. In fact the patch and his black beard gave him an even more dashing appearance than before the operation.

On one occasion Irène and I were dining with him, when he suddenly rose to his feet and imperiously called over the maître d'.

"What's that?" he demanded in a voice that could be heard all over the restaurant.

"Sir?"

"Look at that!" he repeated, pointing dramatically to the plate in front of him.

The poor man dropped the bottle he was holding, and uttered a high pitched cry. By now we were the centre of attraction.

Staring back at the maitre d' from the centre of a bed of rice was Alan's glass eye.

"Oh, I'm so sorry, old chap. It must have dropped out. I'll soon put it back."

Indelibly imprinted on my memory is the occasion when the consultant at Guy's Hospital asked Irène and me to come into his office. One look at his face and my legs turned to jelly.

"I'm afraid the liver is affected, and, unfortunately there's no more we can do."

"How long do we have?"

"About six months."

Heroic in his acceptance of the terrible news, against my advice Alan insisted on sharing it with our mother.

"I can't live my last few months as a lie. Not to Mum."

"You've lied to her all your life!"

Incredibly he grinned: "That's different."

When the end came eventually, I had to break the news. She opened the door of her flat, took one look at me and opened her mouth, without being able to utter a sound. All I needed to do was nod. It was an appalling experience. I loved her so much, and I'd just inflicted on her the most unbearable pain of her entire life. I held her close, and she reverted to the language of her childhood. After an agonised entreaty to her own mother she spoke nothing but Yiddish for about ten minutes. It was heart-rending, yet had a strange tragic beauty.

Twenty years later she herself lay dying in a hospital bed, and on what proved to be my last visit to her, I brought my Aunt Bea. She and my mother had been inseparable.

"I've brought you a visitor, Mum. Who would you most like to see?"

Despite her stroke, her mind and speech were unimpaired.

"Alan," she said.

Without the influence of my brother, I wonder what kind of person I'd have become. Although my junior by six years, his personality was so strong, and we were so close, that it had a major effect on mine. From the beginning we shared a room. My mother said she always knew exactly when we fell asleep, because that's when the laughter stopped. Once, when he was only two years old, he laughed so heartily that he bounced up and down in bed until he cracked his head open on the marble mantelpiece above it. Naturally I was the one to be punished, but, even at that age, it was Alan who instigated the clowning.

My store of jokes - always vast and usually very rude - has had few additions since he died. As a cure for insomnia I developed an unfortunate habit of telling myself some of the fruitier ones to enliven the gloom of sleeplessness. If they're rich enough, I burst out laughing in the small hours. On one occasion, when I awakened Irène, and she asked me what the hell was going on - or words to that effect - I tried to share the joke with her. Never again. I should have known she hasn't our brand of humour.

Under Alan's influence I grew to love boats, caravans and open sports cars. Joint holidays were the most fabulous of our lives. We just never stopped laughing.

On one of our trips we stopped for petrol. Unbelievable as it may seem, my entire family plus our dog, were squashed into what was supposed to be a two seater sports car - a red Triumph Spitfire - with the hood down, pulling a caravan much too big for it. While I was filling up, a passing couple stopped and stared at us.

"I've never seen such a beautiful car load!" exclaimed the woman.

Her husband scratched his head: "How the blazes did you squeeze them all in?" he asked.

Similarly equipped behind me, my brother told him:

"He piles them in one at a time. Just puts one hand on each buttock and heaves. Once he's shoved in the missus and the dog, the rest is easy."

Alan's good humour never failed him. By chance he happened to pull up beside me once at a red light. It was mid winter. Each car had the roof down. We were both swathed in warm coats, wearing scarves and ridiculous woollen hats. The sun was shining in a cloudless sky. It was bitter cold.

"Isn't it a wonderful day?" he called over to me. Before I could reply, the lights changed. He waved a gloved hand, and roared away at high speed.

Nearly all days were wonderful, as far as he was concerned. In the fifty years of his too short existence, Alan had more fun than most octogenarians in their entire lifetime.

Visiting him in the hospice, where he knew he was spending his last days, we were directed to a bed in the corner, by a large window. Autumn sunlight was filtering into the room through trees, the foliage of which was a breathtaking blaze of colour. He greeted us with, as always, a broad smile. In a weakened but still musical voice, he said:

"I'm so lucky to have this beautiful view."

The same pretty nurse who had administered his "heroin", and seemed - like so many women in his life - in love with him - brought him a cup of tea, and propped him up in bed. Solicitously she waited for him to sip. Again his smile flashed, and he said:

"Thank you, darling. It's a lovely cup of tea."

A few weeks later I saw that same nurse at his funeral. She was weeping.

On his tombstone should have been an additional inscription:

"There is now much laughter in heaven."

As a special anniversary gift, our daughters have

arranged a weekend break for us in Bournemouth, so here we are in a hotel favoured by elderly Jewish couples. There are a few other people with wheelchairs, quite a number use walking sticks. I notice a zimmer frame or two, and Irène's chair doesn't stand out like a sore thumb.

At dinner we are delighted to discover that our friends, Cyril and Anita, are spending a week in their favourite hotel, and we're taking coffee in the lounge, when a doddering old man, who must be at least ninety, staggers unsteadily to a halt beside our table, stares at Cyril, and stammers:

"I know you."

My friend looks at me from the corner of his eye. Seen frequently in the theatre, films and on T.V, he's used to this situation. Anyway he's too good-natured to be anything but kind to the old boy. So he smiles and nods.

"Yes, I know who you are. You're... you're..." From the deepening furrows on his wrinkled brow the man is visibly searching back along memory lane. Then his face lights up:

"Yes," he exclaims triumphantly. "You're Myer Tzelnicker." He's named the most celebrated actor of the Yiddish theatre in the time of my grand-parents.

"No," says Cyril gently. "Myer Tzelnicker's dead."

"Yes," replies the old fellow. "I know." And dances off singing to himself.

Could there be a happy component to dementia?

But it isn't so amusing when we go back to our room, which is pleasant enough, and our girls have ensured its facilities are convenient for the disabled. Unfortunately Irène is distressingly disorientated by the different surroundings, especially during the small hours, which become a waking nightmare.

At last the morning comes. Regretfully we take leave of our friends, and make for the familiar environment of home.

The social worker suggested we have a visiting "carer" in the mornings to relieve pressure. I have to admit this morning isn't looking too good. We've been up half the night

- or so it seems - heaving, wrestling, and falling about between the bed and commode.

"Michael!"

Drowsily: "Yes, dear?"

"What time is it?"

Irritably: "Three minutes past five."

"Do you think you ought to get up?"

Emphatically: "No, dear."

I try to settle down...

"Michael!"

Wearily: 'Yes, dear?"

"What time is it?"

Even more irritably: "Fourteen minutes past five."

Urgently: "I need to go to the loo!"

Resignedly: "Yes. dear."

"No, not the commode - the loo!"

An unpleasant side effect of one of Irène's drugs is recurrent constipation, and it's been three days since her last bowel movement. This time she really does mean business.

"Hurry up! It's urgent!"

More wrestling, and now her feet seem glued to the floor.

"Say one. two..." That sometimes helps. Not now.

"Go on!" she commands: "Walk!"

"If I do, I'll just pull you over. Lift your foot."

"I can't!" That's true. So now what?

"No, Michael, not the wheelchair. There's no time!"

I contrive to half carry her into the bathroom, and plant her appropriately.

"It's no use. The urge has gone."

She's back in bed. I begin to settle.

"Michael!"

"Yes. dear?"

"What time is it?"

"Five thirty."

"Isn't it time to get up?"

Not really, but I'm too tired for a discussion. That might become an argument, which - given the way I feel -

could become a full scale row. So getting up seems to be the best option. I stagger to my feet.

"Is breakfast ready?"

"I've just got out of bed!"

As I move to get my gown... "I'm cold. Where's my dressing gown?"

"I'm just getting it."

"Well, hurry up. I'm freezing!"

I'm stark naked, and not exactly warm myself, but, putting my own discomfort to one side I slip the robe over her shoulders, fumble around to slip her arms into the sleeves, more or less heave her into the wheelchair, and - still naked - begin to wheel her into the kitchen.

"I'm not going in there."

"Why not?"

"Can't you see them? About half a dozen, and..."

"I'll go and get rid of them."

"No! Don't!" "Aren't you ashamed?"

"About what?"

"You've got no clothes on, and there are women there! And two men with the long plaits. You said you got rid of them last night. It's disgusting. The men are lying on top of each other."

"Shall I get a bucket of water and throw it over them."

"It isn't funny."

"I agree with that."

I slip on my robe, deal with the cavorting intruders, and take her into the kitchen where I proceed to prepare breakfast - cereal, milk, dishes, orange juice, glasses, crackers, butter, morning tablets...and we begin to eat.

"Michael!"

"Yes?"

"There's a big fly in my orange juice."

"I can't see it."

"Look! There it is floating on the top."

There's no sign of it.

"Throw it away!"

"Yes, dear."

"Michael!"

"Yes, dear?"

"I need to go to the loo! Now!"

Fortunately, she sits at the table in her wheelchair, and we can move fast. Her visit is successful, so we can now relax over breakfast. Then I wheel her to the bathroom, where I am able to leave her while she cleans her teeth. That gives me the opportunity to clear the dishes...

"Michael!"

I can hear she's in distress. Without pausing to dry my soapy hands I hasten to her side.

"What's the matter?"

"Look! I'm bleeding!"

"Where?"

"There's blood on my toothbrush!"

"It's just a spot. The dentist told you it's only your gums."

"It must be my kidneys. I'm sure it's my kidneys."

"But..."

"Make an appointment with the doctor."

About to argue, I change my mind. She'll have forgotten about it in ten minutes.

"Yes, dear."

Her obsession with kidney disease dates back five years, to the time her right kidney was removed. Since that memorable occasion, when she had me driving back and forth to the hospital in the middle of the night, although assured and reassured with two unnecessary X-rays that her remaining kidney is perfectly sound, she is convinced they'll remove that one too.

"I'm sure it's my kidney," she says, whenever she has a twinge in any part of her body, irrespective of the location of discomfort.

"I think it's more likely to be testicular cancer," is the kind of reply she invariably gets from an unsympathetic husband.

Perhaps it's lack of sleep, perhaps she is in an awkward mood, but dressing her this morning is particularly difficult.

"She can't help it," I tell myself over and over, or:

"She doesn't mean it. It's her illness that's to blame."

Then I have the idea of taking her out - anywhere - just to cheer us both up, and we drive to a shopping precinct. Perhaps if we spend some money on something frivolous - indulge in retail therapy... and I always enjoy wheeling her round the shops...

"Hello!"

I feel a tap on my shoulder, turn and find myself face to face with our two daughters. The children are in school, and they appear to be on the same mission as ourselves. We spend a pleasant hour together, followed by a delicious lunch, during which Irène, as usual in the company of the girls, is sparkling.

On the drive home she snuggles as close to me as the seat-belt will permit. I put on her favourite CD. She sings along with it. I take her hand.

Things aren't so bad.

TEN

After his death my mother often spoke of Alan. I believe it helped keep him alive for her. She rarely spoke of my father after he passed away a few years following his admission to Napsbury Hospital on a permanent basis.

In his fifties, and in the prime of life, Dad had his skull smashed by a thief, passing himself off as a customer in the shop. As my father turned his back the thug took a heavy object from beneath his jacket, brought it down hard, rifled the till for what amounted to about ten shillings, and made off. His victim staggered to the door, and collapsed on the pavement in a pool of blood.

After a week in the London Hospital, Whitechapel, my father was discharged, apparently recovered from injury, but, about a month after the incident he had returned to work, and, on his way to open the shop, fell heavily down the steps of Aldgate tube station, cracked his head, and again spent a few days in the London Hospital. For the second time he was sent home as fit.

About a month later we noticed that he was dragging one foot as he walked, and then he developed a spasm on one side of his face. Furthermore, his already odd behaviour was becoming more and more eccentric. Clearly he was no longer fit to commute or consider work, and my brother made arrangements to sell the shop. Our father, whom we expected to voice violent opposition to the proceedings, to our surprise showed little interest. There were further developments in his condition. At odd times during the day, and for no apparent reason, he would emit short shrill screams, followed always by the remark: "Steady boy!" More disturbing was the fact that his violent rages were becoming more frequent, and never with any obvious cause.

His smoking was now dangerous, and there were a few minor fires. So my mother was frugal in dispensing cigarettes. Amazingly he barely noticed, and, to our relief, before long had completely stopped smoking. A steady and rapid progression towards complete insanity was under way.

There is nothing like dementia for the destruction of

social relations. Thanks to my mother our parents' home had always been a focal point for the Goldberg family, and, especially at weekends, full of uncles, aunts and cousins. No more. As the disease takes hold, the patient's behaviour becomes an embarrassment to visitors and carer alike. Even though her brothers and sisters braved the situation, Mum found ways to dissuade them. It was no joke when he made an appearance with his flies wide open and a large stain down the leg of his trousers, emitting weird unintelligible sounds. Very soon, apart from Alan, Irène and myself, almost nobody came.

My mother used to hurry down to the shops and back. One day shereturned to find him standing outside the front door, naked from the waist down. From that time she could only venture out when Alan or I relieved her.

She found herself virtually isolated.

But Mum had guts. Despite the efforts of Alan and myself to persuade her to let us make alternative arrangements, she soldiered on. She knew that we'd been turned away by various "homes" as soon as they learned that he was verbally violent and subject to rage. No establishment where the residents intended to end their days in peace was prepared to admit him. Our options had almost run out.

Then, bad as it was, the situation became even worse. Mum had been hiding from us the fact that he was now doubly incontinent, needed constant lifting, and was, of course, too heavy for her to manage. Yet, incredibly, she kept on trying.

One morning I found her at the sink, washing his badly soiled pyjamas. The stench filled the kitchen. One side of my mother's face was beetroot red . Clearly she was on the verge of a nervous breakdown.

"How long has this been going on?"

No answer.

"I'm not allowing you to go on like this."

Only once in my whole life did my mother raise her voice to me or swear. This was it. She flung the pyjamas down into the soap suds and yelled at me:

"If you've got something to do, then bloody well do it!"

Then, uncharacteristically again, she collapsed in tears.

That afternoon I drove him to Napsbury. It was a beautiful summer's day, and the top of the car was down. We drove through Radlett towards Shenley along an almost deserted country road, and he was enjoying the drive. He hadn't said a word all the way, until he broke the silence with a simple question that has haunted me for years.

"Where are you taking me, my son?"

It was like a knife through my heart. All at once I realised the enormity of my act - my betrayal. Silencing the voice of my conscience I drove on. I was, in fact, taking him to the only place which would accept him... the geriatric ward of a mental hospital, and the nearest thing to hell I've ever seen in my life of over three quarters of a century.

The building itself was forbidding enough, but my wildest stretch of imagination hadn't prepared me for what was inside. The walls had those manure coloured tiles so beloved of the designers of Victorian council schools and institutions. There was the constant clang of gates, and "nurses" with the appearance of prison warders stamped around jangling keys. A stale smell of boiled cabbage pervaded the corridor down which we walked, as we entered the ward, accompanied by an overpowering stench of vomit, urine and shit, only faintly enhanced by the aroma of disinfectant.

Worst of all, I saw the walking dead.

It was as if all the patients were clones of the same tramp. Dressed in colourless rags, it seemed to me they all had skull-like heads, hollow cheeks, walked with an identical shuffling gait, showed the same degree of physical and mental decay... and they all stank to high heaven.

I was about to drag my father out of there, but, as I stood transfixed and stunned, he was whisked away by an attendant. Dazed, and as if in a nightmare, I found myself in an ante-room. where I was shortly joined by some kind of head nurse, who was holding out a paper bag.

"There are two things we can't manage here," he said,

nodding towards the bag, "Glasses and false teeth."

Illogically the only thought that came into my head was: "What the hell am I going to do with them?"

"I must also tell you," he went on, "that he won't be able to keep his own clothes. They have to be washed regularly, and it isn't possible for us to identify who wears what. We just give out something that fits."

The rest of what he said fell on deaf ears. Through all my senses I absorbed just about as much as I could take, and, after a hurried farewell to my father, who was mercifully oblivious to his appalling surroundings, I got out into the fresh air as fast as my legs would carry me.

I hear Irène crying in the lounge, where I left her having an afternoon nap, which normally lasts about an hour and a half. Once she's fallen asleep I tip-toe into my study for some private therapy with this manuscript, careful to keep a wakeful ear in case she calls. Hearing her sounds of distress I hurry next door. She's sobbing and reproachful:

"You left me all alone."

"I'm sorry."

"Where have you been? I've been calling you for half an hour!"

Not true. But why argue?

"You left me alone - with her!" And she points a trembling finger at the television set, which is switched off. Then she startles me by screaming at the blank screen:

"Go on! Tell Michael what you just told me!"

"What was that?"

But her features are set like a mask. Oh, God, she's sulking. I know she won't say another word until she gets over her resentment at my being away from her side for more than five minutes. But I'm not in the mood for a row, and I keep my mouth closed too.

So we sit in silence ... No sound except the rain pelting against the windows. Side by side we stare at the wall. It's exactly the way my father used to sit, until I took him to Napsbury.

Maybe I'm going crazy too!

It might have been a guilt trip, but I visited Napsbury regularly every Sunday. Alan hardly ever went. He couldn't take it. Our mother accompanied me from time to time. I wanted to spare her the ordeal as much as possible, but she surprised me by her philosophical acceptance of an inevitable situation. She did say repeatedly:

"He doesn't know where he is. Thank God he doesn't know."

In fact he rarely recognised us, although he knew we were bringing him sweets, which he would cram into his toothless mouth, and choke himself, unless we carefully rationed him.

What upset my mother most was the way he was dressed, virtually in rags. He'd always been a dapper dresser, and I only remember him in happier times wearing a hand-made suit, immaculate shirt and tie, highly polished black shoes... never anything remotely resembling casual attire.

She knitted him a cardigan - for his "birthday."

"Mum," I said, "you're wasting all that work on something he'll probably only wear once!"

"So? Then it will keep some other poor man warm."

In point of fact, either because he hung on to it for dear life, or because the nurses realised it was something special, he did retain the cardigan, and wore it until it was threadbare, and as colourless as all the other clothes in the ward, but, as long as it did keep its colour it made him recognisable whenever I arrived. Without it he would have been just another zombie, indistinguishable from the rest.

On one of our visits he thought his wife was actually his mother. She'd died when he was only four years old! His brain was a scrambled mess, and his memory completely gone. But something uncanny had happened to our relationship.

I wondered if it was because he was no longer wearing glasses. The victim of extreme short-sightedness he used to sport very thick spectacles, with lenses like the base of a bottle, and which more or less concealed his eyes. Unlike those of the rest of the family they were grey-green.

They say the eyes are a mirror of the soul, and, on the rare occasions when he recognised me, I had the strangest feeling that I was seeing deep into the real man as never before. I was no longer afraid of him. There was pity, of course, but apart from that, I felt something for this pathetic wreck of a human being who happened to be my father, and whose face lit up when he recognised me, a fact which I had difficulty in believing... Was I seeing the real human being, as he might have been without the trauma of his own dreadful childhood...? Was I actually feeling *love*?

ELEVEN

What's wrong, Dad?"

"Wrong? Nothing... nothing in particular..."

Mandy is, of course, unconvinced.

"Come on. I know that look." She's worried. "What happened?"

"I told you. Nothing."

"You had an appointment with the social worker this morning."

"That's right."

I don't want to tell her, but I know she wont give up. I'll try and bluff.

"Well? What did she say?"

"She's going to arrange for someone to come and relieve me for a while twice a week, so that I can start swimming again."

"But that's good." Suspiciously: "What else?"

"There's also the possibility of a night nurse once a week to give me an uninterrupted sleep."

"That's even better."

For a moment I think I might get away with it, but my daughter knows me too well.

"So why the long face? There's something you're not telling me."

With a sigh I accept the inevitable. Anyway, if I keep it to myself any longer I feel as if I'll burst.

"She asked me for details in order to brief the night attendant. How, for example, do I cope with the commode? So I told her about getting Mum up from the bed, first into a sitting position, then to her feet, turning her round, settling her, and reversing the procedure to settling her down again. She wanted to know how long it took, and how much movement she could manage unaided..."

"What comment did she make?"

"She said it sounded like a wrestling match."

"And then?"

Mandy's prised it out of me at last. She always does.

"She said that the nature of the disease means that

before long it will need two people to move her about, and then, when I come to social services for help, it will entail placing her in a 'home.' And it will almost certainly be a 'home' that we don't like."

"Oh, my God. What did you say?"

"Over my dead body."

"Yes. I knew that would be your answer. So? Did she suggest an alternative? Well? What was it?"

"You don't want to know."

"Oh yes, I do."

"She says that rather than be forced to accept whatever social services can offer, we should begin preparations - and inquiries - for a 'home' of our choosing."

"Oh, my God!"

"She wants to do it now!"

"You didn't agree?"

"Of course not. Actually we had a bit of an argument - quietly, because Mum was in the other room, and the last thing I wanted was for her to overhear this conversation - and she made an appointment for next month to reopen the subject."

At this point Mandy bursts into tears, and, after a minute:

"You haven't told Elaine?"

"Now I'll have to."

"Well, tell us when the social worker's coming, and at least one of will be here."

We stare at each other for a long moment.

"You see what you've done?" I say. "Now we're both miserable."

Just after my fifteenth birthday war was declared against Germany. Reluctantly I confess that, at that age, I could not repress a tingle of anticipation. Nurtured on adventure stories which were more concerned with heroics than massacres, the future held some prospect of excitement. Of course I should have known better, and my suppressed emotions of that time were trivial, compared with the massive relief I felt six years later in a military hospital when the fighting was over.

September 1939 did indeed mark a great change in my life. I left home: that is to say I left behind me the unwholesome environment of Limehouse and docklands, but, more significantly, the unpredictable rages of my father, who actually acted with great presence of mind to keep the rest of his family together. He discussed the problems of evacuation - the scheme whereby all schools in the danger area of London were to be removed with their teachers and pupils to places in England considered safer from air raids - with his uncle, Abe Hyams, who was headmaster of the Robert Montefiore Junior School in the heart of the East End. Uncle Abe was at the time looking for a "helper" to assist the teachers in the more domestic care of his pupils, and suggested that my mother accompany him, and that my brother, Alan, should enrol in the class of his age group. Mum said she couldn't leave me. Unfortunately, at fifteen, I was too old for Junior School, said my uncle, at which point his wife, Aunt Fanny, had a brainwave:

"You could be Michael's tutor."

"Of course. I'd like that."

So it was decided, and shortly afterwards we found ourselves in Haddenham, a delightful village in Cambridgeshire. The three of us were assigned to our "billet", a pretty house owned by an elderly couple, brother and sister, who gave us a warm welcome, possibly relieved at having a mother and two sons aged nine and fifteen rather than a trio of screaming little ones. At all events they showed us nothing but kindness and friendship throughout our stay. They became very fond of my mother - who wouldn't? - and perhaps for the only time in his life - it could be because he was miles away from our father - my brother behaved impeccably. Another reason might have been the fact that he was given permission for unlimited access to the orchard and its apples - marvellous that September. Moreover he quickly made new friends in his class, and they were all - town bred and starved of greenery as they were - enraptured by the freedom and space of their new environment.

Ironically the first few months of the war may well have been the most peaceful I had ever known. Born and bred in the heart of London, all my senses had been assailed by emanations from the slums, grey stone, ugly buildings, the clatter of trams from the terminus outside the bedroom window, hooting of ships' sirens from the nearby docks, persistent smoke, snarling traffic to and from the dock gates and the hovels of Limehouse's Chinatown emitting smells I found offensive, and not a tree or a blade of grass to be seen within miles.

The Cambridgeshire countryside offered a blissful change, in all its autumnal glory, with vast stretches of the most incredible shades of green, beautiful skies which were not obscured by endless rooftops and smoking chimneys, and, most remarkable of all, the silence of night, broken only by the whispering of leaves, the chatter of crickets and the early morning song of the birds.

Moreover we were extremely fortunate in our designated billet. I had never known people like our host and the maiden lady who was his sister. Until now we had been completely absorbed as a family in the life of the East London ghetto, virtually barricaded against all influences from the multi-racial squalor, unfriendliness, poverty and ignorance with which we felt surrounded and threatened. Our new hosts were from a group as alien to us as if they came from a different planet. It was our first experience of English, Christian gentility... which we appreciated, respected and grew to love.

Our hosts were reserved and shy of us at first, but invariably solicitous and kind. In a very short time they were completely charmed by my mother. In fact I had a suspicion that the crusty old bachelor had fallen secretly in love with her, while his sister very soon dropped her reserve and confided in her as a friend. The difference of religion had no place in our relationship, except as a source of interest. The only problem might have been food, since, at that time, we were all strictly kosher; however that difficulty was solved by the simple fact of our becoming vegetarian ... no problem at all, since Horace and his sister were distributors of fresh vegetables and fruit, with which we were liberally supplied. My young brother, Alan, was particularly happy with the abundance of two favourite items of his diet - apples and tomatoes.

The picture of our host which springs most readily to my mind is his ritual at the end of each meal. He would unfold his snow white, starched table napkin, use it to take two sweeping and vigorous swipes at his flowing white moustache, one to the left, then to the right, carefully refold the napkin into its original crease, replace it on its former place; then he would nod first to my mother, then to his sister, to me and finally Alan, before rising from his chair - with never a hint of a belch or - heaven forbid, a fart. None of us would have dreamt of leaving the table before the ceremony was complete.

His sister was amused by the fact that Horace insisted on Mrs. Shocket cooking his morning bacon. Only my mother had the gift of preparing this with exactly the right amount of crispness, without burning and spoiling the meat.

"It does smell marvellous," said Mum. "I sometimes feel tempted to try a bit ... just once."

But, of course, she never did.

Or did she?

Uncle Abe and Aunt Fanny bring into the story my father's family, which requires some introduction.

My paternal grandfather, a butcher, was an austere and - for me - remote character. Widowed when my father was four years old, in accordance with ancient tradition, he married his dead wife's sister. Perhaps the practice originated with the thought that an aunt would make a more sympathetic replacement for a natural mother than a stranger, but this certainly did not apply to my father and his older brother, for whom Aunt Minny became a fairy tale *step*-mother. I believe she bore considerable responsibility for my father's mental instability, and remember her as a silly, pretentious woman. Mum, a wonderful mimic, used to give a hilarious impersonation of her, satirising her absurd snobbery and peculiarities of speech to perfection. Aunt Minny had a lisp, and an inability to pronounce the letters "th". Furthermore, although a kosher butcher's wife, and herself from a long line of butchers, she was no inhabitant of 'Befnal Green," her original family habitat, of which she would speak in comically derisive terms, but conducted her business in "Hammerthmiff," frequently removed in her conversation to the more prestigious area of "Kenthington."

Both my grandfathers were deeply religious and completely orthodox - but there the similarity ended. As a child, I was constantly perched on Zeida Goldberg's knee, and my face agreeably scratched by his beard. He was forever telling me stories, and invariably smiling. But I can recall no physical contact whatever with my other grandfather. Never a week passed without my seeing my maternal grand-parents, and I spent many of the happiest week-ends of my life in their house. My other grandpa I wouldn't see for months at a time, and was kept at arm's length on the rare occasions we paid him a visit. I can never remember his coming to our home, whereas I have cherished memories of Booba getting off the tram on Zeida's arm, invariably carrying a large bag of goodies, and my grandfather holding a gigantic French loaf on his other shoulder. Zeida Shocket was a different kind of man altogether.

He had two sisters, both of whom were married to headmasters. The younger woman, Fanny, we have already met, and the older, Leah, was married to the head of the most celebrated Hebrew school in London, a reputed innovator in direct method language teaching - *"Ivrit b'Ivrit,"* and a leading figure in early twentieth century Zionism. My father loved to bathe in his reflected glory. I found the Reverend J.K. Goldblum just a lovable old man, much more demonstrative and openly affectionate than his brother-in-law. His son, Herzl, was to play quite an important role in my future, responsible, in fact, for the most momentous event in my life.

Grandpa Shocket's youngest sister, Aunt Fanny, had none of the austerity of her older brother. She had an impish sense of humour, and was on the same wavelength as my brother; it was if they had a secret form of silent communication, which would send them both into peals of laughter. After Mum returned to docklands, and I rejoined my old school in its new location, the unique couple who had organised our enrolment in the school virtually adopted Alan, and contrived to keep him trouble free, except for the time he broke his leg, whereupon Uncle Abe carried him around as if he were a baby.

In the early days when we were all together, the war was an anti-climax. Our gas masks remained unused, there were no air raid warnings, no sounds of gunfire, and I was exceptionally happy, especially with my first experience of country life. Entranced by my surroundings, armed with the sketchbook and pencils provided for me by my uncle, I attempted to copy nature's magnificent sculpture of tree-trunks, massing of variegated foliage, and wanted desperately to capture the colours of autumn, but with little success. I was never happy with water colours, and found the powder paints I'd used at the club under the guidance of the "missus" uncomfortably "scratchy". As with the paints given to me now, I only achieved either a wishy-washy or muddy effect. It was years later that I experienced the thrill of using oils, to which - mixing metaphors - I took as a duck takes to water.

On our first morning at Haddenham, Uncle Abe needed to hold a staff meeting. Hesitantly he turned to his "helper" - Mum.

"Pearl, is there any way you could possibly keep an eye on all these children for about an hour?"

My mother gaped at him. She'd been compelled to leave school at the age of fourteen with the outbreak of the first world war, and the prospect of taking on the role of teacher-in-charge must have been daunting. Then, as she looked round the hall her eyes fell on the piano.

"Can you find me some music? Songs? Hymns? Some I can improvise..."

"Marvellous!"

Inspired by the example of this lady I hardly recognised as my mother, I had the audacity to offer my services too.

"Can you also find some poems and stories I could read?"

"We've plenty of those."

And it worked. The kids had a wonderful time. So did we.

The harmony between my great uncle and aunt enfolded them in an aura which was almost tangible. I asked Uncle Abe to propose the toast to the bride and groom at my own wedding. Implicit must have been the wish that our marriage would involve as remarkable a bond as theirs. When he was ninety I paid him a visit. He had an appointment to give a tutorial to a semi-literate adult in the vicinity.

Aunt Fanny handed him his walking stick, and brushed a speck of dust off his lapel.

"Be careful how you step off the kerb, dear."

They exchanged a kiss. He shook my hand, smiled, and off he went.

The couple were without doubt influential in my acquiring the reputation of an incorrigible romantic.

To the dismay and incomprehension of Alan and myself, our mother decided to return home to docklands. How, we wondered, could she choose to go back to *him*? Shortly after her departure, arrangements were made for me to rejoin my old school in its new site at Fakenham, Norfolk, as a member of the fifth form preparing for the first University examination, which we then called "Matric." Since there had been no sign of any German bombers, as an intermediary stage, I followed Mum back to our home in West India Dock Road.

A few weeks later I was in Fakenham, a busy town in Norfolk, where I rejoined Central Foundation School for my fifth and final year. I have pleasant memories of this little town, mainly because I secured a place in the same billet as my great friend, Pip, and we were lucky to find ourselves with a delightful family in - of all places - a bakery!

What I most clearly recollect is the heavenly smell of freshly baked bread which pervaded the place each morning. Our host and his eldest son, Jack, began their day at four a.m. We grew accustomed to the bustling sounds of their early activity, followed by the waking noises of the town outside the window of our cosy bedroom on the bright mornings of late autumn, 1939, as yet undisturbed by the dreaded hubbub of anti-aircraft fire and German bombers.

Breakfasts were great: hot rolls and newly discovered bacon, all the more succulent for being - as far as we were concerned - strictly forbidden. It was a fine start to each day, and school, now that we were fifth formers intent on passing the all important end-of-year examinations, was no longer an imposition. With a common aim, we were no longer at loggerheads with our teachers.

Traditionally, boys at Cowper Street School fooled around, intent on having as much fun as possible in the early years, but when the crucial university exams loomed ahead, underwent a complete change of attitude. Faced with the probable fate of their fathers, who toiled for a pittance in the virtual sweat shops of East End clothing factories as "pressers", "under-pressers" and, at best, tailors, they became hell-bent on acquiring some professional qualifications. Consequently, Central Foundation School had a splendid academic record.

Pip was a typical example. His father, an immigrant with no special training or trade, virtually killed himself in underpaid menial factory work to keep his large family alive in conditions of the most abject poverty. Pip has three sons, all highly qualified academics, and from my own classmates in 5A, over half reached universities; one became my family G.P., another my accountant, one a reputable consultant, and I had the proud privilege of one day watching my friend, Cyril, on stage beside Laurence Olivier.

At Fakenham, Cyril and I were selected to represent the school, and given prime roles in a performance at a national drama festival. I'd already been on stage in club concerts and a one-act play, and, in fact, until our paths were divided by national service, acted later with Cyril in a couple of amateur productions. The feminine lead on two occasions was a pretty fifteen year old - Fenella Feldman - who later adopted the name "Fielding." Even at that tender age her performance was remarkable for a honeyed voice, an almost excruciating drawl and the fluttering eyelashes - all of which would make her famous. In those days she was terrific fun - a lovely girl... After the war Cyril went to R.A.D.A. and began a distinguished career. I went to Cambridge on my way to an academic future. We've remained close friends all our lives, and, the other day, when he phoned me, having just returned from filming in Moscow - at the age of seventy seven! - I have to admit to a spasm of envy, and the thought: "There but for the grace of God..."

Over sixty years ago we were not yet at the threshold of our respective careers, with a common objective, but, unlike Cyril, I was in deep trouble. The minimum requirement for entry into the sixth form, and continuing education, was a pass in five subjects of the General Schools Certificate, with obligatory English, mathematics, a foreign language and a science included. I knew there would be no problem with English, French and German, but, after that I would be in trouble.

To cut a long story short, by dint of intense study and considerable luck, I eventually achieved the minimum requirement by the skin of my teeth. It was a miracle that I succeeded in maths. I owed my success to the brilliant teaching of a martinet we called "Taffy" Evans - a fiery Welshman, who would, under normal circumstances, have murdered me, but, somehow, having taken a liking to me after my comic stage performance, gave me a lot of attention. Taffy had the reputation of being an absolute bastard, but never lost his temper with even an idiot like me - as long as I made an effort to understand. Tyrant though he was, Taffy never lost his cool if you asked him to repeat or explain something.

Although I chose the wrong school, considering the one-sided working of my brain, if I'd been educated at one of the so-called top establishments in the country, my education would have come to an inglorious end when I was barely sixteen. Intent on statistics they would never have allowed a potential failure like me to sit the exams in more than three subjects, whereas, in fact, I was awarded three distinctions and two bare passes - a pathetic result, but it put me on my way.

In June 1940 I left Central Foundation School, left Fakenham, and, since the threat of air raids on London had not materialised, made my way back home to docklands.

It seems that the Luftwaffe had been waiting for just that.

I'm driving Irène to the day centre in Edgware. She looks even prettier than usual; she visited the hairdresser yesterday, is wearing a sky blue top which I particularly like, set off to perfection by a little silver necklace I bought for her last week, and a long, almost diaphanous floral skirt in honour of the brilliant summer sunshine. Momentarily I take my eyes off the road to steal a glance at her... the same beautiful profile of over sixty years ago. The stereo is quietly playing one of her favourite love songs. There is no need for words between us. Traffic is light, and I wouldn't mind driving along like this all day.

We arrive at the centre. She arranges herself in the wheelchair with some difficulty, because of the flowing skirt, and I wheel her inside towards the table she has been allocated. Surrounded by her elderly and generally faded companions she glows like a ray of sunshine. Small wonder that she's so warmly greeted.

I say good-bye.

"Don't I get a kiss too?" asks her neighbour, Fay.

"With pleasure."

On her right, Simon, a great bear of a Russian immigrant, shakes my hand.

"Don't worry. I'll look after her for you."

He will too.

A grouchy old sourpuss opposite grumbles about the wheelchair inconveniencing her foot. Fay wipes the floor with her.

On my way out a smartly dressed, middle-aged

woman stops me. It's the welfare officer.

"May I have a word?"

"Please."

"You know that we're closing down for a few weeks ... holiday time..."

She pauses, clearly uncomfortable.

"I really don't know how to tell you this... I hate having to do it... but...I'm afraid we can't accept Irène back after the holiday."

It's as if she's hit me with a brick.

"We're really very sorry about this, but she does need one to one attention. I have four volunteers and over sixty people to look after..."

I hardly hear the rest: liability, lack of professional staff, insurance... My first reaction is anger. I have the kindness to leave my lovely Irène to light up their existence; her presence brings the place to life - she's literally welcomed with open arms, and now...

Then common sense dissipates my unreasonable irritation. Her mobility problems are increasing alarmingly. I have difficulty in manipulating her physically at home.

"I wish I didn't have to say this to you."

I realise she's telling the truth, and nod unhappily.

"I understand."

I do indeed, and the implication is disturbing. I turn and look at my wife, shining like a star at her table. She's so pretty. My heart turns over.

What next?

TWELVE

The name of the film eludes me, but I was alone in the Troxy, a cinema in Stepney, nearly a mile away from West India Docks, the location of our shop, over which we were living at the time, when all hell broke loose. Exactly what happened is something of a blur, but I recall a kind of stampede, and running like mad towards home - and what appeared to be a high wall of fire.

This was September 1940, and the Blitz had just started. Naturally the docks were a prime target. Our home was about fifty yards from the dock gates, behind which there was a raging inferno.

At this point I'll ask my Uncle Joe to take up the story.

He came to see us a few days ago, sprightly and trim as ever at the age of eighty-seven. How fortunate he is to be genetically blessed.

Irène is less fortunate, having a family with several members blighted with severe neurological disease. My mother's family, on the other hand, was blessed with longevity: she and six of her seven siblings enjoyed "rude health" into their eighties and nineties... so, with luck, I'll have time to finish this book. And Uncle Joe still has no difficulty finding willing partners at his weekly sessions of ballroom dancing. Here, in accordance with Jewish tradition, I have to mimic spitting three times - "*Tu tu tu*' - to ward off the evil eye.

During his visit he couldn't stop talking about his latest toy - a computer - at which he spends hours every day, and he showed some interest in mine. I explained to him that I only use it as a word processor, and, in the course of conversation I let him have a brief glance at this manuscript.

"Perhaps I could do something like that," he said thoughtfully.

Then the idea struck me:

"Why not write about your experiences during the war as a member of the Auxiliary Fire Service?"

My suggestion was received with enthusiasm, and

acted upon the moment he got home. So, at this point of my narrative, I would like to whet your appetite for reading his projected autobiographical work: "Fireman Goldberg," by quoting a page or two, dealing with the first day of the Blitz, witnessed from the other side of that blazing curtain towards which I was running home from the cinema on that sunny autumn day.

* * * * * *

As a member of the Auxiliary Fire Service, apart from several minor fires and false alarms, my experience was limited to drills at the main fire station at Shadwell, then in the heart of the docks, where we were sited right next to a building we called "The Brandy Vaults," containing 50,000 gallons of spirit. They warned us that if ever it was hit in an air raid, our only chance of survival would be to dive into the twenty two feet of water in the docks... and swim for our lives!

The Blitz hit London on a glorious September day.

I heard a distant hum, increasing to a roaring crescendo, as the sky simply filled with planes. Adding to an enormous build-up of ear-splitting noise came the "Crump! Crump!" of exploding bombs, the staccato of anti-aircraft fire; then suddenly overhead was a titanic battle between R.A.F. fighters and enemy planes.

I honestly don't recall fear as one of my emotions, but I was certainly intoxicated with excitement. There was too much for us to do to leave room for fear. In pairs we tackled blaze after blaze, each one of which would normally involve an entire fire station. For the rest of the day and night we fought the inferno - and "fought" is the operative word. An amateur boxer - I use the term "fire-fighting", and leave no doubt about who has to win. However long it takes there must be only one outcome.

The resources were all there - and, given the location, no shortage of water for dousing the incendiary bombs, and preventing re-combustion afterwards. We had no time to look around, but we thought all London was ablaze. For seventeen hours - without a breather - we were up and down ladders, atop them as they sometimes swayed precariously, hammering with our axes, and constantly fighting fire with endless jets of water.

I have no recollection of sirens sounding the "all clear", but I do remember the blessed relief in the morning when, our battle almost over, we were able to have our first taste of food and drink. In the ruins of a warehouse, among the debris we found cans of pineapple and peaches. Using our axes to break open the tins we slaked our thirst and assuaged our pangs of hunger with their contents. Most delicious of all I found the tins of Polish pickled cucumbers - "just like the ones mother makes" - and how wonderful it felt to stretch our strained muscles under a clear, momentarily quiet sky.

On a subsequent raid the adjacent "Brandy Vaults" were indeed hit by a bomb. We were spared the challenge of leaping into the water to swim for our lives by the miraculous fact that the missile did not explode. I remember our being half drunk the following day, and kissing the bloody thing before the bomb disposal unit arrived to deal with it.

The morning after the first raid we heard that the R.A.F. had shot down one hundred and sixty seven Luftwaffe machines, but realised that this was just the beginning of a terrible struggle. It wasn't very long before we were almost overwhelmed by disgust and horror, as we pulled severely burned, dead and dying civilians out of buildings in the East End, and were sickened by the lines of blood-stained stretchers at the London Hospital in Whitechapel.

* * * * * * *

While Fireman Goldberg, on the other side of the dock gates, was striving manfully to hold back the flames, here was his nephew, running as fast as his legs would carry him, seemingly straight into the inferno. Amazed at last to see my father's shop still standing, I flew inside, straight into my mother's arms. To say that we were pleased to see each other is quite an understatement.

Clearly it was no longer possible for us to live over the

shop, and I have only vague memories of spending that night with Mum in an air raid shelter, with minimum luggage, half way to the home of Uncle Pop, who had recently moved house from one end of the Northern Line tube to the other, and had implored us to get away from the danger zone to take temporary refuge with him in Edgware. I remember that our journey was interrupted mid-way by the air raid sirens, but don't recall much except being very uncomfortable, and hiding my face in embarrassment when Mum went to pee in a makeshift toilet - and it sounded like Niagara Falls.

Dusty and tired we arrived at my uncle's house to the warmest of welcomes and a delicious breakfast.

My father was to join us later, with the intention of commuting daily to business, and subsequently surprised me by his unusually quiet behaviour, while a guest in my uncle's house.

I spent only a short time there, because it was the beginning of the school year, and I travelled off to Bedford, to join the sixth form of Owen's School, evacuated from Islington, in London.

This afternoon I get the electric chair.

Elaine suggested we try out a kind of small wheelchair, designated for indoor use, powered by rechargeable batteries, and easily manoeuvred by a disabled occupant. The zimmer hasn't been much use so far. Irène tries to make it walk for her - and, of course, that's impossible. As she pushes the frame forward her feet remain glued to the floor; instead of making progress she leans forward more and more, and, unless I straighten her up, would fall flat on her face.

"Don't push! Walk!"

But that's the problem. She can't.

Unfortunately she hasn't the strength - or co-ordination - in fact the slightest desire - to propel herself in the wheelchair we use outdoors, but prefers to lean on someone - me, it goes without saying - to prevent herself from falling. Since I constantly haul her about and wrestle her either upright or to turn her around, my ancient back is beginning to give signs of strain, so my daughter came up with this idea of a simply operated mechanical chair. Now, like a child expecting a new toy, I am eagerly awaiting its delivery for a trial session. Irène, I have to say, does not share my feelings. Pessimistic by nature she hates "gadgets", as she calls them, convinced they won't work before she even sees them. I suppose that's natural enough. She resents needing assistance for what she thinks she should be doing naturally. But understanding her negative attitude doesn't make it easier for me to live with... or perhaps, as my younger daughter, Mandy, delicately puts it, I'm just "an intolerant old bugger." Hopefully, however, this afternoon, if the demonstration is a success, we'll be left with a contraption which will allow Irène free and unassisted movement within the flat. What does she think?

"I won't be able to use it."
"They tell me a child can manage it."
"Children don't have Parkinson's."
"People who've got Parkinson's use them."
"Well I can't."
"How do you know till you try?"
"I just know."
"You used to drive a car."
"I used to do lots of things."
"I'm sure you'll manage."

Well, here comes the technician, a nattily dressed, quietly spoken, middle-aged man. And here too is the machine. When my wife sees it she gives a gasp of horror.

"Is that it ?"
"Quite smart, don't you think?"
"I'm not having that monstrosity in here!"
I wink at the gentleman.
"Don't worry. That's just her sense of humour."
He smiles uneasily.
I offer him a cup of tea, and retire to the kitchen, leaving Irène to charm him, as I know she will. Yes, it's a good move, because, when I return, they're both chatting like old friends, and eventually he persuades her to sit in the

chair.

I'm not sure to what extent she's playing up, but she shows great difficulty in learning how to press a button in order to switch the damn thing on and off. But the chap is unbelievably patient, and eventually moves on to the next stage, and we come to the business of the joystick - a lever no bigger than her little finger.

"Nothing could be simpler."

Is he kidding?

"All you have to do is decide which way you want to go and just point the joystick with your finger - left, like this, right, like this, forward... You see how easy? Now back... and it moves quite slowly...O.K?"

And here's where I make a stupid mistake. Heartened by the simplicity of the whole procedure, I poke my nose in, and try to help. She'll understand me much better than a stranger. It must be a lot easier than when I was teaching her to drive... And that's where I ought to pause, and reflect... and remember.

It was many years ago, and, although we'd been happily married for ages, during this period she revealed rather unpleasant aspects of her character I'd never discovered before. Until I had the belated good sense to hand her over to a professional, we were getting closer and closer to a divorce. Some snippets of conversation still make me shudder as I recall them:

"Turn left."

"Why?"

"Too late. You're going the wrong way up a one way street."

"Why didn't you say so?"

At a roundabout: "Turn right."

"Are you sure?"

"I said so. Turn right. No! You bloody idiot! We're not in France! You can't go this way round a roundabout!"

"You said: "Turn right!"

On another occasion: "You're on the wrong side of the road, dear... the wrong side of the road!"

"Mind your own business."

That's the way it was, and I forget too easily, because here I go again, several years older, but none the wiser, as I try to direct her in the battery operated chair.

"Turn left, darling."

"Why?"

Bang! Then a clatter of broken glasses. That's the bar.

"Turn left... left... left!"

Crash! That's an armchair on its side.

"Stop! Reverse! Pull the blasted knob back towards you... No! Not that way... Watch out for the television! That's better... No... Back!

Careful! That's the gentleman's foot. Sorry... Left! Left..."

Bang!

"For God"s sake! You're wrecking the fucking flat!" Whereupon the technician, after wiping his eyes, intervenes... none too soon.

"Do you mind if I take over?"

"Please."

I have to admit that my pride is somewhat redressed when he doesn't have much more luck than I did, although I have to say, he remains calm and amazingly courteous. But eventually, much as he would love to sell us the chair - a mere two thousand pounds worth, in this case "practically new at half price," he has to call it a day and admit defeat.

"First and foremost," he says apologetically, "we have to consider the safety of our customers."

Shortly after his departure Elaine telephones.

"How did you get on, Mum?"

"Quite well, dear, as a matter of fact."

"You passed?"

"Not quite. I failed the test on a three point turn."

Tranquillity slowly returns to our flat, now clear of wreckage. Irène, rid of the "monstrosity", is asleep in her armchair, which is again upright, apparently undamaged and in its original position. The half smile on her face gives me cause to wonder whether she staged the whole performance. After fifty-four years of marriage she still keeps me guessing. On the other hand she can always read me like a book.

At all events I'm going to take advantage of the fact that she's likely to be out for the count for at least an hour. And return to my adolescence in war-time.

THIRTEEN

My change of school at the age of sixteen was due to the fact that my original choice, Central Foundation, not only specialised in maths and the sciences - at which I was hopeless - but so scorned the arts - at which I excelled - that no advanced level courses in languages were on offer. Having won the Rothschild Modern Languages prize, in order to further my academic career, I had to enrol in the sixth form of another school, preferably with a good reputation for teaching French and German. My favourite teacher, Mr. Hollingworth, gave me excellent advice, and I was accepted at Owen's, evacuated from Islington in North London, to Bedford, where I fell on my feet, sharing a billet with a delightful chap called Charles Schiff. Unlike my previous schoolmates he didn't come from the slums of the East End. I found he had a certain quality of "class" - reflected in aquiline features - which made me feel, by contrast, like a peasant. Nevertheless we became the best of friends.

At first I didn't like the school at all. Discipline was much tighter than at C.F.S. and I soon fell foul of authority. For the first time in my life I found it compulsory to wear school uniform. That would have been acceptable, except for the fact that it entailed wearing a school cap - a practice I had discarded at about the time I started shaving every day at the age of fourteen. Its resumption represented a reversion to childhood at the very time I was desperately trying to prove myself a man. After all it was possible I'd be called up for military service before long. Furthermore, I was becoming more than a little interested in young ladies, and found the idea of parading in front of them with a ridiculously childish cap perched on my head utterly abhorrent.

I had the misfortune of being seen in the town by a particularly unpleasant member of staff without the requisite headgear, which, apparently, he would have liked me to doff with due respect. The following morning I was summoned to his presence - and quite a presence it was too. He was well over six feet tall, and must have weighed about seventeen stone. Towering over me he glared down. I am so filled with shame when I record our conversation and my abject submission, that I must permit myself the indulgence of talking back through time, no longer diminished by his size and the fact that he was twice my age. I'm now over twice as old as he was then - older, yes, and wiser too.

"When I saw you in the street you were not wearing your cap. Is that not so?"

"Yes, sir."

He roared: "Speak up, boy. I can't hear you!"

You heard perfectly well. I suppose you want to show right now who's boss.

"Well?"

"Yes, sir."

"Presumably you've been with us long enough to know the rules?"

"Yes, sir."

If you weren't a natural fascist you'd know that excessive rules are counter-productive, and the imposition of unnecessary laws detract from the respect due to the good ones.

"So why weren't you wearing your cap?"

Something about his attitude really got up my nose at that point, and I looked straight up into his eyes and said:

"Because somebody of my age looks a fool in one."

Ah! you didn't like that, did you?. Good for you, young Michael. Just for a moment there you sounded like your brother, Alan. Mind you, he could get away with it, but you...? Watch out! I can tell he's thinking of something rather unpleasant.

"I'm putting you in detention - not because you weren't wearing a cap - as I would have every right to do - but for insolence."

Whereupon he permitted himself a nasty smile, turned on his heel and walked away.

You sadistic bastard. Sixth formers never get put in detention. You'll make me a laughing stock. But, of course, that's exactly what you want. - that's just the kind of bullying which gives you a kick - probably because your father beat the shit out of you when you were a kid.

And I bet my younger brother, Alan, would have told

him - just that, and would have added:

"So what are you going to do now? Expel me?"

And that is exactly what would have happened to him. Again.

After my initial shock at the enforcement of stricter discipline than I'd experienced previously, and my humiliation at the hands of someone who should never have been given authority over anybody younger and smaller than himself, I learned how to keep out of trouble, and fortunately my tormentor was in the science department, so I was able to keep out of his way. Academically I soon realised that I had fallen on my feet. Form-master of the Lower Sixth was a gentleman called "Dickie Dare," who taught us English Literature, and was able to fire us with enthusiasm with the poetry of Keats. The French master, known affectionately as "Gus", was equally inspirational about French romantic literature, while German romantic poetry, to which I had already been introduced at C.F.S. was sheer bliss when taught by Mr. Pearce. Due to exceptional planning by the Arts department, I was able to link the literature of three European countries. It provided me with a love of romanticism which would remain with me for my entire academic career and be the subject, years later, of my Ph.D thesis.

Despite my irritation at the irksome discipline of the school, I shall always be deeply indebted to Owen's for the excellent education I received. Furthermore I was introduced to Latin, passed the school certificate examination which was at the time essential for entry to Oxbridge after only nine months study, and "Dickie" was responsible for planting a cultural seed which would bring me immense pleasure for the rest of my life.

At that time the B.B.C. Symphony Orchestra was broadcasting from the Corn Exchange, Bedford, quite close to the situation of our school, and Mr. Dare had the idea of taking us along to rehearsals, which he followed up with lively discussion of what we heard. Malcolm Sargent was conducting and took the trouble to talk to us about each item they were about to perform. The first piece of classical music I ever heard "live" was Mendelssohn's Hebrides Overture.

Hearing a full-bodied, full-blooded symphony orchestra was a completely new experience for me and had an explosive impact which I recall as one of the greatest emotional experiences of my life. If I close my eyes now, I can hear those opening chords, and visualise a turquoise sea.

Gus, apart from teaching French, was also responsible for the annual school play. In my first year at Owen's his production was set in a Gothic interior, and I offered to design the set. It involved quite a lot of panelling, and I remember my difficulty in mastering the technique of painting wooden scrolls. The following year I again undertook a novel theatrical experience, and played a ballad singer.

One event which cast a shadow over my stay in Bedford was the news of my beloved grandfather Goldberg's death. A letter from my mother said that he'd died in her arms, looking radiantly happy, and with the words: "I'm better now."

That evening I went for a solitary walk, and spent a long time staring up at the starlit sky.

Could his spirit be up there, I wondered? Is that where he'll find the God with whom he communed devotedly so many hours for every single day in his life? Grandpa had been ill for months, and was his dying cry a glimpse of the paradise he so deserved?

I remember the tight feeling in my chest, due to the emotion I'd been holding back, and I tried to reach out for his soul... Was it way up beyond the stars in the impenetrable sky? I did know that it was eternally a part of mine. I spoke aloud to Zeida's spirit, and cried a little. Then the tightness in the region of my heart relaxed.

A few weeks later I said goodbye to Bedford. Although I was thrilled that my schooldays were over, it was not altogether a happy homecoming. The family which welcomed me was mourning a great loss.

I am deeply grateful for my two year's experience at Owen's of English grammar school teaching at its best. My immersion in study - really more enjoyment than hard work - was rewarded with an exhibition to study Modern Languages at Cambridge, where I began the course in

September 1942.
  But first of all I was to meet my first real girlfriend.

FOURTEEN

I'm about to do my morning chore: take down the rubbish, bring up the morning mail - usually unsolicited offers to give me a huge loan, or telling me that I've had the unique good fortune to be selected for a free gift and the possibility of winning an enormous sum of money, if...

On some days in the lift I meet my next door neighbour on a similar errand - hopefully not this morning. After last night's shenanigans I wouldn't know what to say to her.

The social worker's main argument in suggesting the consideration of residential care was her contention that in the not too distant future we'd find it would require two people to lift or move Irène. I told her that if that happened I'd somehow think of an alternative solution. But last night I was made painfully aware of the fact that we do have a problem. Several times I was disturbed: twice to get rid of some extraordinary nocturnal visitors, one of whom somehow found her way into our bed, once to make sure that the curtains in the lounge were properly drawn - don't ask me why - and several times for her to use the commode.

What I'd only give for just one uninterrupted night's sleep! I can sympathise with a mother suppressing a homicidal urge, when she has to pick up time after time, night after night, a screaming child. It's one thing to lift a baby, however, but quite another to haul a woman weighing nine and a half stone to her feet and hold her there. Whenever Irène needs to pee we have a performance. Without going into explicit detail, the difficulties should be obvious if I say that I'm moving an inert weight. Many sufferers from Parkinson's disease cannot turn, and their brains have a problem sending the appropriate message to their rear ends in which direction they should be aimed, the designated target area for discarded toilet paper ...enough! Suffice to say that according to the large luminous dial on our bedroom clock, the procedure each time now lasts from ten to fifteen minutes, at the beginning of which my eyes refuse to remain open, and, at the end of which, they persistently refuse to remain closed.

Last night was a lulu. The fourth time I was roused from slumber - having only just lapsed into sleep, we engaged in a veritable wrestling match to get her to her feet, when - alas - I lost my grip, and she began to fall. With the reflex action of a passenger in a lurking train she reached for something to hang on to - and grabbed my exposed manhood, hanging on for dear life. At that point I emitted a yell that must have awakened half the occupants of our block of flats Then, to offset the force of gravity, I tried to hold her up by seizing her shoulders, whereupon she let out a scream which probably woke up the other half.

"You're hurting me!"

And she's the injured party!

"I'll be black and blue!"

I express indifference to the impending colour change.

"And how about you using my willie like a straphanger?"

"It isn't funny, Michael."

And that's a fact.

As far as London children of the lower and middle classes were concerned, in the early part of the century, the actual location of our homes was the decisive factor in out-of-school friendships. In the confines of Cowper Street and within range of the overwhelming smell of its biscuit factory, we had our circles of pals. Once through the school gates, relationships depended on the area in which we lived. Every morning I was joined on the sixty five tram by boys from the East End Jewish ghetto, many of whom were fellow members of my club. The majority of other pupils in my year travelled to school southwards on the forty three tram from the slightly more salubrious district of Stamford Hill, and the two groups had virtually no chance of contact after school hours.

The pal with whom I had most in common during the day, Cyril, travelled on the forty three, putting paid to any extra mural association we might have wished.

By 1942 the situation changed. Pip and I were by now swept apart by the tides of war. He was in the R.A.F.

and, eventually deeply involved with our careers and families, we would regrettably not meet again for too many years. When, after my Higher Schools examination I went to live again in my parents' home, it was in Edgware. My father had bought a house there, close to most of Mum's brothers and sisters.

In the forties and fifties, like ripples in a pond, Jewish families moved outwards, away from their ghetto in the East End, regrouping either northwards in Golders Green, Hendon and Edgware, or further east in Ilford. The ripples, incidentally are still moving north and west of the centre of London, with the constant building of new synagogues for newly burgeoning communities. In the wake of these outward moving circles are those of later ethnic groups. I would like to think that eventually the ripples will give way to an even surface - an amalgam in which racism simply disappears.

Be that as it may, in 1942, in search of a social life in the neighbourhood, with a typical clannish attitude I made my way to the local youth club, attached, of course to the synagogue. To my delight I met my old friend, Cyril, with whom I've always had a great amount in common. A few years later he was best man at my wedding, I reciprocated when he married Anita, and we've been close ever since.

He introduced me to a group of young people, all keen on the theatre and staging their own performances. I couldn't take my eyes off one particular girl, and, if I close them, I see her now: slim figure, well shaped, pretty features, tip-tilted nose, enormous eyes, generous lips perfectly curved for laughter... Cupid cast his arrow. Off balanced with its impact, when she spoke to me I stammered,
couldn't find my words and felt like a slave in the presence of Cleopatra.

I'd just met Stella.

From that first meeting we were inseparable, and wrote endlessly to each other when we were apart. I couldn't wait to see her whenever I came home - at first from university, and then on leave from the army. It would belittle our relationship to say she was my girl-friend. Stella was one of the most intelligent people I've known. I not only opened my heart to her, but my mind. It seemed that we'd be together forever.

Again I was swept away on the tide of war. Shortly after I'd enlisted, she met a glib, hulking brute who apparently swept her off her feet, and I learned that she'd become engaged. I was devastated. Before long she found that she'd made a terrible mistake and broke off the relationship, but, by that time I still smarted too badly from her uncharacteristic betrayal to renew old ties. Years later I heard that she'd gone to Australia. In fact, I haven't seen her for nearly sixty years.

You were very special, Stella. I hope you're well, and have had a good life. I'd dearly love to see that tip-tilted nose again.

My romance with Stella occurred at the crossroads of both our lives; we had emerged from adolescence and were about to be caught up in the havoc of a world apparently hell bent on self destruction. Stella donned the uniform of ENSA, the unit responsible for entertaining the armed forces, and looked good enough to eat, and I, with a gown flowing in my wake, was riding a bicycle through the streets of a university town.

In many ways Cambridge surpassed my expectations. Academically it fell short. Perhaps the forties were a low spot for staffing: young men were involved elsewhere, and their replacements appeared to have been dug out of retirement and recruited from old age homes.

I was to discover that lecturers performing once a week - and one day I was to become one myself - are, with rare exceptions, crashing bores, and attendance at their hour-long sessions a sheer waste of time. To be of any value a lecture should fulfil one of two criteria: afford live contact with a man or woman of exceptional personality, or provide the audience with information not readily available elsewhere. Nearly all my teachers at Cambridge satisfied neither requirement, and their lectures were perfect examples of what a wit described as "a series of notes travelling from the lecturer's desk to the student's notebook, without passing through the minds of either."

It didn't take me long to realise the absurdity of it all: straining my ears to hear some old fart mumbling a rehash of a text book - not necessarily written by himself either - which was readily available in more coherent form in the library. Instead of breathing stale air in an overcrowded hall and fighting sleep, I could glide happily along the Cam in a punt, enjoying the sunshine, browse among the bookshops, chat with friends over coffee, or study in the comfort of my room - my very own private room! - and, having worked during the day, enjoy a film in the evening, or - best of all - take part in rehearsals for a play or revue. When I wasn't involved with the dramatic society, my friends and I would argue far into the night, changing the face of the world - and this is where my real academic development flourished.

To be fair I have to admit that a few - very few - of the staff were excellent, and I derived a great deal of benefit from seminars, confirming my belief that, to be of value, teaching cannot be one-way. But there were two gentlemen, at least, who should have never been uprooted from peaceful retirement. First there was my personal tutor for French. He was, in fact, a charming old boy - off duty. Over dinner, with a glass of wine, he could be entertaining and funny. In a tutorial he was a joke.

Once a week I climbed the rickety stairs to his study - how he ever navigated them himself I'll never know - where he was waiting for me, invariably with a glass of milk on an otherwise bare desk. During our session he would lift the glass to his lips every few minutes, the sips interspersed with faint belches and gurgles from his protuberant stomach. The tutorials, which never lasted the full allocated time, always followed a set pattern. Sitting opposite him I would read an essay he'd set the previous week. Nodding from time to time - and I could never tell if it was a sign he was dozing off - he gave the impression of listening, although he rarely interrupted with any comment, and, when I came to the end, he'd say:

"What are you reading now?"

Either I'd tell him, or occasionally ask for guidance,

whereupon he stirred into a semblance of life, sat upright for a moment, and cast his eye along the well-stocked bookshelves until it lighted on a work falling within my field of study.

"Ah, yes..."

He'd read out a title and his memory clicked almost visibly into action. From a vast list of examination questions he'd set or marked in the last century he'd fish out a chestnut, which would be my task until the following week. Not once was I given any indication of a grade, and there was no sign of his making any notes... yet he contrived to give me a mark on an end of term report. And it was always the same as the one given me by the German tutor. Of course.

But the most flagrant instance of resuscitating the dead was a doddering ninety year old - no exaggeration - who lectured on seventeenth century French literature, and I almost suspected that his familiarity with the subject was due to personal acquaintance with the authors concerned. Having reached the lectern - no mean feat in the circumstances - and got his breath back, he snuffled and mumbled too quietly to be heard beyond the first couple of rows. His English was barely audible, and when he had the audacity to quote in French, his pronunciation merited his being sent to Devil's Island. One day I would be a university oral examiner for the language, and I failed students at A Level with better accents than his.

Uninspired as I was by most of the university teaching I couldn't complain about my social life. On my first night in hall for dinner, a happy chance landed me at a table for six - a lucky twist of fate indeed, because we were to become a group of close friends for the entire year, before we went our various ways into military service. My nearest neighbour in college, Paul Vafidis, had a Greek orthodox background, there were two provincial chaps who were fervent Christians, a farmer's son, and one fellow Jew, a Scot studying mathematics.

From each other, over coffee, or tea and cakes, we learned more in each other's rooms - often in the middle of the night - than in any of our various lecture theatres. Fate, alas, sent us on different paths during and after war service, but I was able to organize a reunion, placing them together at a noisy table on the occasion of my wedding.

Divided by a not very glorious army career, my course at the university was in two periods, the first of which was the exciting beginning of a voyage of discovery. Brimful of preconceived convictions, I learned to question them, and open my shuttered mind to give access to the ideas and traditions of my friends, coming from different backgrounds. It was a kind of liberation from a fixed ethnic programming. And I've never moved back.

I was also able to immerse myself in reading. I spent many happy hours - and a small fortune - in the bookshops. To give him credit, my father, whom I'd always considered the meanest of men, never quibbled about the money I was spending on books. For the first time in my life he encouraged - even approved... Was it the distance between us, I wondered, which was responsible for the improvement in our relationship? Was it a vicarious exculpation of his own thwarted academic aspirations? Whatever the cause, my university career marked a changed in his attitude.

However my greatest moments at Cambridge were unquestionably on the stage, where I had sizeable roles in English and French. The best performance I gave was in a revue, for which some wit had written a sketch involving Hitler depicted as a spy in an English household in the guise of a gas inspector. I had the part, for which I was allowed to compose a tirade in German, with the instruction:

"Take the piss out of the language."

Forsaking the sweet sounds of my beloved lyric poets, I delivered a harangue in the most guttural, staccato, lavatorial and ferociously animal sounds I could produce. The speech - expectorating insults at Churchill, Roosevelt, Stalin, Bolshevists and Jews - culminated in my standing in a profiled, mock Hitlerian pose, with my right arm raised in a Nazi salute. It brought the house down. But, after all, that was 1942.

In that same year relatives of Irène and myself from Brussels and Paris were crushed into cattle wagons, gasping for air, en route to extermination camps in Poland.

A gifted linguist, my cousin Herzl was in the Intelligence Corps, and on a course in Cambridge. He was a frequent visitor during his time off duty, and, despite a considerable age difference, we became close. Our friendship managed to survive his attempts to proselytise. An ardent Marxist, he was forever inundating me with communist literature in which I found too little to deflect me from more important reading. I accepted the fact that his extreme left wing convictions had only the most humanitarian motives, but I was already influenced towards generally liberal ideas by the views of my small group of friends, and unimpressed by all extremist factions at the university. As yet we were unable to accept hook, line and sinker any ready-made manifesto.

Long before the media presented selected facts to the public, a Greek philosopher quipped that the first casualty in war was the truth. In the forties, Churchill, Roosevelt and Stalin were presented as the world's champions of freedom - our greatest defence against the evils of dictatorship and the cruelty it could inflict with impunity. Stalin - a fictitious benevolent "Uncle Joe" - was portrayed as a heroic freedom fighter almost worshipped by my cousin, who should have known better. Herzl was unable to convert me, although I still feel twinges of guilt at pretending to read his books.

The course he was on, and the military work in which he was involved were, of course, secret, and outside the bounds of our conversation, but I was sufficiently intrigued to decide that when I enlisted I'd try to be, like him, in Intelligence. In fact, that is what happened, and our next encounter, in the event momentous, would be two years later in Brussels.

FIFTEEN

People were banging on the front door.
"N'ouvre pas!"
Paris, 1941, and my mother's cousin, Esther, looked fearfully at her husband. She motioned to the adjoining bedroom. Kiwa nodded and slipped inside. The hammering started again. Holding the little one, Sacha, in her arms, and her ten-year old, Albert, by the hand, Esther reluctantly opened the door to be confronted by a group of French policemen, who demanded to see her husband. In barely comprehensible snippets of French - Yiddish and Polish were her only languages - and mime, she intimated that he was not at home. To her surprise they left, but her relief was short lived when they returned shortly afterwards, accompanied by a German soldier - resplendent in SS uniform. Knowing that her Yiddish, with its great similarity to German, would be understood, she said that her husband was ill - "*krank.*" This was actually true.

The German barked his orders: she and the two boys were to turn and stand with their faces to the wall. He then strode purposefully into the bedroom, slamming the door behind him.

Kiwa Israel Graber left Warsaw a few years before the outbreak of war to establish himself in Paris, where he would be joined later on by his wife and baby son, Albert. There are obvious similarities between his situation, that of my grandfather Goldberg, and of my father-in-law, Chaskiel, thus becoming a sort of "Tale of Three Cities," Paris, London and Brussels. All three gentlemen were from deeply religious backgrounds in the ghettoes of Poland, but only Zeida Goldberg retained a deep pious commitment. Kiwa, in particular could find no place in his essentially rational philosophy for the talmudic brainwashing of his early years.

His sons have hazy memories of him: Sacha recalls bouncing on his knees on the bed and tumbling through as his father opened his legs.

"It used to make me laugh," he says. And it's the only

time there's any mention of laughter in any talk of his childhood. Albert remembers that his father had a splendid voice, sang as soloist in a choir, and how a neighbour expressed delight at hearing him singing while he worked.

A psychiatrist might find it significant that any mention of their mother has to be virtually forced from them. Sacha, in particular, although he was five or six, at the time, old enough to store events in his conscious memory, says he has no recollection of her whatsoever.

The tailor worked round the clock in his effort to scratch a living after Esther arrived with their little son. Then, to their dismay, his wife discovered she was pregnant. There was half-hearted discussion about a termination, until Kiwa declared that somehow they'd manage, and Esther returned from the Saint Louis Hospital with a fourth member of the family to be squeezed into their one room.

Albert went to his first school, *l'école maternelle*, and spent one of the most wretched days of his young life. Speaking no French he was completely isolated from the other children, and unable to communicate in any way with his teacher. He went home in tears, flatly refusing to go back and face another day in school. His father, like many immigrant parents, was almost fanatical in his concern for education within the national framework, and insistent on the boy's return. There was a family dispute in which Esther sided with the child, and, of course, she won. After Kiwa miraculously taught his son to read French - partly using the Hebrew alphabet! - Albert made a more successful start at primary school, and, of course, in a very short time, was chattering in French like a native, and able to help prepare his brother for much more comfortable assimilation.

The family moved to comparatively spacious accommodation, in the rue Saint Maure, naturally within a Jewish neighbourhood. A large gate led into the courtyard where their building was situated, and the first entrance on the right led to their flat, half way up the building, overlooking the yard. There was a view across the rooftops, and the boys often saw chimney sweeps at work. They also recall the frequent presence of beggars, singing in the courtyard, and recall throwing them coins wrapped in scraps of paper from their parent's window. The entire Graber abode consisted of three adjoining rooms - there was no corridor - a kitchen, a workshop and a bedroom. The floors were of bare wood and the walls a sort of muddy brown.

The German occupation meant growing fears, and increased privation, since Kiwa found it impossible - as a Jew - to ply his trade. Esther actually worked for a while for the Germans, entitling her to an "Ausweis," a permit granting limited freedom of movement. The two boys queued for their yellow star, which became their badge of humiliation. Influenced by propaganda, they were concerned to hide their Jewish identity as a shameful secret. They wore their school satchels across their chests to hide the star, just as my father-in-law would conceal his with a folded newspaper, tucked beneath his arm.

There were stories circulating about outrages perpetrated in Germany. They terrified Esther, but, her husband insisted that they had to be exaggerations. This was the twentieth century. People were civilised.

Nevertheless he'd taken the precaution of hiding away a nest-egg, and confiding its whereabouts to their non-Jewish concierge, Mme Braconnier. It was an act which would save the lives of his sons.

Then came the day when the French police were hammering on his door.

Waking from a deep sleep I become aware that my wife is screaming. Hallucinations again? Not this time. She's been having a nightmare, and she's shaking... shaking... shaking from head to toe, and can't stop.

"They're banging on the door!"

It's her usual nightmare.

"Nobody's there, my darling. You've been dreaming..."

She seizes my arm in a vice like hold:

"My sisters! Where are my sisters? I can't see my sisters! They've taken my sisters!"'

"I've got to get inside the wardrobe. Help me!"

"There's no need to hide. Nobody's here except for

you and me. It's just a nightmare."

"The *rafle*?" - meaning a round up of Jews for deportation.

"Only a bad dream."

Gradually she calms down, but can't stop trembling. I help her off the bed, steer her with difficulty to the commode, eventually back on her feet, on to the wheel-chair and into the lounge. It's just after two o'clock in the morning. I make us a cup of tea. At last her shaking has stopped. We talk about the experience being no more than a dream.

"But it's so real!"

"Like your hallucinations?"

She ponders.

"No. It's different."

"How?"

Again she thinks for a while.

"A dream can be very frightening. But then you wake up and know it wasn't real."

I'm about to pursue the matter, but fortunately realise the futility of going down that road again. I've tried so many times, but it always ends in frustration - or worse, anger and tears. Even when I read her the definition of "hallucination" from the dictionary, asking her if she understood the explanation and word "illusion" - "What does 'illusion' mean?" I can tell from her expression that however clear - however rational the explanation, her creatures making their way through locked doors, flying up fifty feet or so to our window, finding a way through the glass, emerging from a cushion too small to house them, polluting the fruit with their filthy hands, and leaving a bad smell on the furniture ... all this is not a projection from her own mind. The "creatures", as she calls them, are alive. I must be seeing them, despite all my protestations. They can and do affect their surroundings and other people in their vicinity, their presence is malign, and - most difficult of all for me to accept - is her occasional assertion that I am in league with them in a conspiracy to cause her harm. Fortunately, this idea crops up rarely. However, when it does, she has a rather crazy look in her eyes that frightens the living daylights out of me. I pray fervently that this is no presage ... no forecast... Could I take it? Will I ever be put to the test?

We are back in bed at half past three. I hold her close, and soon she is asleep. I can only doze intermittently, haunted by visions evoked by her nightmare.

Esther tried to imagine what was happening behind the closed bedroom door. Voices were raised; the German barking like a dog, and her husband's plangent Yiddish. Then came the unmistakable sound of blows, cries of pain and an ear-splitting scream. Turning her head as much as she dared, she saw the SS man framed in the doorway, brushing his hands together with a grimace, as though to remove some form of contamination. She gasped, made a move towards the bedroom, but one of the Frenchmen snarled at her and pushed her back roughly with her nose against the wall.

The soldier gave an order to his accompanying thugs, who went in to the adjoining room, and emerged shortly after, carrying Kiwa, wrapped in a blanket.

The men stamped out of the apartment, one of them laughing, and Esther was about to run after them, but, to prevent the children following her, she put a potty on the table, planted the little one on it, and told Albert to hold on to his brother, and prevent him falling. By the time she reached the street, the vehicle carrying her husband was out of sight. The courtyard was eerily silent and deserted.

When Albert was recently asked to give his account of the incident, his interviewer asked - with some naiveté:

"What effect did this have on you?"

He answered dryly: "Twenty years of psychiatric therapy."

They took Kiwa to the infamous Drancy prison, which was to become the departure point for Auschwitz. He was one of the first Jews to be taken there, because at this time only those who were considered "foreign" were being victimised. So his stay actually lasted a few months.

The family "visited." That is to stay they stood outside the walls, and signalled to him, where he stood high above their heads on a balcony. With bribery they contrived to send him parcels of food and a few creature comforts.

But persecution increased, and, fearful for the safety of her boys, Esther made arrangements for them to be hidden in the country. Albert was old enough to understand, but the feelings of abandonment and betrayal which were presumably felt by the little one, defy imagination.

Their new "home" was in a village called Arou, near Chartres, about a hundred kilometres west of Paris. It was a peasant's hut of one room, accessed by a stable door, owned by an aged couple: the man was bent double, with his back almost horizontal. He and his wife slept in an alcove curtained off during the day. They were neither kind nor unkind to the boys - apparently without emotion, leading the most primitive existence one could imagine. There was no toilet - they used the woods - no electricity, no water... The brothers remember half skinned rabbits hanging around, headless chickens running until they dropped... insects falling out of their hair on to the table...

But the elderly couple did save the boys' lives. Of course they were paid. From his meagre earnings their father had somehow contrived to hide some money, which was sufficient to satisfy the peasants, carried regularly by the concierge, Madame Braconnier's, daughter. And it was this girl who brought them news of their mother's arrest and deportation.

But as far as the younger boy was concerned she'd been dead from the day he was sent away.

My cousins, Albert and Sacha, are two of the gentlest, most civilised and fastidious people I know. It's difficult to envisage them living for months in a situation of virtual bestiality. Impelled by the instinct to survive it is amazing how one can adjust to seemingly unendurable conditions.

SIXTEEN

Lack of sleep last night leaves me feeling like a wet rag. Irène is demanding my undivided attention, and I shall try hard not to be irritable. We have to face the problem of finding another Day Centre. Our previous social worker, in the service of Jewish Care, has withdrawn from the case, as our G.P. wishes to involve local social services. We are now awaiting a replacement.

Restive at any delay, my daughter, Elaine, phoned the duty officer at the local authority, who suggested we look at a few places in the vicinity. From the scant information available she recommended one about six miles away as suitable for our needs.

Well, as an Irish friend of mine is fond of saying:

"Not to worry. One door shuts and another one closes."

So, with renewed hope, off we went, Irène, Elaine, Mandy and I, to the Centre, having made an appointment to see the head nurse. We drove up to an attractive, modern building, with pretty gardens. Encouraged by the location, we trundled our wheelchair through the main entrance.

"It looks very nice, Mum," said Mandy, trying to reassure the visibly frightened occupant of the wheelchair.

We were greeted with a warm smile from a motherly looking, neatly dressed nurse, who began to show us round. The entrance hall was invitingly furnished and spotless. So far so good. Then we trooped into the lounge.

In varying attitudes of dejection were several very old women: one with a running nose, one slumped wide awake half out of her chair, another snoring loudly, while a much younger woman was dancing, out of time with loud music blaring from the sleeper's portable radio. Elaine, more able to hide her feelings than the rest of us, maintained a semblance of conversation with our guide, and, eventually, as quickly as courtesy allowed, we made our way back towards the front door... to find our way blocked by an old man, grinning at us and holding out a claw-like hand. The front of his trousers was freshly stained, and he stank of urine.

My eyes met those of my daughters, and they simultaneously mouthed the word:

"Grandpa!"

Finally we were outside gulping fresh air. I dare not look at Irène. Mandy was openly weeping.

"We can't let her come here!" she said.

"Not in a million years," I replied.

Both girls sighed. We drove home in silence.

"Coming up for a cup of tea?"

But no. They had somewhere to go. Understandably they wanted to put the horror of the afternoon behind them. But to my surprise they were ringing our doorbell barely two hours later. In they came, flushed with excitement.

"We've found it! We've found the place!"

"What? Where?"

"Just down the road!"

David is perplexed. I know he won't let the matter rest. When my grandson is confused, he worries about the problem, researches it, bombards me with questions - most of which I can answer to his satisfaction, except where God and politics are concerned.

At the moment he is fascinated by war. Good history lessons have sparked off his interest. I wonder what's bothering him.

"You were in the war, grandpa. Right? You were in the army. Right?"

I nod.

"Then you must have had a gun. Did you?"

Another nod. Now I think I know where this is going.

"But you hate guns. You don't even like toy guns."

That's true, and he knows how much I deplore the appalling video games he enjoys so much - all involved with blowing people's heads off, explosions and the most sophisticated means of mass murder on an inter-galactic scale.

"So how come you were in the army?"

I give him the usual *spiel* about the necessity to defend one's family, about a threat by the forces of evil... and it all goes down very well. David perhaps like most of us needs a clear differentiation between the "goodies" and the "baddies." Then out he comes with what's bothering him.

"Did you shoot anyone?"

"No, David."

"So what did you do?"

Not a lot, I suppose. But I know he needs to see me in some sort of heroic role...

"I was in 'Intelligence.' "

His eyes widen, and he whispers: "Were you a spy?"

"No way. Actually I was a rather unimportant member of a unit involved with the decoding, translation, and passing on of enemy wireless messages, which were sent to us after being intercepted by the Royal Corps of Signals. It was a good way of finding out information about troop movements, locations and sometimes intentions of enemy forces."

He thinks that one over. Then, of course, wants an example.

"Well I remember once we decoded and translated a message which gave the exact position of a large German ammunition dump. The C.O. told us to listen for the planes which would be going over above our heads any minute now to blow the place to smithereens.

I can see David's imagination working overtime. Naturally he casts his grandfather in the role of personally deciphering the message, telephoning the R.A.F... and getting a medal! Well, I let him preserve his illusions. It's good to have somebody think you're great - even if it is only a ten-year-old boy.

"I just did my bit," I tell him with appropriate modesty.

Memory is selective as far as I am concerned. Odd phrases - sometimes trivial - I hear in their original speaker's voice, half a century after they were spoken, certain images from many years back remain vivid; brief moments are forever imprinted on my mind, yet entire months have been completely - mercifully perhaps? - obliterated.

I have very little recollection of nearly all my army career. No way can I claim: "It made a man of me." It would be nearer the mark to say that it practically turned me into a nervous wreck. Yet the memories I do have are not unhappy ones. Presumably that's why they've been retained.

The horrors of primary - that means "infantry" - training were mitigated by the fact that our company, for some reason I don't recall, had a large proportion of young men half way through a university course. The captain in charge was a "ranker" - which we took for rhyming slang - and meant that he was a professional who had come up through the ranks - in his case, rather slowly. The fact that, with our academic - and in many cases athletic - background many of us seemed likely to achieve fairly quickly the commission he'd earned the hard way, and that we didn't speak with his working-class accent, did not endear him to us. Moreover the sergeant in charge of our group, by the name of Flynn, was cast in a similar, though coarser, mould. He too was a professional, with a very low I.Q., a vile temper, and the foulest tongue I'd ever heard. One of his favourite preambles to a string of insults was:

"Just because you can speak French and play the piano..."

On one occasion, when he was inspecting me closely from the rear and spotted an unpolished smear on the back of one boot he informed me that proved to him I was not and never would be a "good soldier." I was tempted to tell him that I could live with that.

A common educational background strengthened our resistance to the frequently brutish authority to which we were submitted, and we became masters in practising the art of what the army calls: "dumb insolence." If we were tormented by day, the barrack room was great fun at night. The endless stamping, drilling, snapping to attention and polishing were a standing joke.. except in the case of one creep - a toady always currying favour, and forever polishing - polishing - slapping on "Dubbin"...

One evening, just before lights out a group of us decided to teach him a lesson. We shoved him face down on the bed, bared his backside and proceeded to dubbin his arse, urged on by the cheers of the entire barrack room. We'd just about finished when a giant bellow drowned the hubbub. Framed in the doorway was Flynn.

"What's goin' on 'ere? Talk about a row! This aint no bleedin' row! This is pandy-fuckin'-monium!"

He caught sight of the highly burnished rear end, and his mouth dropped.

"Cor blimey!"

He shook his head, as though to rid himself of a vision, picked on one of us who couldn't contain his laughter and said:

"I'll 'ave you on a fizzer for this!"

But, in fact, nobody was put on a charge. I think he was baffled how to write in plain English an account of what he'd seen.

"Your best friend is your rifle," he told us. We learned to clean it, shoot with it, drill with it. God forbid we should drop the bloody thing on the ground... I wondered if, like my old rabbi with a prayer book, he'd make me kiss it after I picked it up... we learned how to take a Bren gun to pieces and reassemble it in record time - something none of us - mercifully - had to do for real, how to throw a grenade... and above all how to march, stamp and pirouette like a robot. We could accept the necessity for basic infantry training, but "square bashing" remained a joke.

There was one chap called Butterfield a brilliant mathematician with thick pebble-glass spectacles. "Butters" had two left hands and two left feet. Everybody liked him - except the N.C.Os in charge. On one occasion he nearly killed himself. On another he nearly wiped out the entire platoon.

Butters should never have been allowed on the assault course. He survived about a quarter of the way round. Then we came to a five foot leap down, over a coil of barbed wire. He took it bravely, and, to everyone's relief, cleared the wire. Over he went. Then the sergeant screamed:

"No!"

And covered his eyes.

Instead of holding his "best friend" - rifle with bayonet fixed -horizontally away from him, he clutched it upright. As he landed heavily the butt of the weapon slammed into the ground. The point of his bayonet shot upwards, missing his nose by a couple of inches, and the rim of his helmet by a hair's breadth.

"Fuck me!" gasped Flynn.

His other brush with sudden death involved us all. It occurred on the grenade throwing range. When it came to his turn, the sergeant, knowing his man, but not well enough to forbid him trying, advised him:

"Throw it high! Sling the fucker high!"

So he did. Straight up. Vertically.

"Run like fuck!" yelled the N.C.O. And led the field.

The grenade exploded just the other side of the sandbags. Miraculously there were no casualties - except for Sergeant Flynn, who cut his lip as he hurled himself precipitously to the ground.

One especially gruelling day he was in an even fouler temper than usual. He kept us square bashing until we were fit to drop, maintaining a torrent of abuse, during which he exhibited his mastery in modifying the "f" word to an impressive variety of the parts of speech.

That night we just fell into our beds, too exhausted for conversation. Our nerves were stretched to breaking point. Christopher, in the next bed to me but one, was something of an oddball - a classics student I believe, and seemingly the most intellectual of us all. He was extremely effeminate, but far too likeable to be teased. We were all too edgy to sleep, and could feel suppressed anger in the air. Suddenly Christopher sat bolt upright in bed, and in his precise, lady-like tones exclaimed:

"I am acutely miserable."

It broke the tension, and remains one of the unimportant phrases indelibly engraved in my memory. Christopher didn't take kindly to primary - infantry - training. Neither did I.

Relieved to be transferred to the Intelligence Corps, I was delighted to have part of my training in London. Eventually, assigned to 21 Army Group, we crossed to France shortly after D. Day. I have not the slightest recollection of crossing the Channel, or disembarking in Normandy.

There are vague memories of cider, apples and Calvados, but little else, except of moving into a building just vacated by the retreating Germans, and finding, right in the centre of the room to which we'd been assigned as a dormitory, a large pile of human shit left as a parting gift from the previous occupants.

Eventually we reached Brussels. The city was celebrating its liberation with a wild, protracted party. It was the most exciting city in Europe. And that's where we found ourselves, quartered in comparative luxury in the district of Moelenbeek, at the Hospice Saint Jean.

Of course our operation was top secret, and the C.O. was not amused by a cartoon which appeared in the local newspaper. It featured a pretty girl in conversation with an English soldier. The caption below had her speaking in halting English, whereupon the soldier replies:

"*Ne vous en faites pas, mademoiselle. Je suis de Moelenbeek, Saint Jean.*"

We had it made. Hordes of beautiful girls, looking for fun, and over-anxious to express their gratitude to their liberators. Speaking the language fluently, we even had the advantage over the rather more glamourous and better paid Yanks. One of my married friends, a dour Scot, was startled out of his wits - and confessed he had difficulty in keeping his marriage vows - when he discovered that the Belgian girls kissed - "and stick their tongues half way down your throat!"

Clanging trams vied merrily with the music pouring out of the numerous cafés lining the streets, and battle weary soldiers suddenly found themselves having the time of their lives. The whole city was having fun ... except for those desperately waiting for any news of their nearest and dearest deported east.

And there I met my cousin, Herzl.

There it goes at last - the buzzer on the entry phone. The bus is back. It's been Irène's first day at the new centre. The last time I felt like this was when I waited at the gate for

Elaine to come out of school for the first time. She was in tears.

"I hate it," she said, "and I'm not going back."

Will history repeat itself?

Peter, who drives the bus, delivers her to me at the door downstairs. He's all smiles. She isn't. My heart sinks. We transfer my wife to her wheelchair. Peter pats her hand, says a cheerful good-bye and leaves. We go up in the lift in silence, and I settle her into an armchair.

"Cup of tea?"

No answer.

"Would you like a cup of tea, dear?"

Shake of the head.

"Did you have tea before you left?"

Grunt. Then silence.

"I had a swim. It was great."

No response.

"I met Mandy and Richard (our son-in-law) at the pool."

Why is she giving me that nasty look?

"We went for a pub lunch."

And that's an even nastier look.

"It was very good."

"How was *your* lunch?"

Now that stare is positively malevolent.

"Uneatable."

What's the matter with her? I'm only trying to cheer her up with a little conversation... Then realisation hits me. Every time I open my big mouth I put my foot right in it. Now I can read her mind:

"You rotten bastard. You pack me off to the bloody centre, while you go off and have a whale of a time... "

Of course, what I should have said was: "I've had a miserable day, sweetheart, and I've missed you dreadfully." Unfortunately it's too late now, and the best thing I can do is maintain a discreet silence... which I manage for about ten very long minutes.

I tell myself that it could be worse. I recall how she was quite happy at the Jewish Care Centre on Thursdays, when she grew to like the people at her table, but found excuses to avoid going on Tuesdays:

"I don't feel well today. I ought to stay at home." It was exactly the same excuse Elaine would use to avoid going to school - at the age of five!

I draw comfort from the fact that she isn't actually complaining. Deciding to avoid saying more of the wrong things, I take refuge in the kitchen. Giving her the benefit of my most winning smile I announce:

"I'm just going to finish preparing dinner. It's your favourite, darling."

"I'm not hungry," she says.

SEVENTEEN

"Did you see the documentary on the B.B.C. last night?"

Elaine is on the phone.

"Which one?"

"About the last days of the war in Europe."

"What time was it on?"

"Eight thirty, I think."

"No. I didn't see it."

At that time? How could I? And it occurs to me that evenings are no longer a part of my life. We usually finish dinner at about seven. It takes me about twenty minutes to clear up, and then Irène usually has her agitation period. "What time is it?" she asks again and again, keeps needing to go to the loo - mostly false alarms - and suggests over and over that it's time for her evening tablets and to prepare for going to bed. By eight o'clock I normally give in, and it does take an hour before she can be tucked up in bed, by which time I'm too exhausted to do anything but tumble in beside her.

I may have been lucky enough to catch snatches of the news on T.V. between interruptions, always at crucial points, but television is no longer a viable source of after dinner entertainment.

The fact that Irène is no longer able to sustain interest in a film, follow the story, or recognise characters as they reappear is evidence of the deterioration in her condition. Ah, well, most of the stuff isn't worth watching anyway. Furthermore, I no longer have to endure the mindless game shows to which she became addicted, but which now no longer hold her attention.

However, I find great pleasure in music, and console myself with the thought that a few hundred years ago an emperor would have given half his kingdom to be able to enjoy - as I do - wonderful music without stirring from his armchair, merely by pressing the button on a remote control.

Another part of my existence which has disappeared with the progression of Irène's illness has been our social life, outside the limits of the immediate family. We no longer have much use for our best china. There aren't any visitors.

I remember how my mother became isolated, as a result of my father's condition. Irène is not unpleasant the way he was. Far from it. But our friends are upset if not embarrassed by the change they cannot fail to notice.

"People who matter don't mind," says Mandy, "and people who mind don't matter."

That's all very well, but, sadly, even those who matter seem to have made themselves scarce.

"Ah well," I say to myself. "Who needs people? We've got each other, and, when all's said and done, there's nobody else I'd prefer to have sitting beside me. Even if my evenings disappear, I must admit that when we're tucked up in bed - albeit at a ridiculous hour - I'm more than ready for sleep. The bed is so comfortable. I take your hand, and wouldn't choose to be anywhere else in the world".

"Line up in single file. Shortest in front."

That put Sacha first in line.

"No talking now! We're going into the bathroom to clean our teeth. Ready? Left! Right! Left! Right!"

The morning ritual at the orphanage in Gormay was more military than my primary infantry training. Even to the ten-year-old inured to harsh conditions the treatment seemed crazy.

"Stand by your beds!"

Routine inspection followed.

"You dirty little boy!"' This to Sacha's neighbour and new friend. "You've wet your bed again!"

Then a furious: "What's that? That unspeakable, filthy mess?"

To Sacha: "Is it that disgusting animal you brought in?"

He'd found a stray kitten, carefully tended it, house

trained the tiny thing with a box he and his friend had lined... It was the first pet he'd ever had, and he adored it. Now someone in authority had removed the litter, and the kitten had peed in its customary place, but on the floor.

" Somebody took away her box..."

He picked up the kitten and held it protectively against his chest. In vain. It was snatched away. His protestations fell on deaf ears. He never saw the creature again, and - strangely more than any previous loss - it nearly broke his heart.

"Liberation" had no meaning for Sacha. It was as if he was in prison.

Ferried between the orphanage and the apartment of his only remaining paternal relatives in Paris, the Burland family, to whom he and his brother were an embarrassment, he led a wretched existence. Then M. Burland succeeded in contacting the family in England. And here's where I come into the picture, supplying Booba with a series of "French letters".

"My sister's grandchildren," she said tearfully, over and over again.

Eventually Uncle Joe - ex-fireman Goldberg - and Aunt Sophie's husband, Dave, went to Paris on Booba's behalf to see what could be done for the two orphans. They learned that the older boy, an earnest student, was intent on continuing his education in France, come what may. The younger boy they found to be in a pitiable condition - a physical and emotional wreck. Uncle Dave, with no children of his own, was deeply moved, and strongly drawn to the little boy.

Monsieur Burland, anxious to be rid of an unwanted burden, and wishing to ingratiate himself with the Goldberg family, insisted that his visitors should take a present to London, where he thought the inhabitants were practically starving. Ceremoniously he presented Joe with a huge breakfast sausage.

"*Voilà! Un saucisson pour madame votre mère.*"

My uncles left the flat, making their way back towards their hotel through a street lined with street-walkers.

"That sausage stinks," said Uncle Dave.

"I know."

"Let's get rid of the bloody thing."

Uncle Joe stopped in front of one of the Parisian ladies of the night.

She eyed the two obvious tourists with professional interest and forced a smile.

"*J'ai pour vous un grand saucisson,*" said Joe hesitantly.

The lady stared at him a moment, sniffed, and named a price.

"*Non, pas payer,*" said my uncle.

Haughtily the woman spat a few Gallic curses, turned and sauntered off on high heels, expressing disapproval with the exaggerated swaying of her rear end. Uncle Dave was helpless with laughter, and, as soon as he was able to collect himself, took the parcel and dropped it in the lap of a beggar, half lying in a doorway.

Back home things were put into motion. Eventually a bewildered Sacha arrived. There were problems of communication. Sacha's memory had blacked out his mother tongue, Yiddish, and he knew not one word of English, so Irène and I acted as interpreters, and Booba, thrilled to bits to have the child with her, was vastly amused at the French, which she called "*kutchker looshen*" - duck language, because all she kept hearing was:

"*Quoi? Quoi?*"

Then came a family conference at which Uncle Dave expressed a wish to take the boy into his home.

It wasn't long before they decided to adopt him legally. And that is really, he says, where his life began. Indeed for a while he did regress, luxuriating in being "babied" and generally spoiled rotten. Nevertheless, he made remarkable progress, linguistically, educationally, emotionally and physically. Within a short time he was given a place at a reputable grammar school, and eventually won his way to Trinity College, Cambridge. His brother, incidentally, was doing equally well in Paris.

Suddenly fate stopped being kind to Sacha. His adoptive father dropped dead with a heart attack. The boy was devastated, and even blamed himself:

"I bring bad luck to everybody," he told me.

It was hardly surprising that he made a mess of the end-of-year exams. Aghast to learn that he was being sent down as a consequence, I wrote to Trinity, explaining his tragic history, and that his adoptive father's death was actually his third parental bereavement. In these exceptional circumstances I asked for a sympathetic review of their decision. In reply I received a curt note that he had failed to reach the required standard, and his place at the university was no longer available.

Fortunately undeterred, Sacha transferred to London University, and secured an honours degree without difficulty.

For my Aunt Sophie the Jewish New Year is a day of appalling memories. Not only is it the anniversary of her mother's sudden death, when she was about to go to shul, but, by a dreadful coincidence Uncle Dave suffered his fatal heart attack in the synagogue on the same date, during the service for *Rosh Hashonah*. Followed ten days later by the Day of Atonement, these are the most solemn and important dates in the Jewish calendar.

It was a few days before the festival in 1944 that I met up with Herzl, who suggested I request leave and accompany him to what promised to be a historic New Year service, coming as it did soon after the liberation, at the main synagogue in the heart of Brussels.

I never set foot inside. For all I knew it was half empty, but a teeming crowd overflowed into the courtyard. The emanation of mass emotion created an atmosphere which could have been cut with a knife. Men and women were laughing and weeping in each other's arms; there was joy as they found old friends alive after the holocaust, and grief as they learned the fate of others.

Hearing that my cousin was the son of the eminent scholar and Zionist, Reverend Jacob Goldbloom, the dignitaries of the community vied with each other to welcome him into their homes. Herzl waved to me and beckoned. I shook my head. He nodded and was whisked away into the throng.

I must have stared in wonder at the scene for about half an hour, when I noticed a pretty young girl with dark, curly hair and flashing eyes moving from one welcoming group to another. She tells me now that she remembers me standing with my back against the wall. Dora knew enough English to give me a friendly greeting, and was astonished when I replied in fluent French. Naturally talkative - a fact always landing her in trouble at school - and always overflowing with *joie de vivre* - she was irresistible, and soon had me enthralled. Her voice was musical - I subsequently discovered she was a gifted soprano - and listening to her rippling French was magic. Soon we were involved in animated conversation . A couple passed by us, and the man laughingly waved an admonishing finger. He remarked about her flirting, and the woman accompanying him told him he couldn't be more mistaken. She knew the family. There were five girls - all of irreproachable character.

Now over seventy, and with her curly hair snow white, after more than her fair share of tragedy, Dora is still bubbly, full of laughs and as delightful a conversationalist as ever. Her voice is that of a young girl - crystal clear. At the slightest provocation she sings like a nightingale. And I love her to bits. Fascinated by her when we first met, I arranged to see her again on my next free day in the city. We were to meet on the steps of the Bourse.

When she arrived home, and excitedly informed her mother of the *rendez-vous* the good lady was up in arms. No way. At your age? *Noch* a soldier? -- But he's a Jewish soldier? -- No difference - Maman! - I said no! - But....

Papa had a suggestion: suppose she took her sister along, to make sure... well, to make sure...

That was all very well, but the sister had other plans, and they did not include child minding... Then Dora was upset. The older girl grudgingly relented: Very well, but just this once!

So one fine autumn evening I waited on the bottom step of the Bourse. I saw Dora walking towards me. Then I didn't see her at all. I only had eyes for her companion - a red head, and the most beautiful girl I had ever seen. My heart did a couple of somersaults. Dora introduced me to Irène, and I fell head over heels in love - literally at first sight.

"Oh, not that top again, Michael! How about the blue one - the blue with the pretty, cut away neck line? Has it been washed?"

Irène is being fussy about her clothes. I like that. She's rather edgy, but that's to be expected on her first morning at the new day centre. Breakfast is a silent affair. Now she can't keep still.

'What time is it?"
"Five to nine."
"I ought to put my coat on."
"You're not due to be picked up for another half hour."
"I want to be ready."
"You will be. Don't worry."
"Should I wear the white coat or the gray?"
"I prefer the white one."
"What time is it?"
"Not quite nine."
"When are they picking me up?"
"They said half past."
"I want my coat."
"You'll get hot... Here it is. "
Five minutes later: "What time is it, Michael?"

So it goes on, until we hear the buzzer on the entry phone. She's been waiting in her chair for the last fifteen minutes, so, it takes a very short time to wheel her to the lift, and then to the front door, where we are greeted by a large man in his fifties, with a florid complexion and a wide grin:

"I'm Peter, " he says, takes over, has her out of the chair, and over to the waiting bus in no time at all with professional ease, and even up the steps. He's the relief driver this morning, he tells us. At the wheel is an attractive woman, also smiling as she says "Hello."

But my heart sinks as I note that the vehicle is quarter full of passengers who all look so old! I'm even more unhappy when Peter settles Irène beside a woman who looks about ninety years old, with her wrinkles set in one of the sourest expressions I've ever seen.

Then the bus is gone.

Guilt overwhelms me. I should be delighted to have a whole day to myself. Instead I experience a sense of loss. This, I say to myself, is how a mother must feel, when she sees a nervous little girl off to her first day at school.

The flat is dreadfully empty. I come into the study and pick up my manuscript. Although this is a long awaited opportunity to write undisturbed, I haven't the slightest desire to look at the damn thing. My deserted surroundings are driving me outside. Shall I go shopping? I could go out and buy whatever I need to make her a nice dinner when she comes home. Then I can prepare the vegetables undisturbed... And, of course, I can go swimming - for the first time in a year! I used to go every morning, and now I should be able to manage twice a week, while she's at the centre. The prospect cheers me a little.

Nevertheless the hours pass very slowly. From four o'clock onwards I stand at the window, looking down for the arrival of the brightly painted bus. It arrives at half past. Apprehensively I hurry down to meet her. To my relief she looks happy. But is that for the benefit of Peter and the driver? I wait until we're upstairs and then:

"Well, how was it?"

If she doesn't give vent to a stream of complaints I'll know the visit has been a success. There's no reply, so I ask again:

"How was your day?"

"All right."

I breathe a sigh of relief.

"Was the lunch O.K?"

"Not bad."

That sounds encouraging, so I venture on to more dangerous ground:

"I must say I was rather worried when they sat you next to that miserable looking woman on the bus."

"She wasn't miserable."

"Oh?'

"In fact she's very interesting. We've been chatting all day. She shared her chocolates with me."

Better and better. Then, after a long pause, she adds grudgingly:

"The people are very nice."

Wonderful. About to pursue the matter, I decide not to push my luck. Of course, she has to show some resentment at being packed off like a child. But although she wants me within arm's length every moment of the day and night, she needs some space of her own almost as much as I do. I see light at the end of the tunnel.

I've grumbled about social services: difficulties of communication, bureaucratic delays, proliferation of paperwork... but, when all's said and done, where would we be without them?

EIGHTEEN

The first time I stepped into Irène's home in Brussels was like displacement in time and space. This, I thought, must be the way my grandparents lived in the East End ghetto at the beginning of the twentieth century. And Sacha's earliest years in Paris were no doubt lived in similar surroundings.

The Rusak apartment overlooked the tram terminus at the Gare du Midi. It was situated in the predominantly Jewish district - at that time - of Anderlecht, above a grocery store, bearing the name of Jacobovitch. The entire dwelling consisted of three rooms on the first floor. Opposite the front door, across the landing, was a small lavatory. The main living room was the kitchen. One wall, facing the window, was entirely occupied by a massive coal-fired cooker - rather like an antiquated Aga -with its cooking surfaces burnished to a gleaming silver. In the centre of the room was a large table, like my grandmother's, covered in American cloth, surrounded by plain wooden chairs. There was nothing resembling an armchair to be seen. There were two bedrooms for the entire family; the parents slept in one, and, miraculously, all five daughters occupied the other. To compound the mystery even further, this second bedroom also contained their father's work-bench, and was where he plied his trade as cobbler. Everything was scrupulously clean.

In these squalid conditions, despite the privations imposed on all Jews by the German army of occupation, the girls had been raised by an impoverished immigrant and his barely literate wife. They had, however, been blessed with very pretty daughters, and were passionately concerned with their moral upbringing. This was a simple shoe-maker, whose five daughters had the looks and manners of princesses.

Although poverty and persecution had left their mark on Maman, they could hardly detract from the classic regularity of her features, or the combination of gold hair and blue eyes. Her Aryan appearance had served her well during the occupation, when, as long as she concealed the yellow star, she was able to circulate with comparative impunity in search of food, whereas her heighbours dared not venture outside.

As soon as she set eyes on me, Maman exclaimed in Yiddish:

"He looks exactly like Jacques!"

The fact that I resembled her son-in-law gave me good marks for starters. She still had hopes that he would return from Auschwitz. And I scored a lot more points when, to her astonishment, I spoke to her in the fluent Yiddish I'd learnt from my grandparents. To Irène's delight we couldn't have got off to a better start.

Chaskiel treated his wife like a queen, exacting without a problem the same love and respect for her from the children. A strong man, when she became ill a year after I met her, and virtually paralysed, he carried her around like a baby. I sometimes wonder whether Irène is disappointed in me, because I don't do the same with her. Hopefully she realises that I'm not up to it. After his wife's premature death Chaskiel fell to pieces. While she was alive he was so firmly in control - of his family and himself. The change was extraordinary.

The oldest daughter, Eva, had been deported. Her wedding photograph portrays a stunning blond, and, yes, her bridegroom, Jacques, does look something like me at that time. You've already met the next in line, Ida, a deceptively gentle brunette, who kept the younger girls in order with iron discipline. After Irène comes Dora, who captured my interest at the synagogue, and finally I met twelve year old Olga, coming home with an armful of books. She is, indeed, a natural scholar.

All the time I was stationed in Brussels, 40 rue Plantin became my home from home. I wasn't just a "boyfriend." Though still in uniform, heading God knows where, in accordance with Booba's code, I was a *choossen.*

It's half past four in the afternoon, and once again I'm waiting for the bus to bring Irène home. I really have missed her today.

Things could be worse. She's been going to the centre quite willingly. In fact we've been fussy about what she wears, how she looks, and that can't be bad. I've had only one complaint: there's nothing to do. I made discreet inquiries and was informed that board games and other "armchair activities" are always organised but only for those who choose to be involved. Nothing is compulsory. If people simply want to sit and chat - that's fine. and for those who are content to take a nap - that's O.K. too.

I tackled her about the games.
"I can't play."
"Why not?"
"Because of my eyes."
"You've got spectacles."
"I can't wear them."
"Why can't you?"
"They're no good."

I called her bluff and took her for an eye test. As I suspected, the glasses are perfect and there is no problem with her vision. It seems that, although offered an alternative, Irène simply prefers to sleep. "Is it the Quetiapine tablets?" I wondered. It so happened that we had an appointment with the consultant, who was concerned that her medication was making her exceptionally drowsy. Therefore, he prescribed an alternative, which she has been taking for a couple of days. Certainly she is brighter...

There goes the buzzer. I wonder how she got on today. I hurry down, and find her holding on to Peter's arm. They're both laughing. I do believe she's flirting with him!

As soon as she's esconsed in her armchair, I begin teasing her. She joins in the banter. Now this is more like the old Irène. To my delight, without prompting, she begins talking about her day. Words pour out - and she can't stop. Enraptured, I listen to all the nonsense she and the other ladies have been saying to each other. It's music to my ears. Then she says something quite trivial, and I can't understand why it makes me hold back tears:

"Darling, we played dominoes. And I won!"

Sister Thérèse hummed cheerfully to herself as she helped the girls unpack. She enjoyed this part of her work at the convent, welcoming new arrivals, seeing fresh young faces. You'd never guess that these three were sisters. How pretty they were, and in entirely different ways. The oldest - a fourteen year old - was obviously going to be a beauty, the middle one, her head a mass of dark curls, had the cutest dimples when she laughed, as she did most of the time, while the little one - such a solemn face for a child of ten! - had flaxen hair, and the bluest eyes...

"What a pretty dress!" exclaimed the sister, beginning to unfold a party frock in midnight blue.

"Oh! And this delightful pink and blue bolero to match!" she exclaimed, as she turned it over.

Suddenly she sprang back with a little shriek of horror. In glaring contrast to the dark blue material was a yellow star.

Clutching the dress to her bosom, the nun bolted from the room, flew down the corridor, and, scarcely hesitating to knock, burst in on the mother superior.

"Those girls!" she gasped, "The new arrivals..."

Mère Ligori peered at her over the top of her tiny spectacles:

"Well? What about them?"

"They - They - They're Jews!"

Back in the dormitory a terrified Dora clutched her sister's hand.

"What do we do now?" she asked.

"I don't know," answered Irène fearfully, and her mind flashed back two years.

How ecstatic the three girls had been, when their brother-in-law to be - the "*choosen*" - presented them with matching dresses for their sister Eva's wedding.

Monsieur Roger van Overbeke received an odd card via the Judenrat in Brussels. It apparently emanated from Number 759 at Malines, and Transport XII on the way to Auschwitz. But the handwriting was familiar, as was the signature: Jacques Lewin. The card contained a polite request for the gentleman to do his best to send the writer a parcel with some food and clothing, shoe polish, a brush...

En route for the concentration camp, it was characteristic of the man to be concerned about the appearance of his shoes. The French dramatist, Jean-Jacques Bernard, writing about a number of his fellow camp inmates, says that many of his friends retained their dignity and self respect:

"*Ces messieurs sont restés des messieurs.*"

That was certainly the case with my brother-in-law.

According to Irène, he was always immaculately dressed. She also remembers how he never called on his fiancée without an attractively wrapped gift of some sort. Moreover, just as my mother was taught to leave a *peckel* surreptitiously for Booba's impoverished neighbour, Jacques, whose parents were jewellers and at that time well-to-do, was in the habit of covertly leaving an envelope with money on the table as he left.

Looking fearfully at the pretty dress with the yellow star, Irène was reminded of her mother busily baking little *chollas* and other delicacies for Eva's wedding. Now, apart from the two sisters in her charge, all those she loved seemed to be a thousand miles away, and the two years since they had last worn the blue dresses a whole lifetime. Her eyes filled with tears as the memories flooded back.

Soon after the Germans entered Brussels, the persecution began, insidiously at first, as in Paris, then with gathering momentum and ferocity.

At the same age as my cousin, Sacha, Olga was similarly shocked when informed that she no longer had the right to attend her school. A gifted pupil, she actually loved the place. Like Sacha, when she was told it was because of her race, she experienced shame, further compounded by an order to wear the yellow star as a badge of public humiliation.

Rumours began to circulate among the Jewish population, now marked as outcasts for all to see. There were stories about what was happening to their relatives in Poland, and the working conditions of the ones taken to work in

Germany, but nobody really knew what was going on outside Brussels.

An official summons arrived at the Rusak apartment, demanding that Ida and Irène present themselves for "work" outside Belgium. Filled with foreboding Maman hid the letter. But my father-in-law was informed that, if the order was disobeyed, in the first place the entire family would be taken, moreover, as a reprisal, their neighbours and their children would be forcibly collected too. Bowing to the inevitable, despite the distress of his wife, my father-in-law made preparations for the girls' departure. Bags were packed. He gave Ida his most precious possession - a pocket watch - which he placed in an envelope. Then Chaskiel made them new shoes, and, with a sinking heart sent them off to whatever fate the Nazis had in store.

As a forlorn hope he secured a fake medical certificate for the older girl, taking advantage of the fact that she was at that time painfully thin and pale. It stated that she had T.B. If it stopped her being deported, her father enjoined the girl to point out that her sister was only thirteen years old, and perhaps... But he had little hope. In fact his daughters had just enough money for a one-way ticket to Malines.

As they turned the corner of the rue Plantin, Irène took a last look back. She saw her mother lying face down in the road, tearing at her hair. She was crying out: "*Vos hob ich getin? Vos hob ich getin?*" What have I done?

Arriving at Malines the two girls saw silent groups of people, many of them children, wearing the yellow star, sitting with their luggage. On all faces was the same look of despair and fear.

"Do you think they're going to 'work'?" asked Irène.

The other girl made no reply, but clasped her hand more tightly.

In accordance with their instructions they entered the Caserne d'Ossyen - now a museum - and were directed into an office, where a huge Nazi was sitting behind a desk, covered in papers. He barked an incomprehensible order, and Ida handed over the summons. He frowned as he read, then, in heavily accented French, slapping a massive fist on the document, growled that they were two days late. Meekly Ida gave him her false medical certificate. The German's eyes flitted from the paper to the thin, pallid girl, back to the paper, and his forehead creased into a deep frown. At length he sighed, commanded them to wait, and, his boots clanging on the floor, left the room. A few minutes later he returned, handed the certificate to Ida, and curtly told her she could go.

"My sister?"

"There's nothing wrong with her. She stays."

"She's only thirteen..."

The Nazi barked something in German. They didn't understand, but realised that his decision was irrevocable.

Ida had the sweet, gentle disposition of her mother - until there was any threat to her family, when the lamb was metamorphosed into a tigress. Barely five feet tall, and slightly built, she stared coolly up at the Nazi, who had risen to his feet and was towering over her.

"I'm not going without my sister," she said.

The German couldn't believe his eyes - couldn't believe his ears. His jaw dropped.

"I go - she goes," said the girl. "She stays - I stay."

The soldier sank back into his chair. Slowly his features softened into the hint of a smile. He scribbled something on a piece of paper, and passed it across the table to Irène, who was in tears and shaking like a leaf.

For the first time he spoke quietly.

"Go home," he said. "Both of you."

I wonder whether perhaps he had a thirteen-year-old daughter of his own - maybe a pretty red head, too. Or did he just have a belly full of sending kids off to almost certain death? Whatever the reason for his action, when he appears on the Day of Judgment and needs a witness for his entitlement to admission into some Wagnerian Paradise, I'll willingly stand up for that Nazi.

"Run!" he said.

"Come on, cried Ida, "Why don't you run?"

"I can't! Papa's new shoes are killing me."

Irène does not remember how they got home without

179

money, but she does recall that they ran a lot of the way - and that her feet were killing her in the new shoes . She also remembers how her mother went mad when they arrived, and hugged them both so tight that it hurt.

In my experience, whatever is said about the Jewish mother is no exaggeration. In her old age I picture Booba rocking in her chair, and counting on her fingers:
"On Shabbas I saw Michael. Sunday Mannie came with the children, on Monday Isaac *hot areingepoppt* for lunch, Tuesday I saw Aarele, Wednesday...." After she'd ticked off her eight children, all in good health, thank God, she'd sink back in her chair with a contented sigh, and doze off.

My mother, too, centred her life around Alan and me, and Irène just lives for her children. Now, even on bad days - and there are many of those - she becomes almost her old, lively self, whenever the kids are around. As far as all the women in my life are concerned, the well-being of their children and grand-children has been paramount; feeding them is an expression of love, and primitive passions were aroused if ever they were in danger. During the holocaust the feelings of Maman defy imagination.

I know they took their toll - she died one year after the end of the war - and her anxiety left its mark on two subsequent generations.

NINETEEN

Today is Mothering Sunday, and Elaine's husband, Abe, has booked a table for a family lunch. It wasn't easy. Most restaurants have been fully booked for days, and we have certain requirements: either wheel-chair access or no stairs; it must be suitable for the little ones, accommodate ten of us, and - it goes without saying - offer good food. At last he struck lucky.

So here we are, happily packed into two cars, driving up to the hotel through attractive gardens, and admiring the splendid view of a lake, with its surface virtually dancing in the sunshine of a perfect day. Or is it?

We encounter our first problem: all parking bays reserved for the disabled have been taken - almost entirely by vehicles without the requisite badges. I'm used to this, but Mandy's husband, Richard, our driver is not. He begins to fret.

"I'm going to sort out the manager and complain..."

But Mandy dissuades him.

"Don't spoil the day."

That's the last thing he'd want to do, so, like the obedient husband he is - and has to be - Richard complies, stops at the front door, while we pile out, and then goes to park the car in the nearest spot - about a hundred and fifty yards away. There's no ramp, and a high step to negotiate - not easy for Irène - and we wait just inside the main door for the rest of the group. They arrive in a moment, and the maitre d' invites us to follow him into the crowded room to our designated table... and this is our next problem. Set for ten, and with probably the finest view in the restaurant, it also happens to be in the furthest corner of the room, which is so packed with diners that navigation - even for the fittest - requires concentration and dexterity. For my wife, clutching a cane in her right hand and convulsively gripping my arm with the left her feet apparently glued to the carpet, it is a daunting prospect. But, with no alternative, and to the inconvenience of one third of the diners - "Serves them right for pinching all the disabled parking," mutters Richard - we eventually are all seated, with Irène and myself at the head of the table.

This may be a pagan festival, I tell myself, but it is a replica of the way my grandparents presided over half a century ago. The wheel has come full circle.

Presented to us in turn with a flourish, the menu is impressive - but - as I note with some dismay - far too long.

"This is what the French call 'an embarrassment of choice'," says Elaine.

Unfortunately, I anticipate what is about to happen. After allowing us ten minutes lively discussion on the respective merits of all the mouth-watering alternatives, the waiter picks up the signs that we have decided what to order. And we all have - except, as I'd expected - Irène. The girls have gone through the menu with her several times. What they don't understand is that their mother, bless her heart, is incapable of making a choice. I know that her mind cannot retain any one item as soon as she considers a second; as far as the extensive number of dishes on offer are concerned, given the weakness of her short term memory, they might just as well be in Chinese. I usually try to avoid asking her to choose, and make the selection for her. Even with clothes, the most I can attempt is to hold up two garments and ask: "Which one?"

"I'll give you another few minutes," says the waiter, but takes fifteen, time enough for me to select a meal for Irène.

The staff are rushed off their feet today and we have a long wait before the first course arrives. I have a sinking feeling when I catch sight of a certain expression on my wife's face which is all too familiar. No. I'm not mistaken.

"I need to go to the loo," she murmurs, and adds for good measure: "It's urgent!" And at that moment a bowl of soup is placed in front of her.

Of course the toilet is sign-posted at the corner of the room furthest away from us. It takes Mandy an age to steer her there, displacing a quarter of the guests in the process. By the time they return the soup is stone cold, and we've asked the waiter - who wasn't too happy - to take back the main course and keep it hot.

Sadly this is not one of our good days. Elaine coolly takes over as her mother juggles uncertainly with the butter and a roll. All goes well for a while, until Grandma notices that Little Lauren has rather a small portion.

"Would you like some of my chicken, darling?" That's encouraging - my wife seems back to normal.

The suggestion is greeted with enthusiasm by the child, who passes along her plate, then begins shrieking with laughter:

"Grandma! You're putting my dinner on your plate!"

Irène's behaviour for the rest of the meal is reasonably normal, and then, when the little ones are chin deep in their dessert, little George starts roaring with laughter.

"Look!" he says, pointing a cream covered finger. "Grandma's asleep!"

She is indeed, about to fall sideways off her chair...

"This," I say to myself, "is the last family meal we take in public."

Now that she's back in the Land of Nod in the comfort of her own armchair and all the children have left, I'll slip back in time to the year 1942, and I'd like to pick up my story again in Brussels.

However, I'm forestalled by an unexpected phone call. Of all people, it's from the rabbi. If it's convenient he'd like to call in and have a chat. Since I attend the synagogue so rarely I hardly know the fellow, But I agree to see him, and, to my wife's dismay, he tells me that he's on his way.

In light of the current appalling situation in which mosques and synagogues are likewise under threat from a lunatic - but dangerous - fringe, I recently received a letter requesting my services on a rota for sentry duty at the *shul* during services on the forthcoming high holy days. I replied that, with regret, I am unable to volunteer as I am a "carer", confined to the flat in order to look after my wife. This was brought to the notice of our rabbi.

"So," he says, "if the mountain won't go to Mahomet..."

And there he is, at the front door.

Today happens to be an anniversary. Precisely fifty seven years ago, on the third day after Rosh Hashonah, Irène and I met for the first time. So we're both in a somewhat festive frame of mind, and predisposed to receive our guest with a warm welcome. He's a likeable young man, with a sense of humour, a ready smile, and, despite her apprehension before his arrival, to my relief, he and my wife are getting on swimmingly.

In all honesty I have to tell him that, notwithstanding the "*mezuzah*" on my front door, I am, in his book, a heathen. He's unperturbed.

"The *mezuzah*'s good enough for me," he says equably.

Brushing aside my protestations of paganism and excuses for not attending services he gets down to business.

"Never mind about what you do for the *shul*," he says, "I'm here to see what the *shul* can do for you."

Irène looks at me, shrugs her shoulders and raises her eyebrows.

"We have a group of ladies looking for a '*mitzvah*', and I think they can help," he tells me. I prick up my ears. "One of them has suggested coming in occasionally to keep your wife company, and give you - er - a break," he goes on.

His use of that Yiddish word has awakened memories, and I have a wave of nostalgia. Perhaps I've been too dismissive of my religious roots. Have I denied myself the comfort of belonging, believing without question... being part of the group...? Then I pull myself together, reminding myself that two weeks ago, in the name of religion, a small group of fanatics slaughtered over three thousand people in New York.

I share my feelings with the rabbi.

"If ever," I say, "I find myself face to face with your God, I'll challenge him. I've got questions..."

This chap reminds me of my grandfather. He's completely unruffled.

"That's O.K.," he says. "Abraham had the same '*chutzpah*'..."

We go at it, hammer and tongs. Irène drops off to sleep. Time flies.

When he eventually rises to go I realise how much I've enjoyed our conversation, how starved I've been of intellectual stimulation.

And there is where you come in - the reader. It occurs to me that I've been using you as my confidant!

Before she dozed off, the rabbi asked my wife about her own religious background. Unfortunately she was too drowsy to reply coherently. If he could stay here longer I'd love to fill him in. Now that he's gone, if you'll bear with me a little longer, I'll be pleased to tell you. However, before you learn about her immersion in Catholicism, I have to relate the events which brought it about.

Irène and her oldest sister, Eva, were very much alike, in both stunning looks and exceptionally nervous temperament. Recently married and now in a very early stage of pregnancy, the older girl was so terrified of the occupying forces and their abduction of neighbours, that she threatened to kill herself rather than be taken. Her new home was a walking distance from her family's flat in the rue Plantin. Her parents' front door was actually on the corner of the rue Brognier. This fact proved significant.

One night army lorries thundered to a halt the length of the rue Brognier. Soldiers leaped out of the vehicles. They began shouting, banging on doors, and were soon dragging out half dressed men, women and children, whom they threw, screaming, into the trucks.

Dora, who slept with Irène, tells me that her sister was shaking violently from head to toe. She says, with a wry smile at the absurdity of her remark, that she whispered to her to stop trembling so much, in case the Germans heard the bed rattling on the floor.

Presumably their orders specified only the rue Brognier, known to be occupied mainly by Jewish families, because the Nazis stopped at the corner. The Jewish grocery shop, with Jacobovitch in bold lettering on the facia, above which three Jewish families lived, had on the wall a street name which did not appear on their list. Scrupulous as ever in obeying orders to the letter, the Germans left. The Rusak's had escaped - for the moment. But that was enough. The following morning, the parents fled with the three youngest girls to the country.

Their sister was safe. She worked in an exclusive lingerie boutique.
The owner, Mme d'Haen, treated Ida like a daughter, took the girl into her home, and virtually adopted her for the duration of the war.

The country cottage proved to be a very temporary haven. There was nowhere for mother and father to sleep. Dora remembers bugs crawling all over her during the night ... Could that be the source of one of Irène's most persistent hallucinations? And maman, who had heard through the grapevine that some Jewish girls had found sanctuary with certain catholic orders, began making the rounds of convents, accompanied by Irène, like her mother, fair enough to escape observation, as long as they both concealed the yellow stars with a bag or scarf. It was a harrowing experience, as door after door was closed in their faces.

They had almost given up hope, when they pulled the bell at number 13, Place Saint Jacques, in Louvain, the convent of les Soeurs de Charité du Mouvement Saint Vincent de Paul. La Mère Ligori, a diminutive figure received them deferentially. Maman never learned to speak reasonable French, so Irène did the talking. Although she was scared stiff, she remembers how the reverend mother, blinking over her pince nez and smiling, made it easy for her to talk. Eventually she raised a hand, and asked:

"Combien?"

Maman knew enough French to understand - in fact misunderstand. Under the impression that the nun was asking how much she could afford to pay, she began fumbling in her bag.

"*Non, non, non, madame,*" Mère Ligori protested. "*Combien d'enfants?*"

Prompted by her mother, Irène explained that she had two younger sisters. There were two cousins, a few friends... in total about ... Maman hesitated, afraid of being excessive. She took a deep breath, and at last held up all ten fingers. The good nun winced a little, then nodded.

"We have certain requirements," she said briskly. "Black dress with a white collar, black pinafore, hat... I'll give you a printed list... It's very fortunate that we are at the beginning of the holidays, and all the pupils are at home. Please explain to your mother that you will have to integrate completely with the other boarders, and before they arrive for the beginning of term, you will have to learn enough of our religious practices to pass unnoticed."

And so it came about. Aged fourteen, Irène began life as a Catholic.

I suppose I have to face it. Mobility is now a serious problem. Sometimes it takes us five minutes simply to move through a doorway, or from her wheelchair to the toilet seat. In an emergency - and these occur too often - it isn't funny. And it's not only a question of time. For a major part I'm supporting most - if not all - of her weight, and that's beginning to take its toll on my aging body. Her feet remain glued to the floor for increasingly long periods.

Irène can no longer sit down without support and guidance. Even if she were able to move more easily, the loss of her sense of direction - lack of orientation allied to rigidity of movement - create a major operation. Getting in and out of the car can require the assistance of two people, as she needs to be lifted on to the seat, positioned - because she inevitably slumps to one side - and belted in place. Helping her to use the commode at night several times is something I dread more than ever...

I know something has to be done. But what?

I've asked the social worker to call. But I'm not sure I want to hear her advice.

Sister Thérèse came back into the dormitory where three terrified girls were standing like statues. She was holding the party dress to her chest.

Smiling she said: "You've forgotten to remove the label. Don't worry. I'll see to it for you."

And that was that.

It wasn't pleasant kneeling on a stone floor and inhaling the unfamiliar insense at morning prayers before they'd had anything to eat or drink, and conditions in the dormitory were spartan. But all this was a picnic to the girls, after squashing bugs all night in the country hovel and too much in fear of their lives to sleep more than an hour at a time.

Anxious not to betray themselves, they earnestly set about learning the ritual, prayers and establishment rules. Under the guidance of Sister Thérèse in particular, they concentrated on becoming acceptable Catholics, and, indeed, when the other boarders flooded in at the beginning of term, no suspicions were aroused.

Day followed day in a set pattern: chapel, breakfast, lessons, vespers and bed. In the dormitory a chaste routine was expected: there were curtains to ensure privacy, and the girls were not allowed to expose their bodies while undressing or dressing. A pot was kept under each bed. " It had to be emptied each morning and wiped dry with a rag," Irène tells me. "Yuk! We never showered. On Fridays we washed our hair and feet in tin bowls - outside, in all weathers - and every Thursday afternoon, there was a compulsory walk in the country. Whenever we passed German soldiers, Dora, and the other few girls, who were afraid they looked Jewish, used to pull down their hats and hide their faces. But nobody ever stopped us."

Lessons were conducted in both French and Flemish, and the curriculum included German, English, and, for the older girls, shorthand and typing.

"And we had fun!" says Olga. "Sœur Lucienne taught me to play the piano!"

When the same sister heard Dora sing she was entranced, took her under her wing, and had her singing solo for the choir.

Of course, the girls were homesick. Not only did they miss the other members of their family, but, given the situation, weeks went by without news of them. And there was the ever present fear that they might have been dragged off in lorries.

In these circumstances, the girls tell me that an extraordinary thing happened. I'd be curious to know how my rabbi would react to this. After weeks of daily prayers:

"Notre père qui êtes aux cieux,
Que votre nom soit sanctifié,
Que votre règne arrive,
Que votre volonté soit faite
Sur la terre comme au ciel..."

Acquiring the habit of inwardly voicing their own fears and hopes in the sanctity of the chapel, they began to appeal directly to the effigy on the cross and pictures of the Madonna, deriving comfort and hope from spiritual forces, when the powers on earth would have driven them to despair. Furthermore, the influence was by no means short lived.

Dora tells me that, two years after she'd left the convent, when her mother was obviously on the point of death, the girl ran frantically to the doctor.

"I was clutching my rosary," she tells me, "and begging the Holy Virgin to save her."

True to her faith, Mère Ligori was not only saving the Jewish girls' lives, but hoping they might become Catholics. She never actually converted one, but she took good care of their souls. I once asked my mother-in-law how she felt about her daughters' Christian indoctrination. She surprised me.

"It was a wonderful thing," she said in Yiddish. "I wouldn't want my girls to grow up like animals (*behemas*)."

Of course, the refugee children remained at school during the holidays. One day Olga was at the piano. They sang a few hymns. Then suddenly the young pianist launched into a lively Yiddish tune, which her father and sister had performed at Eva's wedding. Delighted, Dora burst into song. Sœur Thérèse, supervising the little group, was fascinated.

"Please teach me that!" she pleaded.

So they did. Olga tells me that she could hardly play for laughing at the incongruity of the situation: this bespectacled nun, in her full habit, letting rip:

> "Choosen, Kala,
> Lomen alle
> Trinken a glesele Wei-ei-ei-ein..."

> "Bride and Groom,
> Let us all
> Drink a glass of wine..."

Another incident Irène remembers is Sœur Bonne Aventure giving out the results of a mathematics test. Most of the nuns were good humoured but this particular teacher was especially so. Olga says she was "*la plus rigolote.*" Arriving at my wife's name on the list, the good sister gave a sorrowful smile, then held up an elegant thumb and forefinger in the shape of a nought.

Irène was never good at arithmetic, and neither, obviously am I.

Yesterday I attempted to complete a form I received from the local authority, inviting me to fill in the amount of time I spend as a carer and house-keeper. The duties specified form an impressive and comprehensive list. Unfortunately, allowing five hours for sleeping, another two for eating, personal showering, toilet, correspondence, telephone calls, and so on, I've filled out a form which credits me with a day of thirty two hours.

Perhaps that's the reason I had an accident this morning. Having left Irène in the capable hands of her hairdresser, I made the most of an opportunity to do the day's shopping. It involved walking from one end of town to the other, and I had to hurry. That was a mistake. I didn't see a low pillar, and went down like a ton of bricks. My trousers were torn at the knee, my face was bruised near the left eye, and my spectacles broken. It took two men to pick me up, but I was, as I assured them, O.K., I'd only smashed my sunglasses. The regular specs were safely in the glove compartment of my car, so I was able to drive home.

The problem now is that Irène wants me to make an

appointment with our doctor. No way. I'm fine.

"At the same time you can tell him how exhausted you get."

"Nonsense. We've been down that road. He agrees that I'm just tired."

"Why should you be tired? You don't do anything," she says.

I gape at her.

"There are men of your age still working. What do you do?"

"Ah, I'll show you," I reply, and begin moving towards my study, to show her the written details of my thirty hour day. The form is on my desk, awaiting amendment and signature.

"Michael!"

"Yes, dear?"

"While you're up, would you get me a tissue?"

That's in the kitchen. I'm in the study.

"Yes, dear."

"Then you can throw my chewing gum in the dustbin."

I leave the evidence of my over-employment untouched on my desk. I don't think I'll bother to show her. What, I ask myself, would be the point?

TWENTY

"Michael!"
"Mmm?"
"What time is it?"
"Twenty to six."
"Is it Sunday today?"
"No. It's Tuesday."
"Then you'd better get up."
"It's too early."
"I want to be ready when the bus comes."
"That's in nearly four hours, for God's sake."
"We've got to sort out my clothes..."
"I did that last night."
"I don't want to keep them waiting."
"Don't worry. You won't."
"What time is it now?"

This is not a good time. We had a difficult night. I can see this is going to be a bad morning, and I'm so tired. Irène is having more problems with rigidity than ever before... and I'm being a right sod. I keep on saying the wrong things, in the wrong tone of voice, and can't seem to help myself. Against my better judgment I tell myself that she isn't making any effort. In the middle of the night I accused her of not trying to help, as I wrestled her dead weight up and sideways - quite a feat of strength for an old man - wrenching my shoulder in the process. As a result I'm in considerable pain, for which I unreasonably consider her to blame, and which I use as an excuse for excessive bad temper.

It's already taken her nearly five minutes to negotiate three feet between her wheelchair and the seat she needs to occupy, and my patience is exhausted.

"You've been standing on one spot, just shuffling your feet for five minutes!" Nasty. "Lift your foot off the floor!"

"I can't!" That's true.

"You've got to. Otherwise you'll be stuck there all day." Exaggeration won't help. "Stamp your foot!"

"I can't!"

"Yes, you can, if you try. Move your foot!"

"Don't you think I want to?"

At last, I use a little sense, bend down, and move it for her.

"Good. Now just one more step..."

"Put the wheelchair in the hall."

"Never mind about the bloody wheelchair! Take another step."

About two minutes later: "Right. Now turn around. Please move. You can't sit down when you're facing the seat. No. Leaning further over it won't help. You've got to turn around."

"I can't!"

"Yes, you can."

Listen to her, you idiot. She really can't. Help her. All right, you've already twisted your shoulder, but just stop making excuses and help the poor woman.

"Michael! you're hurting my neck! Don't be so rough! Do it gently."

I do my best.

"I'm not comfortable."

"That's because you're sitting on the front edge of the seat. Move backwards. You're not moving at all. Put your hands on the arms of the chair, and lift yourself up and back. No. You're not moving an inch..."

I put my hands under her armpits and heave, but achieve nothing except a sharp pain down my already sore back. We end up with a compromise; she is neither comfortable, nor in danger of falling off the seat.

"Michael! "

"Yes, dear?"

"I'd better put my coat on."

"The bus isn't due for another hour!"

"I don't want to keep them waiting."

"You won't."

Five minutes later: "I think I should put my coat on now."

"You'll be too hot."

"Well then, close the window."

"You mean... Oh, never mind. I'll fetch your coat

193

soon."

"What time is it?"

So it goes on. And I regret to admit that I become irritable, impatient, intolerant and unkind. This is the woman I love with all my heart. She's ill, and I'm treating her abominably. Am I no better than my father? A chastening thought indeed! Perhaps I'm reflecting her Parkinson's, in so much as my brain says one thing, and something quite different comes out of my big mouth. At the back of my mind reason - and love - tell me that I ought to be exercising restraint and understanding, then irritability dispels common sense, and, against my will, I find myself being horrible.

By the time her bus arrives to take her to the day centre I've proved myself to be a most unlovable brute and have the rest of the day for remorse - relieved by an hour's much needed sleep after lunch.

From four o'clock onwards I look anxiously out of the window for the bus to bring her home, hoping she'll have forgotten what a pig I was this morning, or, at least, forgiven me.

She's there! I hurry down to meet her, and to my delight, find her all smiles. I give her a big hug and fuss over her, wondering how I could possibly have been unkind to this wonderful person I'm lucky enough to have as my wife. In future, I tell myself, I shall mend my ways. But... haven't I said that before?

Eva fanned herself with the bag she was carrying. It was just like Maman to force these "goodies" on her, when there wasn't enough to eat for her parents, now living alone. It was wonderful how her mother could conjure food out of nothing, turning a few potatoes - and heaven knows how she managed to acquire them - into a tasty and nourishing meal... Now there was a welcome coolness in the air. It was August 1942, and had been a scorching day. She'd spent a large part of it by the open window in the rue Plantin, chatting with Maman about Papa's attempts to avoid capture, the terror of night raids, stories of appalling working conditions for the deported Jews, and unbelievable rumours of an even more sinister fate awaiting them at the end of their journey east, about the girls, now concealed in a convent, Ida living in safety with Mme d'Haen, and, above all, about Eva's pregnancy, now in its second month.

Her mother was confused; overjoyed, as she would expect to be, at the prospect of becoming a grandmother for the first time, but filled with foreboding at the idea of caring adequately for a tiny, vulnerable little soul in the current world of madness, cruelty, and constant danger. She hugged the girl's arm closely, as they reached Saint Gilles, then the Rue de Danemark. They walked towards the girl's flat...were almost there.

Turning the corner, they found their pathway blocked by a small crowd outside the bakery. Recognising Eva, the *boulangère* tried to pull her inside the shop. But the girl let out a cry and jerked away.

"Come inside!" pleaded the baker's wife.

"No!"

Eva had spotted a van outside number 61. Her heart sank as she recognised it for what it was. Then two soldiers emerged, accompanied by a young man. Eva yelled when she saw him:

"Jacques! That's my husband! Jacques!" Turning to her mother, who was standing as if turned to stone:

"Can't you see? They've got Jacques!"

The baker held firmly on to the older woman, but Eva eluded restraining hands and ran towards the vehicle into which the Nazis were pushing their captive.

She clawed at the sleeve of one of the soldiers.

"That's my husband!"

"I don't know this woman," cried Jacques. "She's crazy!"

"I'm his wife!"

Twice she tried to climb into the van, and twice she was pushed back.

"I'm going with him!"

"The woman's mad! I've never seen her before!"

Again she made a frantic attempt to pull herself over the back of the truck. This time she was hauled up beside her husband, who pulled her, sobbing, into his arms.

Stricken dumb with terror, shaking from head to foot, her mother collapsed and fell to the ground.

A family in Eva's apartment block had received summons similar to the one sent to Irène's family, for their children to report for deportation from Malines. They decided to ignore the demand, and had taken flight. As a reprisal the Nazis had raided the building and seized the only Jew on whom they could lay their hands - my brother-in-law.

And now the unfortunate couple found themselves on Transport number XII, headed for Auschwitz.

Jacques contrived to send his message requesting food and shoe polish - I have a photo-copy - and a coat for Eva, who added her signature beneath her husband's.

When it was discovered at the camp that Jacques Lewin was a skilled jeweller, the Germans decided to make use of him. There was a plentiful supply of jewellery and watches to be sorted and repaired for use by the officers and their wives. After a while Jacques realised that the articles were not merely "confiscated", but stripped from their owners before they were slaughtered. Sickened by his task and having lost hope of ever seeing his wife alive, one morning he told a fellow worker that he was too ill to continue and intended reporting to the infirmary.

"Don't be a fool," said his friend. "You know what they do there."

Jacques shrugged his shoulders.

The other man continued working and was eventually liberated by the allied forces. He paid a visit to his friend's family, told them the story...

"He reported sick that day," he said. "I never saw him again."

Eva didn't need the coat he'd requested. Together with all the women and children of that particular convoy, she was gassed on arrival.

The stones on the cellar floor vibrated as another bomb fell very close. It was probably the one which reduced the magnificent library of Louvain to a pile of rubble. Once again allied planes were raining destruction on to Belgian soil. This was the second night of a relentless bombardment and the girls huddled together in terror.

The convent was no longer a safe refuge. In the morning parents arrived to collect their children and the mother superior considered it her duty to get news to the Jewish families that in these circumstances, she could no longer accept responsibility for their daughters' safety. Gradually the convent was emptied of pupils.

There was no regular transport available, so Ida and her mother reached Louvain perched on the logs of a lorry transporting tree trunks to take the three girls home to whatever little security they could hope to provide.

Although virtually in retreat, the Nazis were still indulging themselves with the deportation and murder of Jews, wherever they could lay hands on them ... with certain exceptions. There was a Jewish organisation allowed to function on a limited basis which provided the occupying forces with a few selected tradesmen when their services were needed for the continued prosecution of the war. It so happened that the Wehrmacht required experts in handling leather to fashion articles of soldiers' uniforms out of rabbit skins.

Charles Rusak was one of the first to be recommended. He was granted a certificate guaranteeing his immunity from deportation, and began working in a factory called Lustra.

"Don't write about my father working for the Germans," Irène asked me.

"Don't be silly, darling," I told her. "In his place, I'd have done the same."

Working alongside my father-in-law was a hungry looking young man called Henri Silberstein - now unrecognisable as Harry Silvers, a prosperous citizen of Los Angeles. He took a shine to Dora when they met. He was small, undernourished at the time, something of a runt, and she couldn't fancy him pickled, but then he introduced her to his best friend, Charles, a tall, handsome fellow who'd spent the war in Switzerland. Outwardly cool and laid back, in complete contrast to the effervescent, high-spirited girl, he had an underlying sense of humour. They were a perfect match and promptly fell in love. Irène and I flew to Brussels for their wedding, a year after ours.

With their father working at Lustra, the girls spent the last months of the German occupation in reasonable safety. Irène's friend Toba, renamed Thérèsè at the convent, and her little sister, were not so fortunate when they went home following the heavy air raids on Louvain. Both children were hauled off to Auschwitz with their parents.

On arrival at the camp, as men and women were separated, Hilda and her mother were sent to one side. Toba and her father were pushed to the other.

"Please..." the man pleaded... "Please leave her with her mother!"

An angry guard virtually threw her back into her father's arms... and saved her life. Mother and child went straight to the gas chambers. The other two survived and were liberated.

Shortly after our marriage Irène and I were in Belgium, and paid them a visit. It was an emotional reunion. At that time Toba would not - or could not - speak of her time in the camp. All we know is that her family was denounced to the Nazis by a notorious character known as "*Jacques le moosser*" - Yiddish for "stool pigeon." This was a Jew, who earned only temporary immunity - and, hopefully, a permanent place in hell - by betraying his brethren.

Many years passed before Toba told us what happened and that their survival was mainly due to a young Nazi who secretly befriended them, smuggling scraps of food.

It was only a short time after I met Irène and had virtually become one of the family, that I was involved with the aftermath of the holocaust.

Survivors of the death camps were beginning to reappear, some as walking skeletons, and all with horror stories to exacerbate the anxiety of those awaiting news of deported family members.

My mother-in-law, already showing symptoms of a rapidly progressive neurological disease, and walking with difficulty, dragged herself daily to search the list of liberated inmates of concentration camps for the name of her daughter. The light gradually faded from her eyes together with vanishing hope. When she died a year later, the doctors gave the cause of death as "heart failure." It would have been more correctly termed "heart broken."

There are two dark threads in the tapestry of Irène's family. The first is inherent and the second an interwoven pattern. Intrinsic - on the maternal side - is a predisposition to severe neurological disease. The tragic attached thread is linked with filaments which are all blighted with the stigma of Auschwitz.

This second strain became apparent to me when, as an accepted member of the family, I was introduced to the *machetoonim*. The lives of all of them had been blighted by the holocaust. Ida's prospective parents-in-law were the exception. Chaskiel had no respect for them. He considered the old man to be a *poer*, a peasant, and his wife a *macheshefer*, a witch. Having met the pair, I could not improve on his description. Chaskiel considered it an example of the imponderable nature of divine justice that, of all his in-laws, every one righteous, respected and admired, only this couple, who, as he confided in me, turned his stomach, should have been spared.

From all I'd heard of Eva's husband, Jacques, his parents were no surprise... refined, gentle folk. When I met them, they had only recently had confirmation of their son's death and the circumstances of his imprisonment. They were still in a state of shock, but bore their grief with dignity.

Olga's in-laws were introduced to me a few years later. Even with the extra passage of time they were still visibly grief-stricken; they both shuffled, rather than walked; just middle-aged, they could have been taken for seventy. The father spoke in barely a whisper, as if through a mask:

"We sent them," he said. "We sent them... my son, my daughter..."His voice broke. "We sent them both."

They'd received the same summons which had called Irène and Ida to Malines. In their case it had been on a one way ticket.

"How can we be forgiven?"

Clearly they desperately needed to forgive themselves. Just as clearly they never would. His little grandson, Serge, Olga's baby, was on his knee. Gently he stroked the boy's flaxen curls, but there was no tenderness in his eyes, bereft of any expression - lifeless. He sighed.

"Tell me," he said, speaking in Yiddish, a language in which the words strangely have an added poignancy: "What do you think? Is it better to bring children into this world or not?"

"I'd say 'yes.'"

He shook his head. "No."

Even as he spoke he continued stroking the child's head, and the effect was horrifying.

Vainly I attempted to make the point that the little fellow on his knee could help make the world a better place. It was a waste of breath. Mentally he was years away - back in the past, tormenting himself with guilt. He never lived to see it - died, in fact, soon after our meeting - but Serge is a conscientious and respected social worker in Brussels. We're all very proud of him.

A final look at Chaskiel's *machetoonim* brings me to Dora's husband, Charles. One evening he returned home from work and was settling down to his evening meal when his older sister, Jeanne, announced:

"Tonight I have a special dessert for you."

"What is it?"

"It's a surprise. Just wait and see."

The young man wondered for a moment why his younger sister, Rosa, was hovering behind him, but he'd had a difficult day, was hungry, and eagerly began to tuck in.

"Well?" he asked eventually. "Where's this special dessert?"

An empty plate was placed before him. Charles looked questioningly at each of the girls in turn. As though waiting for a cue, Rosa produced an envelope from behind her back and placed it on the empty dish.

"What's this?"

"Open it and see," said Jeanne.

Even more puzzled, he tore open the envelope. It was an official communication that his mother had been found alive in Auschwitz and was on her way home. Charles folded both his sisters in his arms and sobbed his heart out.

"I knew that if I'd given it to you when you came in, you wouldn't have touched your dinner," said Jeanne.

Their father never returned.

In due course I met the good lady and was struck by the strong resemblance to her son. She was tall, handsome, dignified and reserved - exactly like Charles. Dora tells me she had the same unshakable integrity, and one can imagine her quite unsullied by the bestiality of the death camp. She probably survived by sheer nobility of soul.

Irène's family are haunted by their connections with the holocaust, but only just beginning to become aware of that other shadow cast by genetic brain disease. Of the several cousins affected worldwide, in Belgium, France, Israel, Australia and England, we are most closely in touch with those based in London. Anne recently died in residential care, allegedly a victim of Alzheimer's. With almost identical symptoms, her brother, Louis, has been given the same diagnosis as my wife, Parkinson's coupled with Lewy Body disease. His wife, Barbara, and I keep in touch, and compare notes.

The last time we spoke, she told me that Louis was taking a new drug, *Risperidone*, which had virtually rid him of the hallucinations driving them both crazy. Our own consultant preferred prescribing *Quetiapine*, used for the same purpose. Since it proved ineffective, he has agreed to try the other medication, which Irène has been taking for few days - so far with a slight lessening of the problem.

At the moment her cousin is in his second home in Spain, and, as I haven't heard from Barbara for several weeks, I'll give her a ring.

She answers at once, and we waste no time on small talk:

"How's Louis?"

"Terrible."

She goes into detail, and I am flabbergasted at what she has to say. To date the cousins have been more or less level pegging in the progression of their illness. Apparently for Louis, there has been a rapid progression of dementia.

"How about physical difficulties?"

"I don't think you want to know."

"Try me."

I hear a mirthless chuckle at the end of the line, and she adds:

"I don't think I want to tell you... but I will."

"Please."

"That's the worst part. I have to tell you that I can't cope any more. We now have a day nurse and a night nurse. You wouldn't believe how much that costs, but that's not my worst concern... Are you sure you want to hear this?"

"Please go on."

So she delivers her bombshell:

"He's in nappies day and night."

TWENTY-ONE

A few months before Hitler decided to do the world a favour and blow his brains out, I had an epileptic seizure. But nobody, including myself, had a clue about what it was. When I was whipped into a military hospital, the staff were - understandably - far too busy with bullet wounds, amputations and life-saving operations to concern themselves with what appeared to be nothing more serious than a nutcase. Only subsequently, after a comparable attack many years later, did I realise that I'd suffered a major seizure of recurrent temporal lobe epilepsy.

From childhood I'd experienced minor episodes, all with the same pattern. Due no doubt to my terror of doctors and possible hospitalisation, I'd been able to keep them secret. They were never serious enough to cause a problem. Each attack begins with an odd premonition, followed immediately by a singular sinking sensation in my chest and stomach. I have a dizzy spell. A particular smell, sound or image causes a time slip: I know that this precise moment has occurred before. It is a remarkably convincing sense of *déjà-vu*. My eyes focus on an object in the middle distance, which then appears in micro vision, further away. Normally the sinking feeling subsides and everything returns to normal in a minute or two. Less frequently the attacks last longer and are accompanied by confusion and distress. On three memorable occasions there were varying degrees of amnesia, the worst occurring near the end of the war. Only twice did the seizures warrant seeking medical attention.

About fifteen years ago I was getting into the driving seat of my car. My wife and daughter were behind me. It happened suddenly, and I had no idea where I was or what I was doing. Irène became hysterical, but, fortunately, level-headed Elaine was there:

"Don't panic," she said, and virtually gave me a swift psychological test, during which she discovered that I didn't have any idea of the time, date, year, where I lived - but knew perfectly well who I was and who was with me. She directed me to the front passenger seat, took over the wheel and drove us home. By the time we arrived, about half an hour later I was completely - to everyone's relief - back to normal. But this time I couldn't wriggle out of a visit to my G.P. He was a dear old man - sadly no longer with us - and nobody's fool. After being questioned at great length, I was forbidden to drive for three months. After that time, he said, he'd review the situation. I protested.

"If I report this to the DVLC you'll be banned for longer," he threatened.

"I think you've got temporal lobe epilepsy," he said. "We'd better have you seen by a neurologist for a positive diagnosis."

No way would I open that can of worms just then, if it could be avoided, and, after much persuasion, he agreed to defer everything until our next appointment. Fortunately, apart from a few incidents too trivial to cause concern, I've been trouble free ever since.

The army doctors didn't have a clue what was wrong with me, and probably didn't care either. Cursorily, I was classified "schizophrenic", and I never saw a doctor again until they discharged me. I spent a dreadful night, wide awake most of the time, listening to the weird noises made by patients in a psychiatric ward. By the morning I'd had enough and tried to tell them that my memory had returned; I was now quite well, thank you, and, please could I rejoin my unit... The male nurses smiled at me indulgently and took not a blind bit of notice. After all, I was supposed to be crazy. Unbelievably they went on ignoring me for nearly three months.

A week after my hospitalisation, in Belgium, I had a wonderful surprise. To my knowledge I was the only patient ever to receive a visit in that ward. I was amazed - and delighted - to see Irène and her mother coming towards me, as I was sitting beside my bed. They'd somehow contrived to discover where I was, and, concerned that I might be seriously ill, had travelled a considerable distance to see me. It must have been a Herculean effort for Maman. I noticed, for the first time, that she was not walking properly. She dragged one foot. Then I heard that her speech was slurred.

In fact, I was witnessing the first signs of a rapidly progressive form of a neurological disease diagnosed by her doctor as multiple sclerosis. I was able to reassure them that my illness was all a fuss over nothing, and, not to worry, I'd write to them and keep in touch. In fact it turned out to be a lengthy correspondence, and over a year before Irène and I would be together. Sadly, I would never see her mother again.

A few days later I was shipped back to England in a hospital ship. I noticed on an official slip of paper in my possession an entry which puzzled me: it said "Lying." Ah, I thought. They realise at last that there's nothing wrong with me, and think I faked the amnesia. But then, if they think I'm a liar, why are they sending me home? Is it for some sort of punishment? I compared the note with one in my neighbour's hand. The entry there was "Walking."

They deposited me "lying" - on a stretcher - in the psychiatric ward of a military hospital in Banstead, Surrey. I was perfectly fit, but nobody cared, and abandone to a protracted nightmare. The treatment of mental illness is a popular theme in literature and on the silver screen, invariably involving diligent psycho-analysis and inspired intuition by a practitioner, resulting in his turning a magic key to unlock the patient's deeply buried, willfully forgotten trauma and effecting a miraculous cure. My experience of mental illness is nothing like this at all. For weeks on end I never saw a doctor, and, to my knowledge, neither did any other patient in the ward. We were in the sole care of male nurses, and they provided only one form of treatment. That was what we called "jungle juice."

Left to our own devices, we sank from lethargy into deep depression, roused only by the shrieks of one of our less quiescent neighbours. When this happened, or there was a suggestion of violence erupting, the nurses appeared in twos and threes out of nowhere, sprang into action... then pouf! jungle juice rendered senseless the miscreant who had the audacity to disturb their peaceful existence, and dreadful silence descended again on the ward.

I don't recall any friendship with a fellow inmate, any

conversation above an odd word, any faces... only one very tall fellow, who prowled restlessly up and down almost all day long, never speaking, expressionless... One of the nurses told me that he was a glider pilot who'd made a forced landing behind enemy lines and was found wandering when the allies advanced, completely out of his mind. Like the rest of us - some suicidal, one or two homicidal, and all desperately miserable - apart from being stripped of anything dangerous, like shoe laces, a belt, a tie, he was left alone - very much alone.

I was still there on the day everyone in England celebrated Victory in Europe... Everyone? Not where we were. All the staff vanished, to wave flags, drink beer or whatever. For the whole of that day our ward remained gloomy and silent as a tomb.

By now completely recovered, even before my arrival, from the epileptic attack which landed me in hospital, if I'd been left much longer in that place I'd have really become as bonkers as the rest of them, but eventually I did at last see a doctor, and was careful to give all the right answers, so that I could rejoin my unit, and perhaps, with luck, end up in Brussels again.

" Do you still hear voices?"
Did I ever?
"No, sir."

I succeeded in convincing him I was sane enough to be let loose, but, to my surprise and delight, informed that I was not considered fit enough to continue serving my country, and would be duly discharged - in civilian clothes.

Technically I was still a teenager when I had the cheek to ask Irène to marry me. Despite the earlier objections of her sister, Ida's, ex-fiancé, Bernard, she said yes, and, as far as we were concerned, the matter was settled. In Brussels, the family thought it exciting. In England, when I wrote and told them, my family sent an immediate reply to the effect that I was out of my mind - an opinion confirmed a short while later, when I was locked up in the loony ward.

After my return to the U.K. and civilian life, my parents slowly realised that my resolve was unshaken, and eventually stopped telling me that I should not have been released from psychiatric care. They must have been of the opinion that, now separated by the Channel, I'd soon get over a schoolboy crush and find myself attracted to some nice Jewish girl, too sensible to entertain thoughts of becoming a child bride. Oddly enough, the one person to take me seriously was my grandmother. This surprised me because Booba was a rationalist through and through. Perhaps it was the thought of providing shelter and love to a survivor of the holocaust ... but I came to the conclusion that - with her addiction to reading - she couldn't resist a romantic story. At all events, she was a willing listener to my eulogies of the beautiful girl I'd met, and enthralled by the circumstances of our courtship. Incidentally, when she met Irène eventually, she took me aside and whispered:

"*Mazel tov!* You picked a lovely girl."

A song, popular years ago, has the words:

"They tried to tell us we're too young..."

It could have been written especially for us, because that's just what they all did say. When we decided to marry, Irène was just seventeen years old. I was twenty, in the army, and bound goodness knows where. I hadn't finished my education, never earned a penny in my life... I heard it all, over and over again, and it went in one ear and straight out the other.

Finding me obdurate, my parents suggested a compromise: we should delay an official engagement, until first of all I completed my degree in a year's time, secondly until they had an opportunity to meet the girl and her family, and thirdly Irène should have a while to acclimatise to life in this country before beginning married life. I knew they were simply stalling, still with the belief that my passion would cool and express itself elsewhere. But, knowing my feelings would never change, I agreed. Our love affair would continue to blossom by post.

I wrote more or less every day. And I discovered quite recently that my letters were kept and treasured... not, alas, by the fair maid to whom they were addressed, but by her youngest sister, Olga, who has a more sentimental nature.

It was one of the slowest years of my life. Only the Channel separated me from the one I loved, but it might as well have been the Atlantic or the Himalayas. I ached with longing. In my rooms at Cambridge two of her photographs had pride of place: One in the centre of the top book-shelf, and the other on my bedside table.

All, however, was not doom and gloom. I enjoyed the intensive studying - by dint of war service having the concession of telescoping two years' work into one - and, above all, involving myself in amateur dramatics.

At home my mother's curiosity was truly piqued - especially about one thing: the colour of Irène's hair, which I vainly attempted to describe. Nobody we ever passed in the street had quite the same shade of golden red.

"Is it that colour?"

"No. That's blond - like her mother's."

"Really? As fair as that? Not dyed?"

"Oh no. And she has blue eyes to go with it."

"Are Irène's eyes blue?"

"A sort of amber... a soft..."

"Hm. you mean brown. Oh, how about that gingery...?"

I never saw a match - except one near miss - on a dog, which I pointed out to her and then regretted. One day I had a brainwave. I suggested in my letter that Dora should snip off a fragment - the tiniest lock - which Irène could enclose in the next envelope she sent me. It worked. From the moment she saw the sample, Mum couldn't wait to see the whole real life package.

Before that could happen tragedy struck. I'll never forget the words of the next letter I received. It began:

"*Mon grand chéri...*"

She'd never called me that before. Reading on, I realised that she was pouring her heart out to me on paper. Her mother had died, quite suddenly.

I'm ashamed to say that I did not behave like any self respecting hero in a romantic novel or film and jump on the next flight to Brussels. That's fiction. Life isn't quite like that. I received the terrible news two days before the dress rehearsal of a play to be performed at the Cambridge Arts Theatre. I had a major role and couldn't possibly catch a plane. It was, in fact, only after my finals, that I was able to travel across to Belgium. My parents and my brother accompanied me for what I hoped would be a formal engagement.

When the taxi deposited us at 40 rue Plantin, Irène and her three sisters flew into my arms.

"Each one's prettier than the other!" exclaimed my mother in Yiddish.

"I like ours best!" said Alan.

Chaskiel emerged, and returned the compliment in an aside to me:

"*A shayne mamma!*" he whispered, and began oozing charm - something he could do quite well, if he chose, and my father was clearly impressed by Irène.

It may have been due to the beginnings of Alzheimer's slowing him down, but since the absence from home of my brother and myself, he'd considerably mellowed. Furthermore, there were two women in whose presence he behaved impeccably and never gave vent to an explosion of rage. Those two people who brought out the best in him were my wife and my grandmother. I could never fathom the reason why.

He hit it off well with Chaskiel, who addressed him as "*Mechooten*" and my mother - always with a slight bow - as "*Madame.*" During the few days we spent in the city, the two men reached certain decisions about our future: Irène should stay with my family for a few months, giving her an opportunity to learn English, become accustomed to life in London, and give me a chance to make some start in a career. I had discovered that one way of cutting through all the red tape required for Irène to obtain a visa was to use the subterfuge of inviting her into the country as a domestic servant.

So it was decided. We returned to England with smiles all round.

I thought the day would never arrive, but here it was at last. Irène was on the cross Channel boat, on her way to live with us. I'd never been so excited. Intent on absolute privacy for the tender moment when I'd take her into my arms, I insisted on going alone to meet her. This was going to be like the climax in a romantic film: the train, first pictured in the distance, steams slowly into the station. The hero is standing on the platform. His eyes search eagerly for the appearance of his beloved. Tantalised by the delay he watches passengers descending with their luggage. Scanning the train he catches no sign of her. Then, when he is on the point of despair and is about to turn away, a single, battered suitcase drops on to the platform, followed by a shapely leg... Is it...? Can that be...? Yes! He runs to enfold her in a passionate embrace. Somewhere, the violinists in an invisible orchestra are sawing at their fiddles like mad, playing a rhapsodic melody... The camera closes on the lovers with their lips virtually glued together... and the screen triumphantly announces ... THE END.

Believe it or not, that's exactly how it happened - except for the last bit. I was going crazy with anxiety, and on the point of going away with a broken heart, because she was indeed the last passenger to disembark. Didn't she want see me as much as I was longing to see her?

In fact the poor darling didn't want to see anybody at all. She thought she was going to die. It had been a rough crossing and she'd been sea-sick all the way. Her face was green. There was no orchestra playing - just the raucous din of a busy London railway terminus. I went to take her in my arms and she pushed me away:

"*Ne me touche pas, ou je vais vomir*!"

So much for romantic dreams... "Don't touch me, or I'll be sick!"

Neither does our wedding provide us with an unreservedly romantic finale. I'm sorry, but this is fact not fiction, and, although we had almost all the criteria for a perfect day, there was one large fly in the ointment.

In the first place the weather was fine - a beautiful day in June. Then all the people we loved were there, with the exception, of course, of my mother-in-law, who would have been overwhelmed, and my grandfather. But the rest of the entire Goldberg family were present, fit, and in great form. Booba was *kvelling* and *shepping naches.* Inadequately translated the words mean a combination of ecstasy and pride, which, according to the Jewish laws of cussedness, only *other* people get from their children. Right through the day there were peals of laughter coming from the tables of our friends; Cyril was my best man - a compliment which I repaid by standing up for him and Anita a few years later - and there were no tedious speeches, just a short and witty toast from Uncle Abe. He'd just retired as headmaster, and wished me success at the beginning of my teaching career. The band was excellent. This was before we were afflicted with the present predilection for deafening wedding guests with an ear-splitting cacophony, which renders normal conversation impossible. Among their repertoire came a medley of traditional Yiddish folksongs and the high spot of the nuptial celebrations occurred when Dora walked over to her father, put her face next to his and they both broke into an impromptu Yiddish duet... soprano and bass. Booba clasped her hands together with delight. This was a song from her own childhood, and a tear rolled down her cheek.

So, with all these wonderful things happening what could go wrong?

Why, during the actual marriage service were all the ladies weeping and all the gentlemen killing themselves with suppressed laughter?

The women were tearful because the bride looked absolutely drop-dead gorgeous, we were both very young, obviously deeply in love, and this beautiful girl in the stunning dress had been - so to speak - plucked from the recent holocaust. So what, as far as the gentlemen were concerned, was the cause of stifled mirth?

Well, it was all due to the *ganef* in Bethnal Green from whom I rented my wedding outfit. Somebody had recommended his establishment, at which I duly presented myself, accompanied by my brother, for a fitting.

"How do I look, Alan?"

He was impressed, and, when I looked in the mirror, so was I.

"Like a prince!" exclaimed the owner of the shop.

Indeed, a morning suit does have the ability to transform even the less attractive specimens of manhood into a semblance of royalty.

"I'll have it all delivered to you on the great day... Oh, by the way, payment is in advance, please."

He was true to his word. Just before lunch the package arrived, and, amid all the excitement, I didn't bother to open it until the time arrived for me to dress. Big mistake! To my horror I discovered that these were not the clothes with which I'd been so carefully fitted. The jacket was about three sizes too small and the trouser tops were about three inches above the tops of my shoes. That was not all. Literally the crowning touch took place when I put on the top hat. Perhaps due to a difficult birth I have a small head. My size in hats is six and three quarters. The topper provided must have been about seven and a half.

"It's too late to do anything about it now," said my father, "you'll just have to make the best of it. Nobody looks at the groom anyway."

He had a point. We were standing beneath the canopy, waiting for the service to begin, and all eyes - including mine - were on my beautiful bride. The organ stopped playing introductory music and the rabbi cleared his throat for the opening prayer. There was a moment of anticipatory silence. It was broken by my dear brother's stage whisper:

"Blimey! He looks just like Charlie Chaplin!"

Not content with that, he sang sotto voce, but loud enough for half the congregation to hear:

"Where did you get that hat... ?"

EPILOGUE

Irène has taken her tablets, we've eaten breakfast, and she's now tucked up in bed again. We had a good night, with only two sessions at the commode, and on both occasions it was less a wrestling contest than the opportunity for a cuddle. She'll be sleeping for at least an hour, so this is my opportunity to write the last page.

It's seven o'clock on the morning of a fine autumn day. From the window of my study I see a faint glow on the horizon. Lights are going on in one or two distant windows and a few vehicles can be heard as the town wakes up for the day's activity. I find it all strangely reassuring. The radio is on quietly and I'm listening to the divine slow movement of a piano concerto by Mozart. The comparison is, of course, odious, but, writing my book, I've been feeling rather as he must have done when composing his "Requiem." Now I can thumb my nose at the grim reaper.

The weather forecast is good. Irène doesn't go to the centre today and I think I'll take her for our favourite walk around the lake. We'll crunch the fallen leaves with the wheels of her chair, admire the riot of colour on the trees, and breathe deeply the sweet, fresh air. I'll even take some bread for the ducks and swans. She'll enjoy that.

I woke up very early this morning.

"It's tomorrow," I said to myself. "And it's not so bad. There's nowhere I'd rather be, nobody I'd rather be, and no-one else I'd rather have beside me."

"Michael!"

She's awake.

Tomorrow never comes, they say. Of course it does. And it came yesterday four months after I wrote the last page.

Today I'm on my way to visit Irène and the nursing home is near enough for me to walk. I look forward to seeing her, and half dread the prospect at the same time. At the sight of that beautiful face, my heart will still miss a beat, but then, when I realize that her eyes are fixed in a vacant stare, the pain strikes - just below the rib cage. She's awake - now a rare occurrence - but looks right through me, then past me, without a flicker of recognition.

My daughters took matters out of my hands. At least, that's my excuse.

I'd developed a sore back heaving Irène around. The poor old darling was no longer able to walk a step, or take the weight on her feet while standing. I'd dropped her several times and needed help to pick her up - no easy matter in the small hours. At night, I'd been getting little sleep, and not much rest during the day. The district nurse - a French lady - organized with considerable bureaucratic hindrance the delivery of a 'oist, a massive crane like contraption, so that a "carer" could help me for half an hour each morning and evening. That lightened my burden - a little. Unfortunately, the 'oist required two people to operate it, and was therefore unusable for twenty-three hours in the day. Furthermore, on one occasion when, with the assistance of the French lady, I 'oisted Irène on to the commode, the procedure was inadequate for the emergency, and the patient - alas afflicted with diarrhea - let fly while dangling in mid-air in the 'oist over the nurse's 'ead.

We experienced another difficulty with administering tablets. Irène acquired the habit of clenching her teeth to avoid taking them. To my shame I confess that once or twice, when this happened, I lost my temper. As far as I know the nurses have no problems with her medication where she is now.

Perhaps I'm telling you all this to justify putting my wife in a home. If only I could convince myself!

Alone in my flat, I'm living through a kind of bereavement. With the realisation that she'll never be here with me again, the feeling of loss comes over me in waves. I hide her armchair in another room, can't bear to look at the photographs of her - where she's always laughing. At times I'm tearful, particularly when all around me seems most beautiful. Through the patio doors I see the trees beginning to turn green, daffodils are dancing in the breeze on my balcony, there's Mahler, superbly played, on the radio...

It upsets me that I no longer remember Irène the way she used to be... with her smile which lights up the world, the deep, throaty voice... Have I really lost her? Even in my mind? I must stop this... stop feeling sorry for myself. It will solve no problems, only make things worse for the family if I give way...

Talking of family, both her sisters have visited - Dora from Israel and Olga from Brussels. They cuddled, kissed her, held her hands, without having any visible sign of recognition. There were momentary, fleeting expressions of pleasure, but we couldn't delude ourselves that she knew who we were. Olga, who'd nursed their sister, Ida, through a comparable illness, sustained the ordeal better than Dora, who retreated to a corner, where she cried her eyes out.

Now, here I am, sitting beside her in the pleasant lounge of this establishment, where she is slumped in her chair. I'm vainly waiting for her to open her eyes. At the moment Irène is not looking her best. Her mouth gapes wide open and droops to one side in that characteristic grimace of dementia. She's dribbling saliva from the corner of her underlip, has become much thinner, and, as I feel her thighs, I'm shocked by the loss of flesh. They tell me she's eating very little. I know she has difficulty swallowing - even the puréed food they provide especially for her. Now, not only her brain, but also her body, is shutting down.

At last she stirs. Her eyes open. I call her name. There's no response. I wipe her lips and kiss them. Still there's no reaction. She's a baby again. I sing her a nursery rhyme, try baby talk... Convulsively her hand clutches mine. Does she know me? My heart quickens. Her features are contorted... Is she in pain? Trying to communicate? There's a strong smell... She's having a bowel movement...

"Nurse!"

Two girls whisk her away without any fuss, and soon wheel her back to me, fresh, changed and clearly comfortable - but, unfortunately, fast asleep.

After a while, I leave, with a heavy heart.

Yoko stops me at the main door, which is half open.

The girl is new to us because she's been home to Japan, caring for a dying mother. Yoko's a vivacious, tiny nurse, with a ravishing smile.

"Excuse me," she says. "You Irene's husband?"

"Yes."

"You name Michael?"

"That's right."

"This morning you wife ask for Michael,"

"Are you sure? She hasn't spoken for weeks."

"Oh yes. She call for Michael two, three times."

Through the door I see the sun shining. It's the first day of spring and I take a deep breath.

The girl flashes her teeth and I can't resist giving her a big hug. Bless you, little Yoko. You've made my day.